"I listened... and maybe I'm not as good at understanding out of bed as I am in bed. But I am trying, damn it."

As much as she wanted to cry or rage, at least they were talking, and she wouldn't let temper or tears shut that down.

She stared into stormy gray eyes usually so steady, constant, ever honorable, and the truth deluged her like those storm clouds opening up. In his man-speak way, J.T. had answered her question after all. J.T. didn't lie. He gave sparse accountings, but his words counted. He had told her he loved her in the early part of their marriage. She'd just never listened.

The truth raining over her chilled to a deeper realization of icy, sheeting sleet. He'd said loved. Past tense.

Today, he hadn't said a thing about loving her still. In fact, he hadn't said those words for a long time. And she couldn't help but notice his love had stopped right about the same time as the kisses.

Dear Reader,

Once again, Silhouette Intimate Moments has a month's worth of fabulous reading for you. Start by picking up *Wanted,* the second in Ruth Langan's suspenseful DEVIL'S COVE miniseries. This small town is full of secrets, and this top-selling author knows how to keep readers turning the pages.

We have more terrific miniseries. Kathleen Creighton continues STARRS OF THE WEST with *An Order of Protection,* featuring a protective hero every reader will want to have on her side. In *Joint Forces,* Catherine Mann continues WINGMEN WARRIORS with Tag's long-awaited story. Seems Tag and his wife are also awaiting something: the unexpected arrival of another child. Carla Cassidy takes us back to CHEROKEE CORNERS in *Manhunt.* There's a serial killer on the loose, and only the heroine's visions can help catch him—but will she be in time to save the hero? *Against the Wall* is the next SPECIAL OPS title from Lyn Stone, a welcome addition to the line when she's not also writing for Harlequin Historicals. Finally, you knew her as Anne Avery, also in Harlequin Historicals, but now she's Anne Woodard, and in *Dead Aim* she proves she knows just what contemporary readers want.

Enjoy them all—and come back next month, when Silhouette Intimate Moments brings you even more of the best and most exciting romance reading around.

Yours,

Leslie J. Wainger
Executive Editor

Please address questions and book requests to:
Silhouette Reader Service
U.S.: 3010 Walden Ave., P.O. Box 1325, Buffalo, NY 14269
Canadian: P.O. Box 609, Fort Erie, Ont. L2A 5X3

Joint Forces
CATHERINE MANN

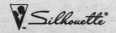

Published by Silhouette Books

America's Publisher of Contemporary Romance

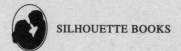 SILHOUETTE BOOKS

ISBN 0-373-27363-0

JOINT FORCES

Visit Silhouette Books at www.eHarlequin.com

Printed in U.S.A.

Books by Catherine Mann

CATHERINE MANN

writes contemporary military romances, a natural fit, since she's married to her very own USAF research source. Prior to publication, Catherine graduated with a B.A. in fine arts: theater from the College of Charleston and received her master's degree in theater from UNC Greensboro. Now a RITA® Award winner, Catherine finds following her aviator husband around the world with four children, a beagle and a tabby in tow offers her endless inspiration for new plots. Learn more about her work, as well as her adventures in military life, by visiting her Web site: http://catherinemann.com. Or contact her at P.O. Box 41433, Dayton, OH 45441.

To my firstborn, Brice. Thank you for being a constant source of joy and smiles. I am so very proud of you, son!

To a wonderful fan and dear friend, Elizabeth Benway, and to all the fabulously fun folks at eHarlequin.com who keep me endlessly entertained and motivated at Catherine Mann's Bunker Bash. Thanks for everything!

And as always, much love to my own flyboy,
Lt. Col. Robert Mann.

Prologue

February: Over the Persian Gulf

"We've been hit!"

The aircraft commander's words popped like bullets through Senior Master Sergeant J. T. "Tag" Price's headset. Ricocheted around in his brain. Settled with molten-lead heat as J.T. sat in his solitary loadmaster perch beneath the cockpit in the cargo plane.

Not that he even needed the aircraft commander's announcement. The teeth-jarring thump still shuddered through the C-17. Yet up to that last second, he hadn't given up hope of a minor malfunction.

Minor? The wash of warning lights blazing across his control panel told him otherwise. "Details," he quizzed, quick. Brief. Never one to waste words even on a good day.

This sure as hell wasn't a good day.

Aerodynamics went to crap. The craft already rattled, strained.

"Missile hit," the aircraft commander, Captain Carson "Scorch" Hunt, answered from the cockpit above. "Probably a man-portable, fired from a boat, I think."

The plane bucked. Shuddered. His checklist vibrated off the console. "Are we gonna have to put down somewhere bad or can we make it to Europe?"

"We're not going to make it to Europe."

Silence echoed for two seconds, cut only by the rumble of engines taking on a progressive tenor of pain.

Crap.

J.T. pivoted toward the cavernous cargo hold containing a pallet full of top-secret surveillance equipment. The technology could not fall into another government's hands. Beyond that, the stored intelligence from monitoring terrorist cell-phone traffic would give away field agent identities. "Plan of action?"

"We'll have to circle back and haul ass toward the coast to land in Rubistan."

Definitely bad. But not as bad as it could be. Relations with the country were strained, yet not outright hostile. Still, the equipment on that pallet made for a serious time bomb if they didn't offload it before reaching land. "How much longer 'til feet dry?"

"Ten minutes until we make the coastline."

Tight, but workable. Scooping his small black binder off the floor, he flipped through to the destruction checklists. "All right, then. Stretch it if you can while I destroy as much of this crap back here as possible before ditching it in the ocean."

Then pray like hell they didn't end up ditching the plane, too.

"Make it quick, Tag. I can buy you one, maybe two extra minutes over the water, but hydraulics and electrical are going all to hell."

"Roger, Scorch." J.T. unstrapped from his seat. "Beginning destruction checklists. Get the back ramp open."

He pivoted toward the man strapped into a seat two steps away. Spike—Max Keagan—also an OSI agent undercover as a second loadmaster on the flight, another potential land mine if the Rubistanians discovered the man's real job. "Stay out of the way 'til I'm through, then get ready to start pushing."

Spike flashed him a thumbs-up while keeping clear, laser-sharp eyes processing from his agent's perspective. He raked his hand over his head, normally spiked hair now in a buzz cut for his undercover military role.

Feet steady on the swaying deck thanks to twenty-four years in the Air Force and five thousand flying hours, J.T. charged toward the pallet. He flipped red guard switches, started hard drives erasing data about terrorists financing operations by trafficking opium out of Rubistan. And somewhere on their own base in Charleston was a leak. Thus the involvement of the Air Force's Office of Special Investigation.

As he destroyed data, J.T. tried not to think about all the government time and money wasted on the trafficking investigation. He hooked his fingers in the metal rings, pulled while also pushing a small plunger. Foam filled the motherboards, seeping out.

The load ramp yawned open. Wind and light swept the metal tunnel. The coughing drone of wounded engines swelled.

Now to finish the last of the destruction the old-fashioned way. He yanked the crash ax off the wall. Hefted back. Swung.

Hack.

What a helluva way to miss an appointment with his wife at the divorce attorney's office. *Sorry I can't make it, babe, but I'm a guest of a foreign government right now.*

Or worse.

He jerked the ax free of the cracked metal, swung again. God, he'd worried more times than he could count about leaving Rena a war widow, knew she had prepared herself for it, as well. But how the hell did anyone prep for a peacetime front-door visit from the commander, nurse and chaplain?

He'd already caused her enough grief over the years, and now to end it this way. Damn it. She deserved better.

But then she'd always deserved better than him.

J.T. hefted, arced the ax over, repeated, again, endlessly. Sweat sheeted down him, plastered his flight suit to his back. Air roared and swirled through the open hatch. Still, perspiration stung his pores, his eyes.

The aircraft's tail end swayed more by the second. His muscles flexed, released, burned until the surveillance computer equipment lay scattered, split into a pile of metal and wires.

"Destruction checklist complete," he reported, then nodded to Spike. "You ready?"

"Roger." The undercover agent charged forward to push, no help forthcoming from the screwed electrical system.

They tucked side by side behind the pallet. Air and ocean waited to swallow the equipment.

J.T. shoved, grunted. Rammed harder. Toward the gaping open hatch yawning out over the gulf. Boots planted. Muscles knotted, strained, until...

The pallet gave way, hooked, caught, lumbered down the tracks lining the belly of the plane, rattling, rolling, tipping.

Gone.

Swiping a sleeve over his forehead, J.T. backed from the closing ramp, avoiding the friction-hot rollers along the tracks. "Quickest you'll ever throw away a billion dollars. Now get your ass strapped in upstairs."

"Roger that." Spike clapped him on the back on his way toward the front.

J.T. jogged past his loadmaster perch, up the steep stairwell to the cockpit. For a crash landing, the higher up, the better. Two seats waited behind the pilot and copilot. J.T. darted right, Spike left, and buckled into the five-point harness.

The clear windscreen displayed coastline and desert meeting, sunrise cresting. He plugged in his headset again, reconnecting to the voices of the two men in front of him. Their hands flew over the throttle, stick, instrument panel as they battled the hulking craft.

Scorch, their aircraft commander, filled the left seat, a fair-headed guy who looked more like some mythological Greek god from the book in J.T.'s flight-suit pocket, a book he'd packed in anticipation of the quiet time out over the Atlantic. Hell. Scorch would need to tap into some godlike powers to get them out of this one.

Bo, the copilot, sat directly in front of J.T. The dark-haired kid must be all of maybe twenty-five or -six. Not much older than his two kids, for God's sake. Nikki was just finishing up her junior year at UNC. Chris was still in high school.

Regret seared. Damn but he wanted to see his daughter graduate, the first member of his family to get a college education. Of course, he'd attended Rena's graduation a couple of years ago, been proud as hell of her honors grades and quick landing of a job as a civilian counselor employed by the Charleston Air Force Base hospital.

But educational successes were expected for her since all her siblings had already sported a few diplomas triple matted on the wall when he'd met her. Hers had been delayed because of marrying him so young.

His head thunked back against the seat. Images of Rena scrolled through his mind on high speed as if to jam forty years more living into the next four minutes in case he never saw her again.

Never made love to her again.

Hell, right now he'd even settle for fighting with her, something they did as well and frequently as making love, which was mighty damn often. *I'm sorry, Rena.* For so many things.

Scorch thumbed the interphone button. "We're not going to make it to an airstrip. We'll have to put her down in the desert. Strap in tight. This one's going to smack so hard your children will be born dizzy."

J.T. braced his boots. And if they survived the landing? The Rubistanian government would detain them. Question them. It wouldn't be pleasant by a long shot, but they would make it home.

As long as the tribal warlords didn't get them first.

Chapter 1

The doorbell echoed through the house.

Rena Price resisted the urge to duck and run upstairs to keep from answering. Instead, she kept her feet planted to the floor for a steadying second while she tipped the watering can into a potted begonia by the sofa.

Yeah, that sure would make a dignified image, a forty-year-old woman cowering under her bedroom quilt. And all because she was scared spitless she wouldn't be able to resist jumping the man standing on the other side of her oak door. But then her emotions had never been easy to contain. Especially around J.T.

Water gushed Niagara Falls style over the sides of the porcelain pot.

"Damn it." Rena dropped the watering can and scooped up a burgundy throw pillow from the sofa to blot the water off the floor. She'd just wash the pillow later.

Sheesh. She wasn't the same eighteen-year-old at an air show all gaga-eyed and drooling over a hot airman in his flight suit. She was a mature woman.

The bell pealed again.

A mature woman who needed to answer her door so her soon-to-be ex-husband could start his weekend visitation with their teenage son.

She Frisbee-tossed the soggy pillow across the room and out of sight into the hall. Flipped her long hair over her shoulder. Whew. Composed? Ha. Not inside. But enough to pass muster outwardly for at least five minutes.

Rena tucked around and past the ficus tree beside the overstuffed armchair. "Hold on. I'm coming. Just, uh—" her eyes fell on the telephone "—finishing up a call."

Liar. Liar. Her heels chanted with each click along hardwood floors, then muffled on a braid rug as she made her way toward the broad-shouldered shadow darkening the stained-glass inset.

Regret pinched, not for the first time. How sad that she'd come to a point in her life where her husband had to ring the bell at his own house. He deserved so much better than this.

Better from her.

They'd sure as hell tried for years until she'd booted him out six months ago. Taken him back once he returned from Rubistan and whatever horrors he'd endured after being captured. Only to have him walk out on her a few days later.

She slowed in front of the door, pressed her hand to the glass magnolia pattern, her cluster of silver bracelets jingling and settling up toward her elbow. He wouldn't think anything of the gesture if he saw her on the other side since she was unbolting the lock with her free hand. But she let her fingers linger on the colored window for a second longer over the place where his body shadowed the pane.

After twenty-two years of sleeping with this man, her body instinctively hungered for the comfort and pleasure she could find in his arms. Her mind, however, reminded her of the heartache.

Her hand fell away from the glass.

She opened the door. "Hi, J.T."

Whew. She got that much out without stuttering or panting over his hard-muscled body in a flight suit. Still, she couldn't stop herself from soaking up the image of him to reassure herself that yes, he had survived the ordeal overseas. New threads of silver flecked his dark hair beneath his hat, adding to his appeal, shouting maturity. Experience.

Stress.

"Hello, Rena," rumbled her husband of few words.

She sidled outside with the company of passing cars, safer than inside alone, and commandeered a spot by a potted topiary reaching shoulder high. "Chris should be home any minute now. His shift ended an hour ago and he knows he has an algebra test tomorrow. He's looking forward to your weekend together."

"Me, too. We'll be camping, but I'll have my cell phone on me if you need to call."

Camping. A shared sleeping bag with J.T. under the stars while their children snoozed inside the tiny tent. So many memories she'd made with this man.

"Great. Just make sure he packs extra bug spray. West Nile virus and all that, you know." Closing the door and hopefully sealing away at least a few more of those tempting memories made in a bed upstairs, she couldn't stop babbling about everything her son should pack. At least she wasn't throwing herself at J.T. as she'd done the last time they'd been alone together.

How flipping unfair that he should look better at forty-two than at twenty. And he'd looked mighty fine at twenty with those brooding eyes focused intently on her while she gobbled up the vision of shoulders stretching his uniform to the limit. Fine enough back then to entice her out of her clothes and virginity in less than two months.

Of course, when he'd returned from Rubistan, it had taken him less than two *minutes* to talk her out of her clothes.

Rubistan. Her heart clenched tight.

J.T. was alive, she reminded herself. Much more than that she didn't know because this man wouldn't talk to her. He never talked to her. Never had, not about anything that mattered, just let her keep babbling on to fill the silences in their marriage.

And just that fast, her words dried up.

J.T. blinked slowly, gray eyes as shuttered as ever. "I didn't expect to see you here. Your car's not out front."

Good or bad? Did he want to see her? After so many years together she still couldn't read him except in bed. There, she knew his every want, desire. And God, was he ever a man of endless desire.

She shivered in spite of the ninety-five-degree spring day. Rena wrapped her arms around herself and strode past him.

"I left work early and had a friend drive me over to pick up Chris's car from the garage." She stopped at the porch railing, reached to the hanging fern to snap off a dead frond. Her marriage might have withered, but at least she knew how to keep her plants alive. A skill she'd developed in their early days together, an attempt to fill an empty apartment.

"A friend?"

Her fingers stopped midsnap. Jealousy? From J.T.? No way. Even considering it started a slow spiral of hope that would lead nowhere. Besides, she wouldn't play those kinds of games.

Shifting to face him, she crumpled dead leaves in her fist. "Julia Dawson took me. Then we had a late lunch."

Rena searched for relief in his eyes even as she told herself it shouldn't matter. She waited. Wanted… What? She didn't know anymore around this man. Although being able to hold on to her pride would make a nice start.

Heavy boots thundered across the planked porch until he stood beside her.

She swallowed.

He hooked a boot on the low rung. "The new paint job on Chris's car looks nice, don't you think?"

Paint job? So much for jealousy. Argh! Couldn't the man even acknowledge a normal emotion and throw her a bone here?

She wanted to scream. Stomp her foot. Even smack him. But that was one line neither of them had ever crossed, no matter how heated their arguments became and how many plates she pitched. Never once had their fights turned physical.

Well, except for the very physical release of sex that inevitably followed.

O-kay. No arguing today. Paint talk sounded good after all.

The story of their marriage, talking about things that didn't matter when so many more important things loomed. Divorce papers to sign. Children to bring up in a split home.

Whatever hell he'd endured during his nine-day detainment in Rubistan.

The capture had left bruises on his body, broken bones on another crew member. Heaven only knew what bruises and breaks on J.T.'s soul accompanied those new strands of gray. Part of her longed to hold his big solid body, while another part of her raged over him shutting her out—again.

He gestured toward the blue Cavalier. "The body shop did well sanding down the rust spot. Can't even see it. Just keep on Chris not to park so near the beach at work."

"He's doing well with his job at the restaurant. He's picking up some waiter duties as well as his regular busboy job. Better tips." She pivoted, rested back against the railing, late-afternoon breeze sweeping her hair over her shoulders. "And his grades are holding steady. He's keeping it together in spite of everything that's going on with us."

"He's a great kid."

Side by side, they looked into each other's eyes. Memories leapfrogged back and forth between them as tangibly as her loose dark curls floating on the breeze. Memories of Chris's birth. J.T.'s pride in his son. J.T.'s stoic features softened by a smile when he'd held their daughter, their firstborn.

And in that special moment twenty-one years ago with his daughter, Rena had thought maybe, just maybe everything would work out after all. Even if he'd married a woman he didn't love—a spoiled rich teenager who didn't know how to cook and clean, much less balance a checkbook or clip coupons.

She brushed the windblown hair from her face, tossing the long strands back over her shoulder, J.T.'s eyes watching her every move. Lingering on her hair.

More memories filled the air between them while countless cars cruised past. Images of her hair draped over his bare chest, of J.T. twining a long curl around his finger, tugging her closer. Closer still.

She swayed. "We did a good job with Chris. And Nikki, too. We got that much right, didn't we?"

So much for keeping things light.

Magnolia-scented gusts whispered around them while the hammock squeaked a taunting song from behind J.T. She thought for a minute he might dodge answering a question that delved into deeper waters. She wasn't sure why she even bothered pushing him anymore, pushing herself as well, because deep waters were dangerous for them, both with so many secrets unshared.

"Yeah, Rena. We did." His broad hand fell to rest beside hers on the white railing, not touching. But still she remembered well the pleasure of his calluses rasping against her bare skin.

She knew better now than to ask him what went wrong. If she did, he would sigh, dig in his boot heels to weather the storm while she did all the talking. Or yelling. She didn't like what she was becoming around him.

And she didn't want him to step away yet.

Oh God, she was so weak around this man when simply exchanging body heat across air turned her on. Rena backed toward the steps. "I really need to go. Chris has my car. I was hoping he'd come home sooner so we could trade, but I'm supposed to be at the base hospital in a half hour to head the support group meeting." Babbling again, damn it. "I'll just take Chris's car."

Then she wouldn't have to go inside with J.T. where no doubt they would end up naked on the floor in under two *seconds*. Maybe she needed to learn to be away from the house when J.T. picked up their son for weekend visits. Every meeting put her heart, her sanity, at risk.

"Rena?" He stopped her with a hand on her upper arm just below the sleeve of her peasant blouse. Skin to skin. Her bracelets tinkled in time with wind chimes to ride the magnolia-scented air in a sensuous serenade of more want, and God yes, she could see the desire smoking through his gray eyes, as well.

It wasn't enough. Not anymore.

Had he ever loved her? Somehow she thought maybe she could handle his leaving better if, for at least part of their time together, he'd loved her. If she'd been more to him than the woman he felt honor-bound to marry because the condom broke.

Yes, J.T. was all about honor, which made him even more admirable in her eyes after her father's "imports" business dealings. A cover for laundering Mob money, not that the feds could ever nail him.

J.T. was a man of honor to trust, and trust had been rare for her growing up.

"Rena?" he said again, his grip tightening.

"Oh, uh…" She startled and stared up at him, a long look even in her heels. "What did you say?"

"Is it okay with you if I wait inside? The temp's cranking up out here."

Just as when he'd rung the bell to the home he'd helped restore, this request to enter their house tore at her. They would need to talk soon, but now wasn't the time, when their son could walk in at any minute.

And not when she was seconds away from losing it. "Of course. Make yourself at—" *Home.* She swallowed down the word like lemonade without sugar.

A flicker of anger snapped in his eyes, a rare display of emotion from J.T., therefore even more potent. Well, damn him, he could get mad all he wanted. At least he would be talking.

The storm clouds in his eyes dispersed, distance reestablished. "Thanks."

"There's tea in the fridge." She inched away. From him. From herself, too, for that matter. From wanting him, hating him, even loving him still a little, which made her resent him all the more. "I need to head back to base. I'll pick up Chris on Sunday."

"I'll bring him back by tomorrow to swap cars."

"Thank you." No arguing. They would be civil about their offspring.

Nodding, J.T. turned away, twisted the doorknob, left her. Her shoulders sagged with her sigh. Rena blinked back tears blurring the setting sun and J.T.'s broad shoulders. She'd already cried countless tears over this man—many of them bathing his bruised body after his return from Rubistan. Yet still he'd rejected her offer of reconciliation. Zipping up his flight suit on the way out of their bed and her life, he'd made his position clear.

They really were over.

She'd spent three months trying to get through to him, to make him talk about something more meaningful than painting a car, if not for a reconciliation, at least to assure herself he was okay. Now, life had left her no choice but to move ahead and make plans for her children.

No question, they would have to talk soon, when Chris wasn't due home and her eyes weren't threatening to overflow. And when the time came for that talk, she would be stronger than the teenage version of herself.

Head held high, she sprinted down the steps on legs more wobbly than her purple high heels.

Punching numbers on the cordless phone, J.T. watched his wife through the lace curtains covering the living-room window. Wind whipped at her white blouse and long purple patchwork skirt, plastering fabric to her gentle curves. Rena's wild dark curls sailed behind her as she unlocked the driver's-side door.

She couldn't get away from him fast enough.

Yeah, that bit. More than it should. He wanted to bury his face in her hair, his body even deeper in hers. And she was running like hell.

He pressed the phone to his ear. It rang once, twice. Ended.

"Flight scheduling. Lieutenant Rokowsky."

Bo? J.T.'s brain stuttered for a second until he remembered the lieutenant had just started working in scheduling to mark time until he recovered from his injuries sustained in Rubistan.

J.T.'s hand gravitated up to his ribs, rubbed over bruises long faded. Bruises bathed by his wife's tears when he'd come home. So much damn emotion, too much to process then or now. He'd only known that no way in hell did he want to put his wife through that again. Since they'd already split, leaving seemed the obvious answer.

"Hi, Bo. Tag here," he said while watching Rena slide behind the wheel of Chris's two-door Cavalier. "I didn't get a chance to check the schedule since we landed late and I needed to pick up my son. What's on the boards for me next week?"

"You're on a training flight. Monday. Showtime 0600."

"Uh, okay. Got it. Thanks." J.T. peered through the sheer lace and still the car didn't leave. He moved closer until he could discern... Rena slumped over the steering wheel. Her forehead rested on her hands.

He forced himself to stay inside when every muscle inside of him screamed for action. "How long's the flight?"

"You're scheduled for five hours local area, instructing Airman Brad Gilmore."

J.T. winced. "Good God, not Gabby. That guy talks more than a four-year-old overdosing on Mountain Dew and Pixie Stix."

Bo's chuckles turned downright wicked. "What'll you give me not to stop by the flight kitchen and sweet-talk someone there into adding extra caffeine and cookies to his lunch?"

"Listen up, ladies' man." J.T. settled a hip against the window ledge, batting aside a flowering something-or-other hanging from the ceiling. Waiting for Rena to go. Hoping it would be soon before he ended up outside. "You go anywhere near that flight kitchen and I'll tell the nurses over at the hospital what your call sign really stands for. We've been letting you get away with that 'Bo stands for Beau, want me to be yours' crap long enough. Hmm, just think if I tell them you're really—"

"Okay!" The squadron Casanova rushed to interrupt. "No need to say it out loud and risk somebody overhearing. These are government lines, dude, with people listening."

J.T. let a much-needed laugh roll free. "All right, then.

You're safe for now. But I'll be double-checking that flight lunch of his for contraband Pixie Stix.''

Why wasn't Rena leaving? His boots started twitching on the hardwood floor. Maybe he would just—

She sat up, started the car. J.T. exhaled a breath he hadn't realized he was holding. The car backed to the edge of the driveway while a steady stream of after-work traffic flowed past.

''No Pixie Stix,'' Bo promised. ''Wish I was going with you Monday. I'd shut Gabby up.''

Hell yeah, they all wished Bo was flying, instead of indefinitely grounded until docs determined if his left hand would be worth a crap in the airplane once it healed. Flying. They all needed it, actively doing something to discover who had sold out their flight plan that day in Rubistan.

Although having Bo sit his butt in scheduling wasn't a half-bad plan for keeping an ear to the ground. God, the thought of one of their own turning traitor... J.T.'s fist numbed around the phone.

Not gonna think about that day. Keep it level before the weekend with Chris. ''Looking forward to flying with you again soon.''

''Yeah, me, too.''

Quiet echoed again, the lines occasionally smattered with the background sounds of another phone ringing, conversations off to the corner. But J.T. was hooked in that experience—linked with Bo and the young officer's fears over never flying again.

J.T. scratched along the neck of his flight suit. Even after twenty-four years in the Air Force, he couldn't imagine hanging up his helmet. Flying also offered an escape and release since his personal life had landed in the crapper. He'd be screwed right now if he couldn't fly out his frustration.

Yeah, Rokowsky must be in his own personal hell.

Age and officer/enlisted realities might separate them, but

the shared prisoner experience transcended all for a more casual relationship. A bond. J.T. searched for something to keep the guy on the line a while longer, until the edge eased from the kid's voice.

The parenting role came easy, and he figured Bo didn't get much of that since the guy didn't have any family. "What are you doing working the late shift?"

"Easier to call the flight attendant I'm seeing. She's in Japan this week."

"I thought you were dating a research tech from the medical university. Hannah something."

"Hell, man, that was last Thanksgiving. I've had my heart broken at least three times since then."

Bachelor days. J.T. shuddered as Bo rambled on about all the ways Hannah had ripped his heart out before trouncing on it a few extra times.

J.T. sank to the arm of the overstuffed sofa, his gaze never leaving the front yard. Jesus, he was too damn old for that crap. Although the thought of indefinite abstinence pinched. Hard. And having Rena in sight—even out of reach in the driveway still waiting to leave—didn't help with all those images of the two of them tangled on the hardwood floor.

A van turned the corner. After that, finally a break in the stream of cars. Soon, she would be on her way.

The van roared, picking up speed.

Irritation nipped. Damn it, this was a residential neighborhood. J.T. reached for a pad to nab the license number on the front while Bo reminisced about heart-stomping Hannah. The van eased over the center line.

What the—

Into the wrong lane.

"No!" J.T. shouted even though Rena wouldn't be able to hear him. Or move out of the way. He couldn't be seeing—

The van surged. Forward. Faster. Rena jerked to look just as—

The van rammed her passenger door.

Chapter 2

Grinding metal echoed.

He'd expected his marriage to end, but please God, not this way.

J.T. spared critical seconds to bark instructions at Rokowsky. "Call 911 and have them send EMS. I'm at the house. Car wreck. Rena. No time to talk."

He jammed the Off button. Tore open the door. Sprinted down the steps, vaulted the hedge. The car pinwheeled across the road. Rena slumped against her seat belt. The van recovered, righted.

Roared away.

Professional instincts? Calm in a crisis? Damn near impossible at the moment. But he scrounged, pulled them to the fore, logged as many details about the van as he could while his boots pounded grass closer to Rena.

Rage pumped through him with every step. The Cavalier slammed against a telephone pole. His wife's fragile body jerked inside like a rag doll. The crash thundered through the ground. Through him. The car bounced off, skidded sideways, tires squealing.

Stopped. Silence echoed, broken only by the hiss of the engine and a late day bird squawking its way out of a magnolia tree.

Glass glinted on the pavement. Jagged edges rimmed the door. Hand steady, his insides not so very, J.T. reached into the car.

"Rena? Damn it, Rena, wake up."

He pressed two fingers against her neck to check her pulse as his other hand yanked at the handle. The door held firm.

Her pulse pounded under his touch. Okay. One good thing to focus on instead of the bruise purpling her forehead. And at least no blood spurted that he could see.

J.T. sprinted to the other side of the car. Mangled. Dented. He gripped, hefted. Nothing budged. He could bench-press his body weight, but couldn't move the crunched metal.

Even adrenaline wasn't going to work this free.

He dashed back to the driver's side, pried the jagged edges of glass off, tucked his head inside, skimmed his hands over her face, shoulders, arms, checking for injuries and chanting, "Hang on. Just hang on and the paramedics will be here soon, but they're gonna need to talk to you. Come on and wake up for me."

Her head lolled toward him. Relief pressed like weights against his chest. "That's right, babe. Wake up."

"Baby?" she mumbled, dark lashes flickering.

Ah, hell. He shouldn't have slipped and called her that. But twenty-two years of marriage and intimacy were hard to shrug off just because his brain told him they'd reached the end.

"Are you okay, Rena?" He forced himself to speak carefully, say her name. Just her name.

Color drained from her face, leaving her deep brown eyes

all the wider, darker. Her hand fell to her stomach. She swallowed hard. "I think so."

Her voice shook. Her teeth chattered. All unusual reactions from his normally feisty wife. Nothing brought her low. She never complained or faltered if illness or life kicked her. She just kicked right back.

Not now.

For her to be this rattled, afraid even, scared the hell out of him. "You'll be free soon. I can't get the doors open. You were hit on the passenger side, and this side bounced off a telephone pole. I can't risk moving you until the paramedics check you out."

She frowned, fidgeted, bit back a moan. "My foot's stuck. I don't think I could crawl out anyhow."

His eyes fell to the floorboards. Blood trickled down her foot onto the plastic mat.

Damn it, where was EMS? Still no sirens. Only birds, wind rustling the trees, traffic on other roads cut the silence, the working-class neighborhood homes mostly empty at the moment. "Just hold still. Help will be here soon. They've already been called."

She blinked slowly. "I should tell you."

"What?"

Her hand drifted over her woozy eyes. "Um, oh God, I can't think and I need the words to come out right."

"You're hurt, and a little shaken up. Nothing more. No need for gut-spilling." He hoped. "This isn't a good time for soul-searching."

What would she tell him anyway? He'd backed from emotional outpourings nearly three months ago when he'd returned from Rubistan. He damn well couldn't handle it now.

"You're right, of course." Her hand fell away from her forehead. "Maybe you should step away. What if the car blows?"

"It's not going to blow up."

"You should step away anyhow. Just in case."

"Like hell."

"Somehow I knew you'd say that." She stroked his face with a limp and so soft, cool hand.

He stilled under her touch, hadn't felt it willingly come his way in months. What a damn inconvenient time to want her. But then adrenaline could screw with a man's better intentions, as he'd found out three months ago when he returned from Rubistan.

Her hand fell away, landing on her thigh. Her eyes flickered to the slowing cars driving past, to the handful of gawkers watching from sidewalks and windows, then back to the car. "Well, there goes the new paint job."

He smiled because she wanted him to. He'd do anything she asked just to keep her awake, talking.

Alive.

"Babe, there goes the whole car." Babe? Damn. "Insurance should take care of it, though."

And by God, he'd wrap his family in a helluva lot more metal and air bags next go-round, no matter how deep it slashed his currently hemorrhaging budget. Maintaining two households with a kid in college while they were still paying off Rena's college debt…

Not the time to think about money, he could almost hear Rena saying.

"J.T.?"

He landed back in the moment. "Yeah, Rena."

"Would you please call the base clinic and let them know I don't think I'm going to make it in tonight?"

"They can wait. Dedication to your job only goes so far." He clamped his mouth shut. End of discussion.

He held his tone level, tougher by the second. "I'm not leaving this car until they have you out, so stop wasting energy trying to maneuver me away."

"I don't want people waiting around for me. Parents arranged sitters so they could attend this particular meeting. We have a guest speaker.''

''Damn it, Rena, the guest speaker can start without you. Or they can just wait and eat cookies for a few extra minutes.''

Hell. Great way to calm her, by fighting. He mentally thumped himself.

She laughed.

Laughed? Which stunned the fight right out of him.

Soft, breathless, her laughs tripped out with a huskiness that would have been sexy any other time but was too weak for his comfort level.

''Damn, J.T. We even fight about who's going to take care of whom.''

She had him there.

Eyelids blinking slowly, holding closed longer every time, she stared back at him. He reached to take her hand from her thigh. Her bracelets slid, chimed, two sliding from her limp wrist to *tink, tink* on the floor of the car.

''Come on, Rena, stay awake.''

Sirens wailed in the distance. About damned time.

She squeezed his hand without speaking, but her eyes stayed open longer at a stretch as she fought unconsciousness. He stared back, held her hand and willed her awake, sirens growing louder, closer. Pain glinted in her eyes, radiated from her tightening grip around his hand. His fingers went numb, but no way would he tell her, instead kept holding while praying the sirens would move faster.

Her gaze fell to their linked hands. Her grip slackened. ''Oh God, J.T., I'm sorry. I didn't mean to cut off your circulation like that.''

''No problem.'' He needed to keep her distracted, talking. ''Reminds me of when you were in labor with Chris and transition hit you so hard and fast during the drive to the hospital. I was trying to recall all the coaching stuff I should be doing. Except I was scared as hell I'd be delivering the kid on the side of the road. Remember that?''

''Yeah, I do.'' Her grip firmed again. Not painfully this time, but holding on in a way she hadn't done in a long time.

Emergency vehicles squealed to a stop beside them. Doors flung open. He didn't want to let go. God, he'd missed her needing him. What a damn selfish thought.

She frowned. ''J.T., I really have to tell you—''

A paramedic jogged toward them. ''Hold the thought, ma'am. Sir, please move so we can get her out faster.''

J.T. backed away. ''We'll talk later.'' He would promise her anything, even one of those conversations she craved. ''Hang on and we'll talk all you want soon.''

The paramedic chanted a litany of encouragement to Rena while crawling through the passenger window to sit beside her. He placed a C-shaped collar to stabilize her neck, draped her with a protective blanket.

Then noise ensued, grinding and groaning of metal as the Jaws of Life pried her free. His wife's every wince sliced through him during the endless extraction.

Of course, he already knew just how difficult it was to cut Rena out of anywhere. Hell, he'd been trying to cut her out of his life for months without a lick of luck.

Christos Price hated whatever dorky unlucky star he'd been born under. It totally sucked being doomed to a life of geek-dom.

Elbow hooked out the open window of his mother's car, Chris finished clearing the gate guard's station leading into Charleston Air Force Base housing. At least with his friends Shelby Dawson and John Murdoch he could be himself without worrying about being cool.

And he was anything but cool.

Chris accelerated past the never-ending pines and oaks lining the street. He could wear double his regular wardrobe of baggy cargo shorts, open button-down shirt over a T-shirt, and the extra layers still wouldn't be enough to pad his bony body.

What guy wanted to be the ''spitting image'' of his short, scrawny mama? Geez. Scrawny wasn't a problem for girls, but it really blew monkey chunks for guys. Especially when all the other dudes in high school were so freaking big.

He was tired of hearing that five foot eight was a respectable height for a sixteen-year-old and that he would hit a growth spurt soon. Easy enough for his dad to say from three inches over six feet tall with more muscles than a linebacker.

Then his dad would ask him to work out together. Like wrapping a few muscles around his spindly arms would help. Can't make something out of nothing. And that's exactly what he was.

Nothing.

Clicking the turn signal, Chris rounded the corner toward Shelby's house. At least he wasn't getting pounded at school anymore. His friend John Murdoch kept the bigger guys off him, the ones who called him a marching-band wimp just because he played the trumpet. Murdoch played the saxophone and nobody called him a geek. Of course he was tall, a senior, tall, a wrestler, tall and had a girlfriend.

Shelby.

God, she was so hot. Nice. Totally hung up on Murdoch.

And, hey, had he mentioned the guy was tall?

Except Murdoch was also a friend, which meant staying away from his girl. Not that she would have noticed a dweeb like him that way.

But man, he noticed her.

Her corner lot came closer. Shelby sat cross-legged on a quilt in the side yard playing with her little brother while Murdoch sprawled asleep. She didn't see him yet, and Murdoch was out for the count, so Chris allowed himself the rare moment to just look at her.

Her silky black hair swished over her shoulder in a po-nytail. And—oh yeah—her bikini bathing-suit top with jean shorts showcased her belly-button ring. Suh-weet.

He pulled into her driveway. Wanted to pull her right to him and kiss her. Of course, he was more likely to grow ten inches by the end of the day.

"Hey, Chris!" Her greeting floated through the open window. "We're gonna order pizza in a minute. Can you stay?"

Even her voice was hot.

"Yeah, sure. Let me dig out my CDs first." And will away the evidence of exactly how hot he found her. Layered clothes weren't helping him much today on a number of counts.

Teenage hormones totally sucked.

But he couldn't go home, not yet. He needed to give his parents time alone. Maybe then his mom would finally tell his old man why she'd been puking her guts up every morning for the past couple of months. Her stomach was already poking out a little and still she didn't say a thing to anybody about being pregnant.

She must think he was a clueless bonehead like his dad.

Chris turned off his cell phone so his parents couldn't razz him about coming home and snagged his CD case. He would hang with Shelby and Murdoch for a while, and pretend everything was okay. Pretend that his parents weren't splitting. That he didn't love a girl who belonged to his best friend.

And most of all, pretend he wasn't hiding from a threat in his life that even tall John Murdoch couldn't warn away.

"Don't move, please, ma'am," the paramedic warned.

Pain jabbed from her ankle up her thigh. Rena gripped the edges of the gurney, taking mental inventory of her body as much as her muddled brain would let her while she stared up at the entrancing sway of oak branches overhead.

An air splint immobilized her foot. Her teeth cut deeper

into her lip to bite back the need to cry out. She couldn't have pain meds anyway because of the baby. Besides, she welcomed the ache that kept her conscious and reminded her she didn't hurt anywhere else, like her stomach.

Her baby.

Rena gripped the gurney tighter. Love and protectiveness for this new little life surged through her until the pain faded. She'd barely allowed herself to think about this baby she and J.T. had made the night he'd returned from Rubistan.

She had to tell the paramedics about her pregnancy soon, but her mind was so woozy. She would explain once J.T. was safely off to the side, rather than risk springing it on him without warning.

Why hadn't she told him sooner? It wasn't as if she was waiting for a miraculous reunion first. She would have to tell him, today, but later in her hospital room, away from the others, when he wasn't about to crack a crown from clenching his teeth.

If only he would step away, but J.T. always did his duty, and being by his wife's side right now would rank right up there as a responsibility.

A car door slammed. She couldn't turn her head to see.

"Tag!"

A voice. Who? Her muddled mind sorted through… Bo Rokowsky, a member of her husband's squadron.

Bo would make the perfect distraction to keep J.T. occupied at the moment.

She patted his arm. "Go talk to Bo. I'm fine."

J.T.'s scowling eyes flicked from the uniformed workers back to her before he finally nodded. "Okay. But I'll only be a few yards away if you need anything."

"I know. Thanks." She tracked his towering body retreating as best she could without moving her head until he disappeared.

She opened her mouth to tell the paramedic about the baby—

"Ow!" Her foot jerked in the paramedic's grasp.

J.T. landed right back in her line of sight. "What's going on? Is it broken?"

"We won't know for sure until we get X rays, sir," the paramedic answered.

X rays? Not while she was pregnant. And especially not during her first trimester. Pain flashed through her foot again. A whimper slipped free.

The paramedic called to his partner, "Seventy-five milligrams, Demerol."

"What?" Rena struggled to understand through her pounding head.

"Just something to help you with the pain, ma'am." The uniformed man swung toward her with a syringe.

"No!" she shouted involuntarily.

J.T. stepped closer. "Yes. Do whatever she needs. Rena, you don't have to grit through this."

Oh, hell. She needed to spit this out fast and quiet to the paramedic. "I can't take any medications."

"Ma'am, really, this will help settle you." The syringe hovered closer to her arm.

Damn. Damn. Damn. No more time for quiet, reasonable explanations.

Rena inhaled a deep breath that stretched achy ribs. "I'm not agitated. Just pregnant."

He'd already taken one missile strike this year. Didn't seem fair a man should get blindsided twice in a few short months.

Boots rooted to the ground, J.T. watched Rena being loaded into the EMS transport. She stared back at him apologetically without speaking. There wasn't time or privacy to talk anyway since the paramedics had moved even faster after her surprise announcement. A whole new set of medical concerns piled on now that they knew she was pregnant.

Pregnant.

The lone word knocked around inside his brain along with anger at Rena for her secrecy—and an undeniable surge of protectiveness for this new child. J.T. braced a hand against the oak-tree trunk, forced his breaths to stay even.

Rena was pregnant. Again. Well, they'd sure celebrated one hell of a reunion after his return from Rubistan. One with apparently lasting results.

More of that protectiveness chugged through him. Five minutes ago, he hadn't known this kid existed. Now he did and that changed everything.

He understood Rena well after twenty-two years, and she was too proud to let him back in the house because of the baby. The woman carried around enough pride to break the average human being.

The EMS truck lights cranked on. He pushed away from the roughened oak, tossed a quick farewell and thanks to Bo before stalking toward his truck.

J.T. slid inside and slammed the door. Shifting into drive, he steered off the curb to follow the fire department's EMS down the tree-lined street.

He would have to tread warily with his wife. Because damn it, he wasn't walking away from her now any more than he would have twenty-two years ago when she'd been pregnant with their daughter. He may not have planned on this kid, but already it lined itself right up there equally with Nikki and Chris in importance.

And what about his feelings for Rena? The gut-shredding fear he'd felt when the van started toward her?

The pine-scented air freshener dangled from his rearview mirror, swayed hypnotically while images of the wreck pounded through his brain.

He couldn't think of that. Not with so much at stake and

convincing her likely to be a hellacious battle. Safer to focus on the work ahead of him.

Priorities in order, he fixed his mind on a dual mission as unwavering as his path behind the emergency vehicle. He had a family to patch together. And a niggling question to solve.

Why had the van swerved deliberately toward Rena's car, rather than away?

Chapter 3

Tucked into her hospital bed, Rena extended her arm for the nurse's routine blood pressure check, antiseptic air making her long for the scents of home and the comfort of her own bed to gather her thoughts. Her foot throbbed from the sprain and four stitches, but her baby was okay and that's all that really mattered.

And J.T.?

She would face the fallout with him soon enough, once everyone left. Doctors, crewdogs, their spouses. There hadn't been a minute to talk between all the visitors and giving police statements during what was turning into the longest evening of her life.

Longest?

Well, except for when she'd waited to hear if her husband had been located after his emergency landing in Rubistan. Since J.T. was the only married crew member, the squadron commander had come to her house along with another flier's wife to tell her...

The plane had gone missing. Shot down. A special ops reconnaissance helicopter had been deployed. Hours had felt like years.

Okay, so this was the second longest evening in her life.

Tap. Tap.

Rena looked toward the door, adjusted her hospital gown. "Come in."

The door creaked open, a blond head peeking around— Julia Dawson, the wife of the previous squadron commander, an approachable down-to-earth woman in spite of their husbands' differing ranks. "Hey, there. Is it okay to visit now?"

The nurse patted Rena's arm. "Everything looks good. I'll come back later for the rest so you can visit with your friend." She circled round the empty bed in the semiprivate room on her way to the door. "Buzz if you need anything."

"Thank you." She definitely could use a friend today more than anything the hospital offered.

Canvas bag swinging from her shoulder, Julia rushed inside and swooped over for a quick hug, already lighting toward the closest chair before Rena could blink.

The leggy blond plopped into a seat beside the bed, one foot tucked under her, casually, just like her unassuming jean overalls. "Are you okay? Really? It scared me to death when I got to the support group meeting and heard what happened. I mean, God, just hours ago we were picking up Chris's car at the shop, talking about the guest speaker for tonight's meeting."

"I'm fine. Really. Just achy and shaken, but okay. I hope the meeting went ahead without me."

Julia waggled her hand. "The speaker talked, but who could listen? We were worried."

A regular at the base support group meetings for parents of special-needs children, Julia attended because her son had been born with Down syndrome. The weekly gatherings had forged a friendship with Julia that went beyond their husbands' shared profession.

The friendship between the two women had deepened into an unbreakable bond the evening Julia waited with Rena for news about J.T. Heaven only knew what it had cost the woman to stay that night, since Julia had lost her first husband to a crash.

Rena's fingers clenched around the sterile white blanket. She could never repay the gift of her comforting presence. Of course, Julia insisted friendship was priceless.

"Oh, before I forget." Julia leaned to scoop her oversize canvas bag from the floor and rummaged inside. She pulled out a lemon-yellow gift bag. "Present for you."

"You didn't need to do this. But thank you."

Julia's blue eyes twinkled as she thrust the bag forward. "Open it."

Rena grasped the top. The bag clanked and she tucked a cradling palm underneath before she peeked inside to find…

"Nail polish?" Lots of it. In a rainbow assortment of colors. "How fun!"

And unusual, but then Julia Dawson was one of the most refreshingly unconventional people she'd been blessed with knowing.

"Soon you won't be able to see your toes." Julia wriggled her toes in her Birkenstocks, blue sparkly nails glinting. "So you might as well enjoy them now."

The bag clanked to Rena's lap. "Word got around about my pregnancy that fast?"

"Bo's a walking megaphone. Half the squadron's out there checking up on you and congratulating Tag."

Great. Just what she needed, more tension heaped on him before their discussion. "How thoughtful."

"Are you sure nothing's wrong?" Julia straightened, her sandaled foot swinging from under her to the floor. "Should I call the nurse?"

"No need. I'm fine. Just worried about J.T."

"He's holding up well. Although he's worried about you, too, and driving the police crazy with his push for more manpower checking out the accident. They're convinced it was probably a drunk driver."

"Hmm." That explained why J.T. hadn't been in to see her yet. His absence hurt more than she wanted to admit when she should be grateful for the temporary reprieve.

"I hadn't told him about the baby yet," Rena blurted. Why had she spilled that? At least Julia could be trusted not to gossip.

"Oh no."

"Oh yes."

"Men don't like secrets."

Rena knotted her fingers tighter in the blanket. "Nope."

Julia looked down and away, fidgeted with an arrangement of daisies and carnations by the bed. "I thought since you were pregnant that meant you two had reconciled."

"Brief reunion when he returned from Rubistan. And well—" shrug "—here I am. A knocked-up forty-year-old."

Julia abandoned the flowers and leaned in for another hug, held tight for an extra minute. "Ah, sweetie, I'm so sorry things aren't happier for you right now."

Rena fought the sting of tears that couldn't be totally attributed to hormones. "He's going to want to come home because of this."

Julia eased back. "And you don't want that?"

"Things were bad before. How will they magically get better when I know he's only there because I'm pregnant?"

"Raising a kid alone is tough." Julia and her current husband had in fact married for their children from previous marriages, both finding single parenthood overwhelming. And somehow they'd discovered love. Except they'd been friends first, with common dreams and hopes.

Rena's marriage of convenience had started with no such foundation.

Still, the woman's words dinged Rena's resolve. So many years had passed since she'd brought a baby into the world. Did she even have the energy to chase a toddler around the house again? And late-night feedings for a newborn. It had all been hard enough even with J.T.'s help.

She couldn't actually be considering...

Of course, her emotions weren't clear-cut. Being ready to sign divorce papers didn't erase twenty-two years of history with the man. He was the father of her children. She'd once loved him.

Now she didn't know what she felt for him anymore. Their marriage had crumbled slowly over twenty-two years from the stress of job separations, financial strains followed by his dogged determination not to touch her income.

She'd been on the fence when she tossed him out six months ago. But when he'd left her at a time they should have clung to each other more than ever, she'd known. They didn't have what it took for the long haul. The children had been their only common link.

Well, that and hot sex.

"J.T. and I *are* getting a divorce. Of course, we'll have to redo the divorce papers anyway to include the new baby."

"You don't have to do anything but take care of yourself. It's been a nightmarish few months for you two. Give yourself time to let it all settle out. Nothing has to be decided today or even tomorrow. Paint your nails to pretty up that injured foot. Let us pamper you." Julia waved the air over Rena's toes peeking free from the Ace bandage wrap. "It's not like you can get around much anyway."

Sit still with nothing to do but count her failures? Ugh. She'd spent years busy bringing up her children, trying to build a marriage, hoping if she filled enough hours of the day she wouldn't see everything that was missing in her life.

In her marriage.

Sitting still with nothing to do but think about all the things she'd worked to ignore was a daunting proposition.

Almost as daunting as the impending showdown with her husband.

J.T. turned the page, reading with a lone corner light while Rena slept. The hospital halls outside stayed silent in the early night but for the occasional rattle of a passing cart.

He couldn't bring himself to wake her yet for the talk. Like he could have roused her anyway. Pregnant women slept like the dead.

Dead.

Pregnant.

Baby.

Breathe, damn it. Forcing breaths in and out, he loosened his grip on the bending paperback. Escape through the words.

Who can control his fate?

J.T. reread the line from Shakespeare's *Othello,* let it roll around in his head for an extra second. He liked the old Bard's take on life. Human nature stayed the same. Warriors such as Macbeth and Othello and Mark Anthony faced universal issues still relevant in modern day.

The horrors of war.

Getting screwed over by a woman.

Which brought him right back to Rena. No escape through reading tonight. J.T. let himself look at her, something he used to do for hours on end while she slept. Not so easy to do now that he parked his ass in an apartment at the end of the workday.

Her dark curls splayed over the stark white pillowcase. Odd how he still forgot how short she was until she slept and he realized what a small portion of the bed she occupied. A few more curves than when he'd first met her, but the softness from bearing their children only made him want to lose himself inside her all the more. She was a striking woman.

Age had been kinder to her than he had over the years. He'd taken much and given little back.

Well, he sure as hell wouldn't let her down when it came to her safety. Again, he studied the even rise and fall of the hospital blanket, reassured himself she'd come through the day alive. Albeit, still pale under her normally bronzed Greek complexion inherited from her family.

Her family…

Damn but they'd been furious that he'd knocked up their little princess Irena. But the minute he'd seen her—so full of energy and fire—he'd felt as if somebody flicked on a light switch. Colors splashed over a world that had been a monochromatic routine of work, eat, sleep, start over again.

For one time in his life, he'd ignored the practical choice and he'd gone after her. Full force. No holds barred, he had to have her.

He braced his boot on the end of her bed. He still wanted her, even when he was so damn pissed the top of his head felt ready to pop off.

Which pissed him off all the more.

Yanking his eyes away from temptation, he opened his pocket-paperback Shakespeare again. Wouldn't the crewdogs have a field day with that? Yeah, he liked Shakespeare, the classics, even poetry sometimes. He enjoyed the rhythm of how the words went together.

Reading did for him what meditation likely did for other folks. Relaxed him. But he balked at the point of the whole woo-hoo yoga idea. Not to mention the loss of control.

No need for yoga. Iambic pentameter would get the job done for him tonight.

He'd started reading more when Rena went back to college and he thumbed through a few of her books, paused, enjoyed. When others were around, he still kept to more pop fiction selections, like a Tom Clancy novel. The Bard, however, he saved for moments alone when he needed to quiet the roaring frustration in his head.

After the crash in Rubistan and his final split with Rena, he'd worked his way through Shakespeare's whole damn historical canon.

Footsteps sounded outside the door seconds before a soft tap, followed by the door creaking open. A slice of light slanted across the room before Chris tucked his head inside. "Dad?"

J.T. snapped his book shut and held one finger to his mouth. "Your mom's sleeping," he whispered, shoving the book into the thigh pocket of his flight suit. "Come on in, but keep it quiet."

An almost comical request given how deeply Rena slept.

"Oh, sure," Chris whispered in response, shuffling inside, untied laces on his gym shoes dragging as he squeaked across sterile tile.

The door shooshed closed. Ball cap backward over his dark curls, his son slouched against the wall between the rolling tray and window. His clothes hung off his wiry body, which wouldn't in and of itself be annoying except for the fact the boy wore his cargo shorts so low it was a miracle the things stayed up.

And being angry about his teenager's clothes made him wonder how the hell he would handle it all over again sixteen years from now. "Hey, pal. Where've you been? Were you working overtime at the restaurant?"

"Nope. Just hanging out with Shelby and Murdoch. Listening to tunes. Eating pizza." His guilty gaze skated to the hospital bed. "Sorry I wasn't around sooner, but Mom's okay, right? Mrs. Dawson wasn't holding anything back when she came home and told me, was she?"

"Your mother's going to be fine. Only a sprain and some stitches. She'll be on bed rest for a couple of weeks, but no long-term problems.'' Relief still pounded through him, fears giving way and making room for questions. ''Why didn't you have your cell phone on?''

''I dunno. Battery ran down, I guess.'' He swept his ball cap off, adjusted the fit and tugged it on again. ''That's probably good for her, huh? Resting.''

''Yes.''

''So everything's okay? With *everything,* I mean.''

Suspicion nipped. ''Everything what?''

''Uh, you know, the baby. Uh…'' He rushed to add a little too quickly, ''Mrs. Dawson told me.''

He scuffed a gym shoe again just as he'd done at nine years old when lying about dumping his sister's makeup into the sewer system. *Squeak. Squeak.*

J.T. pinned him with a parental stare and knowledge. ''You knew already.''

Chris stuffed his hands in his pockets. ''Geez, Dad, and Nikki calls *me* a bonehead. How could you not notice Mom's getting fat?''

''Good God, son. Shh!'' J.T. shot a quick glance at Rena to make sure she was still sleeping. ''Don't let her hear you say the f word.''

''Sorry.'' Shuffle. Squeak. ''I figured it wasn't my place to mention anything and Mom didn't need to be upset in her, you know, condition. Guess this means you're coming home.''

He intended to, but no need to raise Chris's hopes. ''Your mother and I need to talk first.''

Chris slouched, muttering something that sounded like a surly ''About damn time.''

J.T. bit back the urge for a reprimand on a day already full of enough tension. ''Son, I'm sorry to say your car's totaled. The van that hit it wiped it out.''

Chris paled under the bronzed complexion he'd inherited

from his mother along with the head of dark curls. "To-taled?"

"Afraid so. Insurance will cover everything after the deductible, but it may take a while for the check to come through. There isn't money for a replacement until we get the settlement." And didn't that bite a chunk out of his pride, not being able to provide for his family.

"Sure. I understand. It's just good Mom and the baby weren't hurt."

The accident kicked right back to the forefront of his memory. He couldn't let the emotions shake his focus. The cops hadn't been much help and wouldn't be unless he could give them something more to go on. Figuring out what the odd black-and-red emblem on the bumper represented would be a good start.

Once he got his family settled.

J.T. stood, leaned against the opposite side of the window frame as his son. "Are you all right?"

"Yeah. Sure. Why wouldn't I be?"

Chris's tone and chalky face sent parental antennae on high alert. With deployments keeping him away so much, time with his son lately was scarce. What might he have missed? "Is there any reason someone would come after you? A gang from school?"

Meeting his father's gaze dead on, no shuffling, Chris answered, "I'm not mixed up in a gang at school."

Slowly, J.T. nodded, believed. "Okay, then." Still, he wasn't taking any chances on leaving Chris alone yet. "Bo's been waiting at the house in case we didn't find you first to tell you about your mom's accident. He's going to crash there on the sofa for the night so I can stay up here."

Chris straightened away from the wall. Anger snapped from his eyes, his temper another inherited legacy from his mother. "Geez, Dad, I'm sixteen. I can stay overnight on my own. It's not like I'm gonna throw some drug-flowing orgy while you're gone or anything.''

God forbid.

"Bo will crash on the sofa," J.T. restated, unbending. Arguing never solved anything.

His son slouched back again, layers of clothes rippling over his lean body. "Okay, okay, stupid me thinking anybody could have an opinion.''

While he sure as hell didn't intend to justify himself to a teenager, he needed to remember his son wasn't a kid anymore. Some explanation might go a long way for easing tension. "Chris."

"Yeah, what?" He stared at his shoes.

"It's been a crappy day, son. Cut me some slack.''

"Sorry," he mumbled without meeting his father's eyes.

No, his son wasn't a kid anymore.

The teen years hadn't seemed as difficult with easygoing Nikki. But there hadn't been a marriage breakup in the works.

Since he'd be around more helping out while Rena recovered, he also needed to make use of the extra time with Chris. "What do you say when I bring your mom home from the hospital, we take a couple of hours and lift some weights?"

Not a bad suggestion and the only thing he could remember doing with his old man in between double-shift-work hours.

"Lift weights?" Chris shrugged. "Yeah, sure. Whatever."

J.T. fished in his flight-suit pocket and pulled out a ten-dollar bill. "Here, get something to eat on the way home."

"Thanks. See ya." Chris took the money and shuffled across the room, gym shoes squeaking long after the door closed behind him.

Dropping back into the recliner, J.T. snagged his book again, not that he expected to get much reading done, just pass time while he prepped for battle. As much as Rena might prefer full-out confrontations, he knew gaining ground back into their house would call for a more covert operation.

Rena grappled through layers of sleepy fog, blinked until her eyes adjusted to the sparse light in the narrow room that was private only because no other patient occupied the bed beside her. The antiseptic smell churned her stomach, but she welcomed the reminder of a healthy pregnancy.

A pregnancy now out in the open.

Her gaze skipped to J.T. sprawled in the corner chair, reading lamp on, paperback gripped in his broad hands. She couldn't make out the cover, but imagined it was whatever military-action bestseller hit the shelves recently.

J.T. filled her eyes as completely as he filled the chair. Such a large man shouldn't be able to move so silently, yet he did. Always. Magnetically. Until her world narrowed to dark hair, muscles and slow-blinking brooding eyes.

As tempting as it was to stare at his rugged handsomeness instead of dealing with real-life worries, she was through repeating past mistakes. She couldn't hide from the truth any longer. There wouldn't be a more private time than now for their discussion. "Hi, J.T. Good book?"

He glanced up, studied her without speaking for four clicks of the second hand on the institutional black-and-white wall clock. Closing his book, he righted the recliner. Both boots thudded on the tile floor. "I hope I didn't disturb you with the light."

"Not at all." She'd slept beside him in bed while he read many a night.

Gulp.

Where was some crushed ice and a water pitcher when a woman needed them? "How long have I been out?"

J.T. flipped his wrist to check his watch, a gift from their daughter, complete with stopwatch and listings of multiple time zones for his flights. "Just an hour and forty minutes.

Doc says to wake you up every couple of hours through the night. The nurse will check in, too.''

Which gave them twenty more uninterrupted minutes to talk in the quiet intimacy of a bedroom that wasn't packed with memories. The hospital at least made for comforting neutral ground for their discussion. Might as well confront things straight up. ''I'm sorry for not telling you about the baby sooner.''

Guarded eyes almost hid nearly banked anger. He shifted, slow, silent, tucking the book in the thigh pocket of his flight suit. ''Why didn't you?''

Why?

The truth blindsided her while her defenses were laid low from the accident. Because she'd wanted J.T. to come home on his own. For her. Something that, for the first time, she completely accepted would never happen.

The last of her dreams, hope, love died. There was nothing left for her now but to strengthen her resolve to protect her children and her heart. ''I was still reeling from hearing you'd been shot down and whatever happened to you in Rubistan, trying to sort through what happened to us afterward. Pretty difficult to do with so little information from your end.''

Rena's words sucker punched him. Leave it to his outspoken wife never to pull punches. She stared back at him defiantly, daring him to talk about Rubistan.

He didn't need to think about it, much less talk it out. He'd lived it. Dealt with what happened, and wanted to move on, not bring everything up again until the top of his head blew off. He'd walked away before rather than—

Ah, she was pushing him to walk now.

Not gonna happen. ''I'm assuming the baby was conceived after my return then. You don't look far enough along to have gotten pregnant before we split.''

Although, good God, Chris was right. She did have a slight bulge under the white sheet. How could he have missed it?

She would be three months along. While carrying Chris, she'd been unable to button her pants by that stage.

Damn. He *was* a bonehead not to have noticed or even considered the possibility.

"Yes, it was that night. I missed a pill while you were gone. I was...upset. Days jumbled in my head."

Her pain from then radiated just as powerfully now. Pain he'd caused.

He needed to regroup. Now. He turned his back, reached for the water pitcher, pouring a cup for himself, another for Rena.

"J.T.? It was an accident."

"Of course it was." He jerked around to face her, passed her a water glass. "I never thought otherwise."

Did she really think so little of him that she expected recriminations? Jesus. He might have hurt her, but never like that.

Brown eyes wary, she took the cup from him without touching. "You are *not* moving home because of the baby. Let's get that straight right now. Our reasons for splitting still stand."

He leaned back against the wall, crossing one booted foot over the other. "What were those reasons again?"

"Don't be an ass."

"Ah, reason number one." He drank half the cup of water in one swallow, icy cold along heated anger.

She'd called him a major ass during their fight six months ago about the number-two strain on their marriage. Money.

"I'm sorry." Rena's voice softened. She rolled the cup between her palms. "My temper is right up there on the reason list. I drive you crazy. I know that."

"Oh yeah, babe—" a slow smile crept over his face "—you've definitely always driven me crazy."

Well, hell. So much for smart strategies. But the unstoppable spark between them always had messed with their minds. Apparently still did.

"J.T., damn it." She slammed her cup down on the end table beside a basket of flowers. "That's what got us into this mess before. And again now."

His smile faded. "Don't worry. I'm not planning to pressure you about getting back together." No pressure about it. Slow and steady won the day with his wife.

"You're not?"

"No." Think strategy, not how much easier it would be to kiss her quiet. Not about how tight the knot twisted in his stomach over the thought that even if he made it home, they weren't any better off than before. "You made yourself clear when you pitched my barbells and books out on the lawn six months ago."

And the reason for that final fight? They'd argued over the flipping family Christmas vacation, for God's sake. She'd insisted his lengthy deployments were taking a toll, making growing apart too easy. His fault. He knew it.

So he'd offered to take leave. Not good enough. She'd wanted to rent a cabin in the mountains, something she insisted they could afford now that she was working.

Hell. As if he needed it thrown in his face that he couldn't provide for his family on his own. As if he needed reminding of all the things she'd had growing up. Things he couldn't come close to giving her.

A fact that had been stewing in his gut for twenty-two years.

"Well, J.T., tossing those possessions on the lawn was just the start of venting problems years in the making. Three months ago proved that." She gripped the length of her hair in her hands and began twisting it into a knot on the back of her head. "We'll just draw up a new set of divorce papers."

His eyes tracked the moves of her hands against her glossy curls. He'd always wondered how the hell she did that trick with her hair, had watched her hundreds of times, the memory of those strands gliding through his fingers never failing to make him hard.

He finished his water, pitched his cup in the trash. "Not until you're up and moving again. The doc said you need to stay off your feet for at least two weeks."

She paused midtwist. "What happened to doctor-patient confidentiality?"

"We're married." For better or worse, they'd vowed. Vows that were about to be broken if he didn't ignore the chemistry and put a stop to this. "I already logged in a call to my commander for a lighter schedule while you recover."

"J.T.," she warned, arms reaching up as she finished securing her hair. "Remember that *you* left the last time. I'm not the only one who said we don't have a chance."

And that's what he got for talking. All the more reason to guard his words, so she couldn't throw them back in his face later.

He plowed ahead. "I can't be away from the squadron totally now." The drug surveillance flights with the feds were too sensitive to pass off to anyone else. Since he was already in the loop from the overseas mission, he'd been tapped for the flights. Bringing another loadmaster up to speed this late would cost valuable days anyway.

What a helluva time to have a family crisis. "But all my flights will be at night, when Chris is around."

He ignored the burn in his gut that told him those flights would only bring more stress to his wife if she knew the truth about the mission. But there were so many things he could never share about his job.

However, since C-17 night flights were common around Charleston, his wife wouldn't question late takeoffs any more than anyone else in Charleston. All of which made the craft the logical choice to cart the DEA's surveillance equipment—much the same as used during the fateful flight in Rubistan.

With a little luck—okay, a lot of luck—the high-tech equipment loaded down on those pallets would eventually cough up the crucial link to who the hell in the States had sold them out overseas.

And more importantly, how.

J.T. tamped down the twitch of conscience over keeping it from her. After all, he'd had twenty-two years' practice. "I'll be asleep during the day, so you don't have to worry about me being underfoot. But I'll still be on call for whatever you need. Simple. Reasonable."

"I'll manage just fine."

"How do you plan to take care of yourself while Chris is in school? Nikki's exams start next week, so she can't help."

J.T. searched for signs of Rena weakening but she was too preoccupied playing with her hair and driving him crazy. Low-blow time. "You need to be careful for the baby."

Rena sagged back into her pillow. He'd won. "God, J.T., you don't fight back often, but when you do, you sure fight dirty."

"I save it for the battles worth winning." His victory felt hollow as he inventoried the worry, fears, in his proud wife's gaze.

"Fine." Her hands fell back to her lap, a lone curl sneaking free to bob against her chin. "Whatever. You're right and you know it. Thank you for the help."

Where had her fight gone? Seeing Rena deflated, defeated, worried him more than the purpling bruise on her forehead. But he couldn't afford to back down, as dangerous as pressing ahead too hard and fast. "I'll take some stuff back over to the house in the morning."

"Why not now?"

"Because I'm staying here."

Starch inched back up her spine. "But Chris—"

"Bo's staying over." He dropped into the chair beside her bed. "I'm not budging on this one."

Fire heated her brown eyes and J.T. rushed to forestall her argument. "You owe me right now for not telling me about the baby sooner." A truth that seared his gut. Canting forward, elbows on the edge of her mattress, he continued, "Now go to sleep and I'll read my book. It's not like I haven't watched you sleep before."

Her breath caressed his face.

Her face only inches away.

The familiar scent of her favorite peppermint mouthwash and flowery perfume washed through his senses along with images of sharing a bed. And somehow it didn't matter that they were in a hospital, or that divorce papers had already been drawn up.

He wanted her. She wanted him. With an inevitable intensity that had almost incinerated them both three months ago.

Tears sheened her brown eyes. From hormones? Or another reason?

Something cracked inside him and he didn't want to examine the fissure too closely to see what lay beneath. But he couldn't stop the urge to take her in his arms, not for passion, just to hold her—

She flinched away.

And he hadn't even moved yet. Apparently she'd read his intent in his eyes and didn't want his comfort. Fine. Okay. No surprise. His hands fisted against the mattress.

She blinked away moist emotions. "Just so we're clear. It's two weeks. And during that time you won't be watching me sleep."

"Roger." He read her loud and clear. Not that he'd expected to park his boots under her bed—yet—but it still smacked being reminded of the fact.

Emphatically.

Leaning back in the hospital chair, he fished his book from his pocket, the weight of her eyes on him a heavy reminder of all their unfinished business.

He resisted the urge to look back up, which would only instigate a conversation he sure as hell didn't want. Strategy. Too much was at stake here with only fourteen days to persuade her to give things another try. Again. He'd soothed her temper in less than that often enough before. Problem was, the determined glint returning to her eyes made it totally clear.

He wouldn't be able to get naked with Rena to win her over this time.

Chapter 4

Two weeks alone with J.T.? Gulp. Surely, given all that was at stake now, she could hold strong against the temptation to ditch her clothes every time those long legs of his lumbered into the room.

Still, the upcoming fourteen days of intimacy scrolled through Rena's mind as endlessly as the winding roads through her tree-packed subdivision on her way home from the hospital. Brick and wooden tract houses whipped past her passenger window, a much safer view than staring at her hot husband driving. Even peripheral glimpses of him rocked her thoughts like hanging ferns at the mercy of a Charleston tropical storm.

Nope. She wasn't looking at him. Just staring at his reflection in the passenger window.

J.T.'s window open, gusts puffed inside to flap his unbuttoned, loose Hawaiian shirt over a white T-shirt. Unlike Chris's baggy style, J.T. kept his T-shirt tucked into his khaki shorts, neatly leaving his trim waist and flat abs right there for her to admire even in profile reflection.

She pulled her gaze away, down, found no relief there, either. Thickly muscled legs worked the clutch, brake, gas—shorts putting plenty of tanned skin on display. Her fingers curled at the memory of exploring the bulging cut of tendons, the masculine texture of bristly hair.

Rounding a corner slowly, careful as he cruised past an overgrown magnolia, J.T. draped his wrist over the old Ford's steering wheel, a truck he'd rebuilt himself as he'd done with their fixer-upper home. This talented man could repair anything through sheer determination, ingenuity and sweat equity.

If only relationships were as easy to maintain.

Their two-story white wood house eased into view. Vehicles packed their driveway—her sedan, Julia Dawson's minivan, Bo's Jeep, Nikki's compact car. Welcome buffers against the tension so she would spend less time alone with J.T.

Good, right?

And how could she not be touched by Nikki's visit? Her eldest had come home to check on her. So sweet, her easygoing daughter with an oversize heart. The breakup had hurt her most, even though she showed it least. "Nikki's here?"

J.T. eased off the gas pedal, cruising to a stop on the narrow street. "She drove in this morning for the day. She's heading out after supper for an all-night study session. I didn't have a chance to tell you with all the out-processing at the hospital. You ready to go in?"

She nodded, conversation time apparently over for her husband. Looking back, she wondered now if they'd been doomed from the start to a life of miscommunication followed by quiet distance—Tag's family full of stoicism and silence, hers reverberating with chatter but so much of it lies and anger. Even if she knew better now, with her newfound counselor perspective she could see what a shaky foundation they'd built from the start.

For this baby, for her other two children, she would hold strong. She would model healthy relationships in hopes of helping them build ones of their own.

J.T. ambled around the hood of the truck to her side, opened the door, filled her eyes. He extended his arms, Hawaiian shirt flapping in the breeze, crisp white cotton stretching across an endless chest she could lose herself against.

He couldn't really expect to carry her? He waited, arms out. Unmoving.

She knew he could do it, just wasn't sure she could bear the heartbreaking reminder of other passionate trips in his arms that ended oh so differently than this one would. "Would you pass me the crutches from the back, please? I can make it up there on my own."

"Damn it, Rena." His eyes snapped along with his voice. "Is it really that distasteful to have me touch you?"

His arms dropped, hands hooked on his hips, narrow hips, his fingers pointing a direct arrow to—

Her eyes jerked up. Heat delivered a double whammy to her cheeks, then pooled lower. Hotter. "What?"

"I know you can maneuver around on crutches. And I realize the doctor said everything looks okay with the pregnancy. But you know as well as I do that I can carry you inside. The strain will be less than your trying to maneuver with crutches. Why exert yourself? Unless my touching you is so damned awful."

"Oh."

"Yeah. Oh." He hooked a hand on the open doorway, just over her head. "I'm sorry if my touching you is a problem."

"It's not a problem." Not how he meant, anyway.

"Good. We've always put the kids first. This baby shouldn't be any different."

Rena swung her legs to the side and out, waiting. Bracing herself for the feel of his hands on her body, the unyielding wall of his muscled chest against the give of her own softer flesh.

Broad palms slid under her, one arm around her back, the other under her knees. By instinct, her arm glided up and around his neck. Her fingers found the bristly shortness of the hair along the nape of his neck. Only a soft grunt from him indicated any reaction.

And the reaction wasn't from exertion.

Even with the few extra pregnancy pounds she'd packed on, carrying her posed no hardship for her honed husband. He kept in tip-top shape for the physical aspects of his job that even more mechanized cargo holds couldn't completely eradicate.

So many times she'd stood in the doorway leading to the garage and watched him lift weights, his muscles straining and shifting under sweat-sheened skin. Determination and focus. Strength.

She drew in a shaky breath and found the scent of him, fuller, stronger. How could she have forgotten the familiar potency of his smell—pine soap and musky man? Clean. Arousing.

Pure J.T.

What the hell was with the immutable, near-insane physical attraction she felt for this man? Would she spend the rest of her life starving for his touch?

A daunting thought.

His gym shoes thudded along the flagstone path and up the wooden porch steps. Already voices drifted through the door along with someone playing show tunes on the piano. The lace curtains rippled with the movement of bodies inside.

Only a few seconds more in J.T.'s arms. A few seconds more for the memories to tempt her. Unstoppable images so she didn't have to waste energy trying to tamp them down.

Yes, she and J.T. had hurt each other, done so many things wrong, but some things right. And at the moment, all those beautiful, special, right things about her marriage blossomed through her mind. Did he remember them, too? She couldn't change the past, but she had control over the present, and she intended to make sure J.T. carried something positive with him from their years together.

Her hand fell to stop his on the doorknob. "J.T.?"

He peered down at her. "Problem?"

She squeezed his hand, let her fingers linger in spite of his stunned eyes widening. "No doubt we're wrong for each other in a hundred different ways. But never, never have I found your touch distasteful. Far from it."

His fingers twitched against her, tightened, the only sign he'd heard her as his face stayed stoic. Unemotional. Handsome ruggedness carved in granite.

Still, he'd heard her, and her words meant something to him. Her defenses slipped, and she didn't have the heart to recall them, instead allowed the need building during their ride home to bloom.

She brought her hand up to rest on his neck again. "I thought you already knew that, except now I'm realizing maybe with everything else going on, you somehow forgot. Or wondered. And even though we both realize it's not enough, I just wanted you to know that we did share something mutual."

A smile dented a dimple in his face, so incongruous, and therefore all the more enticing. "Thanks, babe."

Her eyes fell to his mouth, lingered on the sensual fullness of his lower lip. She waited, wanted, even as pride wouldn't let her make the move forward. But if he leaned? She definitely wouldn't move away.

J.T. struggled to control the heat surging through him over something as simple as holding his wife. Damn it, he was not going to kiss her, no matter how good her soft hands and softer body felt against him.

He steeled his resolve. Steel? More like tinfoil, which meant he'd better haul ass inside. Pronto.

He twisted the doorknob. Disappointment flickered through her Godiva-rich eyes. Resolve shredded into foil confetti.

The door jerked open beneath his hand, snapping the mood. Thank you, Lord.

Chris lounged in the open portal with a bag of Cheetos clutched in his hand, fingertips deep orange from munching. "What took you so long? I'm starving and folks brought food that I can't eat until you get here."

J.T. looked away, up. "In a minute, son. How about unload your mother's things from the truck first."

"Sure," he answered through a fresh mouthful of cheese curls.

J.T. angled sideways, guiding Rena's trim legs over the threshold first. Over the threshold. Just as he'd done when they were young, nervous, full of plans.

Ready to break in the new mattress in their efficiency apartment.

Her fingers twisted in his cotton shirt, her touch as hot now as it had been then. Except today, she could hardly stand to look at him. She focused on the hanging ivy that, damn it all, he'd forgotten to water.

He stopped in the middle of their overflowing living room. Bo shared the piano bench with Nikki, playing the right hand from the open score sheet while Nikki plucked out the left. Well, if Nikki's plunkings could be called playing, his tomboy daughter always preferring running track to running scales.

And if Bo didn't move his ass a little farther down that bench—

"Mom!" Nikki bolted up with an athletic grace gained from hours on the university soccer field. Thank God for soccer scholarships, even partials. "Ohmigod, are you okay? Dad didn't call me until this morning or I would have come sooner. Probably why he didn't call me. Geez, like I couldn't drive after dark.''

"I'm fine, hon," Rena rushed to interrupt. "The crutches are just awkward right now.''

"Okay, good, that's what Bo said when he filled me in on the latest, but I thought maybe he was soft-soaping things so I wouldn't worry.''

J.T.'s scowl deepened. Bo? She'd been talking with Bo?

So what if Nikki was already older than Rena had been when they married? He wanted his daughter to have a chance to be young. And while he liked Bo in the workplace, no way was Nikki getting near that squadron player renowned for wooing women with his guitar and singing. And apparently the piano now, too.

"J.T., you can put me down now. J.T.?" Rena tapped his chest lightly.

"Where?" he asked.

"Chair.''

"Ottoman?''

"Yes, please.''

As he lowered her carefully into the overstuffed floral chair, he couldn't help but notice how easily they'd fallen back into marital shorthand conversation.

Footsteps sounded from the kitchen, down the hall, soft padding steps, seconds before Julia Dawson strode into the living room, carrying a blond-haired toddler on her hip. "Hey there, sweetie. I've plugged in a Crock-Pot full of chili. There's also a platter of buffalo wings.''

While the two women exchanged greetings and food-reheating instructions, he tried like hell to ignore the warmth of Rena's calf as he arranged a pillow under her foot.

"Don't thank me," Julia insisted. "Thank my multi-talented husband. Zach made it all before he headed in to work for a couple of hours. I'm only the delivery person. A good thing, huh?'' said the lady carpenter, more comfortable with a hammer than a spatula.

Rena inhaled, bringing her breasts closer to J.T.'s face. ''Everything smells great. You really know how to rev those pregnancy cravings into overdrive.''

He finished adjusting the pillow under her foot, his fingers lingering above her ankle. Oh yeah, he remembered those pregnancy cravings of hers well. All of them, especially how her sensual appetites increased, too.

Julia hitched her son higher on her hip. ''Well, I need to hit the road. Patrick's about ready for his afternoon nap.''

Bo swung his legs around the piano bench, rising. ''Little fella looks like he's getting heavy. How about I buckle him into the car seat for you, ma'am?''

A ploy to impress Nikki? Or was he just being a nice guy? Bo certainly seemed at ease with the baby—and with flaunting that ''talent'' right under Nikki's nose with a smile and wink.

Down, Lieutenant.

J.T. followed Julia and Bo out the door as Chris jogged past inside with a small suitcase and basket of flowers in his hands, Cheetos bag in his teeth. J.T. plowed ahead. He might not be able to do much about his wife, but he could make damn well sure a certain lieutenant kept his musical ''talents'' zipped up tight.

Rena watched her husband stride out the door after Bo and Julia, J.T.'s mercurial moods unsettling to say the least. One minute he seemed ready to kiss her. The next he was Sergeant Scowl. Then Mr. Sensitive with the footstool. Then back to Sergeant Scowl.

And she was definitely Counselor Cranky. Knowing her irritability came from pure sexual frustration didn't help.

Nikki plopped down on the ottoman, long legs folded to the side. ''Do you need anything? A glass of water?''

"I'm fine for now, hon." Rena reached to tuck a stray strand of her daughter's chin-length bob behind her ears. If this sleek, earthy changeling didn't look so much like her father, Rena might wonder what rainbow Nikki had slid down into the hospital bassinet marked Baby Girl Price. "Thanks for coming home to check on me with exams starting."

"We don't all get much time to hang out together in the same house anymore," she said, her tone light, her clear gray eyes piercing. "Sorry I have to go back after supper. But where would I sleep, anyway, with Dad's stuff piled up in my old room?"

Easygoing kid? Not always. Nikki landed her sly digs in with the best of them. "Then let's enjoy this afternoon and the chili before you go. Your father's home to help until I'm on my feet since you and Chris have school. Nothing more and you know that. I'm sorry, hon, but that's the way it is."

"Like you helped him through after he got back from Rubistan." She nodded her bob into a steady swing. "Right. Got it. Lots of helping going on for two people who say they don't want to be married anymore."

Rena folded her arms over her increasing waistline. "Back off, kiddo. I'm the mom. You're not. Boundaries. Respect them."

"Sure thing." She reached to put her hand over her mother's crossed arms. "Hey, cool news about the baby."

"Thank you, hon." Nikki might be pissed, hurt even, but she never held a grudge. Rena envied her daughter the ability to let concerns slide off her. "You're okay with this? Not all embarrassed by your old pregnant mom?"

"Old? You've gotta be kidding me." She patted her mother's tiny bulge again. "And of course I'm okay with the kid. If you're happy about the baby, then I'm happy."

Rena placed her hand over her daughter's and let herself enjoy the momentary peace of simply celebrating the new life in their world. She blinked back tears.

"Oh Geez, Mom. Hormones, huh?" Chuckling, Nikki drew her hand away. "Have cravings kicked in yet?"

"God, yes." She swiped the back of her wrist over her watery eyes. "With a vengeance. I can smell those chicken wings from here."

Nikki's gray eyes flecked with sparks of mischief. "Be nice to me and *maybe* I'll fix you a plate once they're done heating."

"Brat."

"That's me. Always in trouble." Always in motion, too, Nikki scooped three granola-bar wrappers—starving Chris's, no doubt—off the coffee table, wadded them into a ball before lobbing them into a wicker trash basket. "How far along are you?"

What a loaded question since it would reveal the full extent of J.T.'s homecoming. Like her adult daughter wouldn't have guessed anyhow.

"Three months," Rena announced, then waited for the smart-ass comeback. Grown-up kids didn't accept quite as blindly as the little ones.

A knowing smile dimpled her cheek, inherited from her father. "A baby in time for Christmas. Cool."

Rena exhaled. Off the hook for now. Nikki pushed to her feet, starting a long-legged strut out of the room. Rena shifted in the overstuffed chair, adjusted her throbbing ankle on the pillow. She just wanted to get through this bizarre family reunion without an argument. One peaceful gathering. Bone-weary, heartsore and more than a little rattled by the wreck and a short ride in her husband's arms, she didn't have the energy for confrontations before a serious nap.

They could all bolt back buffalo wings and chili and pretend everything was fine. Easy enough to do after twenty-two years' practice.

Nikki paused in the archway leading from the dining area back into the hall. She glanced over her shoulder, patting her own not-pregnant belly. "Oh, and Mom? Way to go, keeping those boundaries in place with Dad three months ago."

Winking, she spun away, glossy hair swinging against her ears with each cocky strut out of sight.

Rena wanted to call her daughter on that statement. Call herself, for that matter. But the brat had a point.

Thumping the minivan roof, J.T. stepped back from Julia Dawson's Windstar. She eased into the street and straightened, clearing the way for Bo's blocked Jeep to leave.

Which the young copilot would do as soon as J.T. addressed one pressing matter.

J.T. jammed his hands in his pockets, dodging strategically planted clumps of flowers in Rena's tropical jungle that would put professional tour gardens to shame. He stopped beside the black Jeep. "Thanks for the help, man."

"No problem." Bo secured the canvas roof for an open-air ride. "Glad I could be here for you."

"You were more than just here for me. I won't forget." True. And he would do anything for this fellow crew member. Except give over his daughter. He wanted easier for his kid than the worries of military life.

A big part of the reason he'd left Rena, and now he had to figure out how to resolve all of that.

"Family's about more than blood relations, you know." Bo stared down at his wrist cast, flexed his scarred fingers poking out. Slowly. No wince. Not that showed anyway. His arm fell to his side heavily. "I owe you."

Spring sun baked J.T.'s head with reminders of a February desert sun in another country. "You don't owe me a thing."

God, he didn't want to talk about that time. Especially not now when he needed his defenses up in full force to work his way past his prickly wife.

"Whatever." Bo's fingers continued to stretch, crook, stretch, crook until the strain lines erased from around the corners of his mouth. The old Bo slid back into place as smoothly as his smile. "Nikki sure has grown—"

"Watch it, *sir*," J.T. growled. "That's my daughter you're talking about."

Bo swallowed his laugh. "Damn, but the old master sergeants know how to make 'sir' sound like an insult."

"Then I guess we're even for the *old* comment."

"Guess so."

Tension eased from his spine. "If you're thinking you owe me something, pay me back by keeping away from my daughter."

"You can relax. Just yanking your chain. Jesus, man, you've got hot buttons so big, it's tough not to push 'em sometimes. No worries, though. I want to keep my other hand out of a cast for a while anyhow, only just got the damn thing off. As fun as it was having those nurses feed me, give me sponge baths..." His baby blues twinkled with devilish intent. "Well, eventually I gotta act, and two casts can get in the way."

"Just so you're not acting with my daughter. She's still a kid in a lot of ways. I want her to have the chance to stay that way a while longer."

"Life has a way of throwing curves fast enough."

J.T. sure as hell agreed, but hadn't expected a heavy comment from the carefree lieutenant. Bo Rokowsky had a rep around the squadron. Never serious. Edgy. Great set of flying hands, but reckless.

As much as J.T. respected restraint, a part of him grieved to see that free spirit stomped out of the young man. Only four or five years older than Nikki in years, but so damn much more in experience now. All the more reason for the copilot to keep his distance. "It's nothing personal. I just don't want any crewdogs sniffing after my baby girl."

Baby girl. What about the new baby? Boy or girl? God willing, healthy.

"Message received about Nikki. I really was just razzing you. Lighten up. I'm totally hung up on my flight attendant."

"This week."

Bo thumped his chest with a fist. "But with my whole heart, dude."

Lightness reestablished. Comfort zone reclaimed. "Well, then, get your sorry ass out of my yard and go call her or something."

"Will do." Bo gripped the steering wheel, fingers poking from the cast while he downshifted gears with his good hand.

He was smiling again, but the new partial cast gleamed white in the afternoon sun. A reminder that hell no, J.T. didn't want his daughter marrying a crewdog like Bo, like himself, just going through the motions since coming home. Both still stuck overseas in their minds…

J.T. flung aside the seat-belt harnesses strapping him into the downed C-17. Through the windscreen, desert, scrubs, jagged peaks, dunes sprawled ahead, offering minimal options for hiding after an emergency landing in potentially hostile territory.

But no sign of rebels or troops yet, either.

Tearing off his headset, he looked to the copilot, Bo, for the prepared evasion plan. Different stages of the mission called for different contingencies to escape until pickup by rescue forces. Forces hopefully already en route.

Bo cinched his survival vest tighter. "We'll run to the right, north, toward the outcropping. Haul ass until we drop. Put distance between us and the plane."

Then they would set up a rescue signal. And pray. "Roger." The affirmation echoed in triplicate from the other crew members.

Scorch, the aircraft commander, cleared his seat and headed out first, followed by Spike—the faux-loadmaster, their undercover OSI special agent and personal time bomb.

J.T. tucked into the narrow stairwell behind Spike, down

into the belly of the craft, popped the side hatch. Critical seconds ticked away. His heartbeat ticked faster, louder. His boots pounded down the metal steps. Still no sign of anybody.

One after the other, four pairs of boots landed on hard-packed desert, already sprinting, each man taking only what he carried in the survival vest. A knife. A pistol. Piss-poor protection against the elements and the enemy.

Fear pounded through him as hard as his heart and running steps. Only an idiot wouldn't be scared. And only a bigger idiot would let it immobilize him.

Sun baked his back, his head, his brain. Rays reflected off sand, even February hot as hell during the day here. If they could only buy enough time for a U.S. rescue chopper to locate them...

Grounding in training, he reviewed the facts on his ISOPREP card—isolated personnel report on file. The ISOPREP gave answers to questions a rescue crew would ask over the radio to positively ID them, to confirm the chopper wasn't being led into a trap.

Questions.

The street from his childhood home.

His mother's maiden name.

Rena's first car. A sleek silver blue BMW, where they'd made out. Made a baby.

Damn it. He spit curses out with sand. He couldn't think about her. About being with her.

Run. Harder. Focus on the three most important elements of survival.

Maintain life.

Maintain honor.

Return.

His feet drummed a steady beat across the desert floor in time with everyone's huffing breaths exhaling more grit-filled curses. Each man's favorite cussword chanted, powered feet faster. His own favorite of the moment spilled free—just like when baby Chris had parroted it back at him from his high chair, Rena behind their son, her hand clamped over her mouth to subdue laughter.

Her face, her smile, even her voice so incredible, exotic, different from the monochromatic world he'd grown up in.

Eyes sparkling, she'd brought more of that light of hers to their tiny apartment filled with babies and plants. She'd subdued her smile then into a parental reprimand and skirted around to the front of the high chair to tell their son, ''Truck. Your daddy said tr-uck.''

Well, he sure as hell was truck, truck, truck on his way as far as he could get across this desert.

God, how long had they been running? Years? Minutes? He didn't dare spare the energy for a look over the shoulder.

Spike slowed as they neared a clump of brush, a slight swell of dune. Damn pathetic coverage. The OSI agent stopped, braced his hands on his knees while the others drew up, halted as well. ''Don't think,'' Spike said between panting exhales, ''it's going to get any better than this, guys.''

Scorch, as senior-ranking crew member, could disagree. But Spike's counterintelligence experience, his days deeply undercover during his CIA stint prior to joining the Air Force as a civilian employee of the OSI, offered weight to his opinion.

And the set of his face told them well this seasoned agent thought their odds sucked no matter where they hid their asses. But that wouldn't stop them from trying to buy time for the good guys to get as close as possible.

J.T. dropped to his knees on the desert floor along with the others, scooping out sand, fashioning a trench behind brush. He dropped flat on his belly beside his crewmates. Sweat soaked his flight suit, caking sand to his skin.

Silence.

His heart tried to slow to a regular beat, exertion complete. Adrenaline kept him revved. How long would they wait?

"Damn," Spike whispered. "I'd kill for a ghillie suit right now." Camouflage made of strips of either desert-colored fabric or jungle hues, the ghillie suit was nearly undetectable to the eye.

Instead, they lay with only the scant cammo of desert tan flight suits, better than their regular green, at least. The Rubistan government, American troops and local warlords would all have picked up their landing. Who would arrive first?

The answer came quickly, rumbling from the hazy horizon. Clouds of sand puffed a toxic premonition before the vehicles cleared into sight.

Vehicles. Not an aircraft. Not Americans.

He swallowed more gritty air. Okay. Rubistan's military? Police? Or local warlord rebels?

The sand swirl parted to reveal…a caravan of crappy jeeps, trucks, RVs. Nothing organized about their approach to indicate military training. Damn.

J.T. slipped his emergency beacon off his survival vest, dug a hole in the sand. Tossed it inside. Pitched brush over it. If they were taken, at least rescue troops would have some point of reference and tracks to follow.

"Keep your head down," Spike instructed. "Don't move. Don't even look at them. With some luck they'll drive right by us."

Bo whispered out of the side of his mouth, "Unless they have dogs."

"Zip it, sunshine," Scorch interjected. "We can do without the gloom and doom."

The drone of engines increased with the cloud of sand spitting behind the vehicles, drawing closer, eating up the miles, becoming clearer as they broke through the rippling heat waves. A half-dozen vehicles, as best he could tell by sneaking peeks through peripheral vision. He couldn't risk looking at them directly, but God, it felt as if they were right on top of them. Still driving though.

J.T. quit breathing. His heart slammed his ribs until it seemed ready to explode out his ears.

The vehicles jerked to a stop, one after the other. The pounding in his ears stopped as well. Everything stopped inside him. Stilled.

Maintain life. Maintain honor. Return. Only that mattered. Survival. Returning home.

Voices shouted in Arabic. Movement flickered to the right. At least twenty or so men.

Honor. Life. Return.

Boots appeared in his line of sight. Paused. Stayed. They'd been found. Spit dried inside his mouth.

A shout sounded from above him. J.T. allowed himself to view through peripheral vision. No direct eye contact. No sudden movements or aggressive action to provoke.

The men looming over them weren't wearing uniforms. Mismatched weapons confirmed his fears. Russian-made AK-47 assault rifles. M-16s. Uzis. All weaponry of the very sorts of people they'd been sent to gather intelligence about. Underworld types dealing in opium trade to funnel money to terrorist camps.

J.T. knew. He was in a crapload of trouble.

His fingers jabbed into the sand as if to anchor himself for what would come next. Their captors would establish dominance and control from the start, pummel them to obtain information ASAP to maximize its utility.

He just needed to hold on, stay alive until rescue could come. He stayed on his stomach beside his three crewmates. Flattened his palms by his head, in the sand.

Keep calm.

Out of the corner of his eyes, he saw it. The betraying twitch from Bo, just seconds before—ah hell, don't do it, kid—the young copilot looked up.

Like making eye contact with the stalking lion.

The man over him shouted, stepped on Bo's right hand. Crunching.

J.T. swallowed down bile. Grit his teeth. Struggled for restraint.

Before Bo's echoing curse faded, the rebel raised his AK-47 above his head. Brought the butt down, fast, hard.

On Bo's other hand.

A strangled scream ripped along the roaring wind. Bo rolled to his side, cradled his mangled fingers, distorted wrist to his chest with his other abused hand. His face screwed up in agony even as defiance blazed from his too-young eyes.

Inviting the worst.

The crunch of breaking bones reverberated in J.T.'s brain, breaking something inside him, as well. He didn't remember making a decision to move, act, intercept. Just flung himself sideways while those cracking-bone sounds rattled around in his head.

Stupid. Reckless. Useless. But already the rifle was raised to come down on Bo again and J.T. couldn't stop the man. But he could control the damage.

J.T. shielded his copilot. His comrade in arms. Launched his body between the young soldier and the shouting rebel. Took a rifle butt to the shoulder. Caught a boot in the ribs.

Focused on the big three. Life. Honor. Returning home...

From the comfort of his porch, J.T. watched Bo's Jeep inch down the street, hesitate at the stop sign for opposing traffic. The white cast gleamed in the sun, stark, but not as harsh as the metal rods that had poked from his skin during the early days of reconstructive surgery after their release.

J.T. held tighter to the wooden railing until splinters cut into his fingers with grounding reminders that he existed in the present. In the States. At home.

Easier said than done.

God, he needed to get his head out of the desert. He told

himself Shakespeare had it right again in *Othello* by asking, "What wound did ever heal but by degrees?"

But he wanted this hell over now. Instead, his brain and his soul were still stuck in that time. Which left him less than half here when more than ever he needed his head on straight to fix his life. Salvage whatever was left of his marriage.

Bo's Jeep, his cast, if not the memories, disappeared around the corner. They'd maintained life throughout their capture. They'd maintained honor until their rescue.

Who'd have thought the toughest part would be figuring out how to return?

Chapter 5

Rena propped her foot on an extra dining-room chair and peered across the sturdy oak table at her family. Everyone was together for the first time since the weekend of J.T.'s return from Rubistan. Even if J.T. was in major brood-mode since he'd come in from seeing Bo off, her heart hungered to hold on to the moment more than her pregnant body craved chicken wings.

And that was mighty damned much.

She'd been so grateful to have him home and alive that nothing else seemed to matter. Not even their split.

She'd met him at the base with their children, never discussing where he would go afterward. Both knew and accepted he would come home instead of returning to the studio apartment he'd leased after she tossed him out.

All through that family dinner months ago, they'd sat together amid balloons and banners and favorite foods. And once the dishes were scraped clean of lamb chops, again there'd been no question but that he would follow her into her room. Their room.

Their bed. Two minutes later, they'd been naked.

Now her eyes met his over the Crock-Pot of chili, the platter of chicken wings and—oh yeah—her husband remembered, too, the night they'd made this baby nestled inside her.

J.T. shot to his feet, grabbed his empty plate and glass before hotfooting it to the kitchen, leaving her at the mercy of more memories.

Then when there'd been another night after his first night home, she'd thought maybe, just maybe they had enough to keep them together after all. She'd married him because of his strength, his honor, the reassurance that never would J.T. Price expose his family to men with concealed guns and shifty eyes. The "Price" last name would never show up in the news with reports about questionable acquittals and hung juries.

Once she'd entered J.T.'s world, people stopped whispering behind her back. Good, honest people no longer kept their families away from her.

Growing up, the promise of security had been everything to her, and she'd found security for herself and for her children. For years she'd thought it greedy to expect more. Finally, she'd learned to respect herself enough to demand everything.

But the cost was so much higher than she'd expected.

Chris scraped his chair back from the table, gathering his plate. "Gotta run. My shift starts in an hour. I'm closing up tonight, so I'll be late."

Nikki shoved back from the table, too, passing her plate to her brother on his way past. "Hold on a second before you go, runt, so I can say goodbye. I need to hit the highway soon to make it back up to Chapel Hill for the study session. Just need to talk to Mom for one more sec."

As Nikki rounded to her mother, Rena took her daughter's hand and squeezed. "Thanks for coming down, hon."

Crouching down beside the chair, Nikki leaned in with a

wide-open hug as exuberant as those childhood embraces, even though she now topped her mother by at least six inches. Rena let herself enjoy just holding on to her daughter and savoring those baby-shampoo and gummy-smile memories of her firstborn.

Finally, Nikki pulled away, rocking back on her haunches. "Boundaries are all well and good, Mom. But it doesn't hurt to push them sometimes."

Her free-spirited daughter would think so. And Rena was proud to have brought her daughter up in an environment where she could feel free to explore life, secure in knowing her parents loved her. That even if her father might be over-protective at times, he would always keep her safe.

Nikki would make a great teacher, with her love of children—an open, honest woman. Rena just hoped no one would take advantage of that.

"Well, hon, I want you to enjoy your time at college and exploring all those boundaries. Don't worry about me. I'm fine."

"I'm glad Dad's here, but I'm still going to drop in when I can." She held up her hand. "And no playing martyr-mom. My teammates are already asking when the next squadron picnic is."

"So they can check out the flyboys."

"Do ya' think?" Nikki almost kept a straight face.

Chris loped out of the kitchen, baggy clothes rippling with every step. "Which dude did you pick out for yourself? Used to be you begged off every picnic that you could. Hmm, I wonder who—"

Nikki smacked him on the back of the head. "Enough, motormouth. I'm just enjoying the scenery there."

"Ow, love you, too, bonehead."

While J.T. lumbered out to see their children off, Rena sagged back in her chair, affectionate sibling insults a welcome ritual in the middle of an upside-down day. J.T. stood in the open doorway until the last car faded, then turned to her.

Who would have thought silence could be so loud?

They were alone. Completely alone for the first time in months. No kids. No guests.

No interruptions.

Kicking the door closed, he ambled toward the table, hands in pockets, slow, deliberate, sexy. "Does she really have a thing for one of the guys in the squadron?"

Rena's brain stuttered as she tried to follow his conversational shift. Then it hit her. They always talked about their children to disperse tension and avoid deeper discussions.

A wise course of action tonight with plenty of tension snapping along the air between them.

"Nikki has been coming home more often since we roped her into helping out with the games at the squadron children's Christmas party. And of course she spent as much time as possible home right after..." Rena swallowed, forced herself not to sidestep the hard topics. "After you were released from Rubistan. But she's never mentioned any particular man to me."

"Good."

"Why so?" Had she soured his thoughts on marriage that much? "Don't you want to see your daughter settled? Have grandkids someday?"

"Someday. Not now." He jerked a spindle chair around, straddled it backward. "And not with a crewdog."

J.T.'s words shocked her silly. What an odd statement from him, a man so devoted to the Air Force. "No question, this isn't always an easy way of life. But I would think the load would be lighter for a couple meant to be together, in sync with each other."

She watched for a reaction from him, some sign that maybe this new perception of his might bode well for them on some level in dealing with their future, even if that future didn't involve them as a couple. A thought that still stung.

But she found no softening from him, just his regular closed expression, dark eyes with full-strength defenses in place. It was almost as if the man wasn't even with her. His body was at her table going through the motions, doing what was right, but his mind was somewhere else.

Definitely not with her.

Major sting.

She speared another buffalo wing off the platter, twisted the bones apart. *Crack. Crack.*

J.T. shot up from his chair.

Rena lowered her hands back to her plate. "Something wrong?"

He stared at the broken chicken bones in her fingers. "Are you ready to go upstairs?"

Did he have to sound so ready to get rid of her? "I'm still eating, but if you want to go up, I can maneuver a few steps. You don't have to stay."

He dropped onto the vacant chair beside her. "I'll wait."

His heels were dug in deep. She sighed her surrender, tossed aside the last wing and wiped her fingers. "Okay, fine. I'm ready. Thank you."

He stood, slid his arms under her, lifted her in a smooth sweep. Their faces were inches apart, and this time no one would open a door or interrupt.

J.T. cradled her against his chest and started down the hall. He turned sideways to angle up the stair, his gym shoes padding quietly on the wooden steps. Framed school photos and family portraits lined the walls, up, faces growing younger and happier with every step.

He cleared the top stair. "Do you, uh, need help getting into the shower or anything?"

"I took a shower at the hospital. I'm okay for now. And

I really can use the crutches with no problem most of the time."

"No shower then."

Was he disappointed? She couldn't tell by the rigid set of his square jaw. More frightening, was *she* disappointed?

Their bed sprawled big and inviting and lonely ahead of her with four large oak posts, wedding ring quilt, fluffy pillows in matching shams.

So many memories.

He lowered her to the giving softness as he'd done often before, except this time easing away. "Shout if you need anything. I'll be right back with your crutches, and then right across the hall."

In Nikki's old room, no parking his boots under their bed.

"J.T.?" she called, not sure what she would say, just certain she wasn't ready to see those broad shoulders leave through her doorway yet.

For a reckless moment she wanted to blame on tumultuous hormones, she wondered what it would be like to loosen those boundaries, be sex buddies with J.T. for a few days and take the edge off so much tension.

But she was weak when it came to this man. Even if he agreed, she wasn't sure she could punt him out of her bed a second time.

"Rena? Do you need something?"

A kiss. His solid body on his side of the bed again. A way to erase the image of him walking out the door the last time she'd swallowed her pride and invited him home. "Thank you for staying here with me. I know this has to be uncomfortable for you, too. But in two weeks, we'll have everything settled out, and you'll be able to return to your place. I'm a fast healer."

Liar. But she was learning.

"Wounds need to heal by degrees. Just take care of yourself and rest up. The new kid will have you running soon enough." He backed into the hall. "'Night, Rena."

Once his footsteps faded, she flopped into the fluff of pillows.

The baby. The reason he'd returned.

Funny, but apparently her heart didn't heal as fast as the rest of her.

Chris's stomach clenched as tight as the rag twisted in his grip while he washed dishes over the restaurant's industrial-size sink. An ocean breeze rolled in through the open back door. Not that it did much good sweeping out the fish stink. Heat popped salty sweat down his face, into his shirt.

Great for the acne. Not.

If zits were his only worry.

Chris glanced over his shoulder, checked, found the kitchen empty. He resumed dragging dishes under the spraying water to rinse away fried seafood and hush puppies before stacking each plate in the dishwasher.

Hell no, he wasn't a wuss. He could work out his problems. Face them like a man. He might not look like his dad, but he would be like him when it counted. He would finish up his shift at the restaurant. No big deal. And under no circumstances would he make any more deliveries.

He just wished he'd never answered the ad in the base paper about this job. But his mom and dad were always fighting about money. He'd taken the job to help out as much as to get away from the arguing.

The double doors from the dining area swished open. Sweat iced, then itched along his back. He snapped around to find...the busboy who'd recommended he take this lame job. The fellow military brat dropped off his tub of plates and left.

At least it wasn't *her*. But the swinging door still offered sporadic glimpses of *her* anyway. The hostess, Miranda Casale, smiling her million-dollar smile for the final departing customers. Miranda sure knew how to flash that smile along with a view down her silk shirts to get guys to do anything she wanted.

Even now he went dry-mouthed at the thought of her honey-golden skin with a charm necklace between two perfect breasts.

He tried to swallow. Failed.

Damn, damn, damn! He loved Shelby, so why was he drooling over someone he didn't even like? Teenage hormones so sucked.

One look down Miranda's dress two weeks ago and before he knew it, he'd been on his way out the door to run an errand for her. Just a food delivery for a special client—even though they didn't normally deliver squat.

Sucker.

He didn't know why Miranda had sent along so much money with the food delivery, but the fluky look he'd gotten at a stack of hundreds left him with zero doubts.

The reason couldn't be good.

He'd reported it to his boss, only to be told he must have misunderstood. Or maybe it was all innocent, but thanks anyhow, kid, and he would definitely talk to her. And, oh by the way, if rumors started, damaging business, Chris and his family would be sued and he sure would hate for that to happen and were they on the same page here now, pal?

God. Chris chunked another plate into the dishwasher. He'd clammed up faster than his father that day.

His parents would totally wig out if they knew. His dad was rigid on the honesty thing, and Mom went ballistic if he got so much as a detention for being tardy twice in a semester. Geez. Sometimes he wondered if it might be easier to forget about meeting their expectations.

But his mom was pregnant. And his dad was a freaking zombie since Rubistan.

So he would hang tough. Not be a wuss. And try like crazy to tell himself his mom's hit-and-run accident in *his* car was totally a coincidence.

Chris stacked the last of the dishes and flung aside the rag. Only a few more minutes and then home free for one more day. Maybe Miranda would transfer to another college and take her flashing boobs and smile somewhere else.

At least he knew better than to let himself be sucked in by her again. Jesus, like a nineteen-year-old hot chick would really be interested in him anyhow. But those raging hormones zapped IQ points.

The doors swished again. No Miranda—thank God. No busboy, either. This time his boss raced in, loosening his tie, a laid-back dude in his thirties with only two employee mottos: Don't make waves, and treat his wife and little girl like royalty.

The boss man, Kurt Haugen, definitcly always sided with the chicks. "I have to leave now before I'm any later getting home. Don't forget to lock up behind you."

"I won't, Mr. Haugen."

"Thanks, kid, and make sure Miranda and the other waitresses get in their cars safe and sound. Okay? Wouldn't want anything to happen to them."

Chris stood taller. Okay, so the guy pampered women. Bet he wouldn't get a baby-sitter Bo to stay overnight when a guy was already sixteen. "Sure. No problem, Mr. Haugen."

Of course, now he had to wait around for Miranda, but he could just sit in the car and watch until she left. Yeah. That would work. Doors locked. Eyes on her face, which was more respectful anyhow. Not to mention safer.

"I really need to haul ass, pal. I missed my daughter's gymnastics competition this afternoon. Engine went out on the shrimp trawler, which had me on the phone all day tracking down repair parts. And damn but I hated missing the little princess turn her back flips. Wife's probably pissed, too. Hey, how about pass me one of those chocolate pecan pies. Maybe if I walk into the room leading with that, it'll soften her up. And a candy bar for the princess. What do you think, pal?''

Swinging open the refrigerator, Chris stretched to get the pie off the top rack. ''I think chicks dig chocolate.''

Mr. Haugen winked, lifting the pie from Chris's hand. ''You'll go far with the ladies, my man.''

''Sure.'' Adults could be so lame.

Mr. Haugen snagged two candy bars from the cooking station, Heath Bars for the specialty pies. He tucked one in his sports jacket and tossed the other to Chris. ''Chocolate. For the special chick in your life.''

Chris snagged the candy bar midair and tucked it into his droopy shirt pocket. ''Yeah, whatever. I'll make sure everyone gets out of here fine.''

A half hour later, he stood in the front parking lot, locking the door, taking his time until Miranda revved her engine, the last of the crowd to go.

Finally, Miranda spewed gravel on her way out of the lot. He exhaled long. Off the hook. Alone, just him and waves pounding the dock, sailboat lines snapping and pinging.

He rounded the corner to where he'd parked—away from the shoreline and saltwater so his dad wouldn't blow a gasket about rust.

And pulled up short. A lone street lamp backlit a person sitting on the trunk of his mother's car. *Shelby.*

She perched cross-legged, flip-flops off and beside her as if she'd gotten comfortable for a long wait. She hugged her knees to her chest, her jet-black hair lifting in the wind.

Damn. How could he have ever even looked at Miranda?

He tried not to think about the chocolate bar in his pocket. ''You shouldn't be out here alone. It's not safe.''

She turned at his voice, then rested her chin on her knees without answering. Did chicks practice this silent-treatment stuff to confuse guys? He didn't have much practice on how to handle it since the women in his family weren't ever afraid to speak their minds.

He strode closer, faster, until he could see her clearly. Ah man, her eyes stared back, all red and swollen, puffy from crying. He tried to think of something to say and only came up with, "Want a Heath Bar? Mom says chocolate cures everything."

Her bottom lip quivered.

Way to go, hotshot. "Okay, no chocolate."

Foot on the bumper, he propelled himself up to sit on the trunk beside her. Maybe quiet was good after all, kinda like his dad did. When his dad clammed up, Mom usually spilled her guts. Then a guy didn't have to guess what was going on and risk botching it by actually getting involved in the discussion.

Besides, sitting with Shelby, the ocean breeze puffing by, he could smell her. Be close to her. Why rush ending that? He stared up at the inky sky dotted with stars and just breathed salty air and Shelby.

She shifted beside him, slid her flip-flops back on. "You probably need to get home."

"Nah, my folks know I'm working." He would take the ass-ripping from his dad for being late. Time alone with Shelby was rare since Shelby and Murdoch were so tight.

Or were they?

Another tear glistened in the corner of her eye. From a breakup? He couldn't stop the hope.

Which made him feel like a disloyal scumbag. "Where's Murdoch?"

"Away for the weekend." She sniffled, blinked fast. "Some family-reunion thing."

Okay, not breaking up. "Bummer. Tough luck him being gone right now. You don't have too many weekends left before the moving truck pulls out. Then college."

"Uh-huh."

She chewed off her glitter lip gloss while more waves crashed. He waited and reminded himself he was her friend. Murdoch's friend. And friends didn't take advantage. He was cool with them as a couple.

"I think I'm pregnant."

Her simple sentence hung there and man it hurt. Bad. He wasn't okay with crap.

He'd known in his head that Shelby and Murdoch were probably doing it. They'd been dating for about two years, after all. But it wasn't something he let himself think about too much because it would drive him kinda crazy.

Not much choice but to think about it now. "Are you sure?"

"No." She swiped hair from her face. "Just, uh, late. Scared. I needed to talk to somebody before I totally lost it in front of my folks."

Honor forced him to say, "Shouldn't you be talking to Murdoch about this instead of me?"

She didn't answer, just kept brushing hair out of her face while wind streaked it right back again.

"It is, uh, his, right?"

She jerked toward him, shock, anger, hurt all glittering in her eye like the sparkles in her lip gloss. "God, yes. What kind of person do you think I am?" She started inching down the hood. "I shouldn't have even come here. This isn't your problem, anyway."

"Hold on." He gripped her arm to stop her from sliding off to leave. "Chill. It's just weird that you're talking to me first. But I'm totally cool with it."

The fight crumpled out of her spine. Tears flooded, dripped over. What kind of guy would he be if he didn't comfort her? No big deal. A friend thing. He patted her back. Safe. Still friend stuff.

A really soft curvy friend.

He clenched his jaw tight. Ditch the thoughts, dude. Remember the mess with Miranda. Shelby's current mess. Hell, his parents' mess.

Couldn't anybody besides him keep their pants zipped?

Shelby sniffed, pressed the heels of her hands to her eyes. "It's not like we were stupid or anything. We were always careful, used condoms."

That was so much more information than he needed. "Uh-huh."

"But no kind of birth control is a hundred percent, you know?"

Not really. But now didn't seem to be the time to mention his virgin status. "Says so on the box."

"We haven't even been doing it all that long."

So she'd held out against John Murdoch. Marginal balm for an aching ego. "Oh, um…"

"John wanted me to be sure."

Hell. Now he couldn't even hate the guy. "You must be really important to him."

A small smile broke through for the first time. "That's what he says." Her smile drooped. "But he's already pissed at me because I won't go to the same college as him, and now he's going to use this to make me do things his way. I'm just a senior in high school. I don't want to get married yet."

Married? "Whoa. Hold on. Why worry until you know for sure? No need to get all fired up and mad at him." Way to go, sap. Help the guy. Except in this case, helping Murdoch meant helping Shelby. "Why don't you get one of those home tests?"

"They're not a hundred percent for sure."

"It's a place to start."

"Maybe I don't want to know for sure." She snapped a hair band on her wrist, then again and again. "God, my dad's going to be so disappointed in me. I don't know how I'm going to face him."

"What about your mom? Can you go to her place for the weekend, talk to her first?"

Shelby snorted, yanking the band off her wrist and twisting her hair back. "She'll either totally freak out and just call my dad to handle it, or pretend everything's fine and offer to take me shopping at the mall."

"Maybe you could go to your stepmom."

"Julia's cool," Shelby conceded, giving her hair a final twist in the band. "But she'll tell Dad, because that's the way they are together. Tight, you know?"

"Hmm," he grunted, because he didn't know. His parents weren't that way, never had been, and it pissed him off that no amount of extra "alone time" together seemed to make any difference. "What do you want to do?"

"I want to scream. I want to cry." Her hands dropped from her silky black hair into her lap. "I want somebody to hug me and tell me it's gonna be okay."

"Well, I can help you out with half of that."

Chris wrapped his arms around her, tucked her under his chin and let her cry. Finally, he was holding Shelby Dawson against his chest—and he couldn't do a damn thing but comfort her while she crushed his Heath Bar.

J.T. creaked back in the office chair in his den, rubbed his hand along his stiff neck, stared at his computer screen offering nada, zip, zilch in the way of info. Damn it, that bumper sticker on the back of the hit-and-run van had to mean something, red circle with a black triangle inside. If only he could identify the damn thing and trace it.

The walls of the small paneled room started to close in on him. He needed progress. Action. Anything to shake the freaking inactivity.

He thumbed along the pages of the discarded book beside the computer. Even the Bard couldn't quiet the storm in him tonight.

Dinner with his wife and kids had been near perfect, so close to what he'd planned for himself during his teen years. Nice house. Plenty of food. The conversation was a bonus he hadn't known he was missing until Rena came into his life. Sure he didn't join in much, but he listened. Enjoyed. Like tonight.

And then she'd started cracking those chicken wing bones. Bo's breaking hand had echoed in his head. And...

It was all too much. Too much emotion, noise. Storm.

He'd retreated. Except his quiet office, books, computer weren't offering him much in the way of relief.

A noise broke the silence.

He glanced up at the clock again, pendulum swinging. Rena was asleep—he'd checked. That one look at her soft body curved into her pillow was the source of most of his current frustration.

Chris was due home over an hour ago, but the office window showcased an empty parking spot.

Floorboards groaned. Old house-settling noises? Or something else.

Unease cranked along with his heart rate. He slid the key into the bottom drawer of his desk, opened, pulled out his M9 Beretta pistol.

The sounds could be nothing. The hit-and-run could be nothing. Or it could all be something, and no way would any of it get near his family.

Another squeak of boards and a rustle spurred him to action.

He edged out into the hall, following the sounds. Quiet, stealthy sounds. Should he have called the cops first? His hand fell to his cell phone in his back pocket, pulled it free and ready as he followed.

His footsteps led him to the kitchen. He slipped around the corner, socks silent on ceramic tile until he found...

His hungry intruder head deep in the refrigerator, a mighty fine and familiar ass pertly in view, clothed in a red satin nightshirt he'd given Rena two Christmases ago.

Chapter 6

J.T. lowered the gun to his side and feasted on the luscious sight of his wife's incredible ass while she feasted on whatever held her attention in the refrigerator.

Adrenaline surged through him alongside relief. Lust raged at Mach speed, leaving him totally at the mercy of memories from last summer when he'd returned home from TDY—temporary duty. He'd been on the road so much over the past few years with Afghanistan, Iraq, and regular TDYs to supply troops all around the world, he'd spent little time in his wife's bed. In his wife's arms.

In his wife's body.

He'd eased into the kitchen last summer after his return from Guam, dropped his helmet bag softly to the floor. She'd heard, her spine straightening as she stood on a ladder stenciling an ivy border along the walls.

A smile had tipped her profile, but she hadn't moved, just waited for him to cross to her. He'd stopped behind her, so damn grateful for his son's band camp because—oh yeah—

now Rena was alone in the house and he could wrap his arms around his wife to lift her off the ladder. Slide her back along his front as he lowered her to the ground.

He'd taken the green-soaked paintbrush from her, cupped the gentle weight of her breasts in his hands as she pressed her bottom against the already straining length of his erection.

Seconds later she'd been gripping the edge of the counter, her dress had been up, his zipper open, her thong snapped.

An awesome memory. No chance of repeating it anytime soon, though. He needed to stay his course. No risking sex until he convinced her he should stay.

He crossed, placed his gun on top of the refrigerator.

Rena jumped, glanced over her shoulder. "God, J.T.! You scared a year off my life." She blushed, thrusting the bowl forward like a peace offering. "Want some chili?"

Peace would be nice. Except he couldn't get past the temptation of her unrestrained breasts against the satin nightshirt. Who turned the air conditioner on so cold? "Heard a noise, and since you shouldn't be up at all it never crossed my mind it might be you. What the hell are you doing up, anyway?"

"No chili? Okay, then. More for me." She popped open the lid on the Tupperware bowl, snagged a spoon and started shoveling. She shouldn't have appeared graceful in the midst of a feeding frenzy. But she did. "You seemed so intent on what you were doing in the study, I didn't want to bother you. Can you reach down there for the grated cheese, please?"

She'd been watching him, too? Adrenaline surged hotter, faster, throbbing low and south fast. Kneeling in front of her to find the bag of cheese didn't help. He was at the perfect level to hitch up that satin and—

"Thanks." She snatched the cheese from his hand and sprinkled some on top of her chili. "I woke up to, uh, go to the bathroom. God, I'd forgotten the seven thousand bathroom runs a night that come with being pregnant. And then

I realized I was starving. In the morning I can't eat without being sick, and then I spend the whole rest of the day unable to eat enough. Crazy, huh?''

Crazy? He stood. Yeah, he was definitely going nuts talking about puking when all he could think about was pressing her against the counter and hiking up her nightshirt. Reenacting that memory of a better time before their world exploded. He'd known the split was coming, always expected the end. Considered every day with her another dodged bullet. Nope, he hadn't been in the least surprised when his hand weights sailed out the window and bounced off his book onto the lawn.

However, he hadn't expected another chance three months ago, a chance he'd blown. A mistake he wouldn't repeat. Which meant no jumping Rena in the kitchen.

Her eyes flashed with inspiration. She snatched a pudding pack from the refrigerator door. "Cravings."

"Like before."

"Textbook." She limped to the minuscule kitchenette table. Sighing, she sagged into a seat, swinging her injured foot up onto one of the other chairs. "Hope you don't want any pudding, because this is the last one, so you'll have to pry it out of my hormonally tight grip."

J.T. kicked the refrigerator shut. He dropped into a chair across from her and watched her savor alternating bites of chili and chocolate pudding. She licked the spoon clean every time. Rapture spread across her face.

His knuckles itched to glide across her high cheekbones as a prelude to kissing away the chocolate on the corner of her mouth. Damn, she was beautiful. "I can't believe I missed it."

"Missed what?"

He shook his head at his own blindness the past few months. "That you're pregnant."

He let himself reach, touch just his thumb to the corner of her lush lips.

Ducking his touch, she grabbed for a napkin. "Because I'm eating like a pig? Thanks. I'm now totally reassured you don't want to come back home or you would have never made that comment."

Her hands fell to her stomach. His hungry eyes followed her gesture to the slight swell. He could almost feel the taut skin over the growing proof of their child. Had in fact felt it in days past when she'd carried their other children.

Would he be allowed to feel the roll of their baby under his hand this time? "Lower the hackles. I wasn't commenting on the food."

"Oh, uh, well, you probably didn't notice because I wore loose clothes."

If ever he'd needed the Bard's way with words, it was now. He'd just have to settle for simple honesty. "That still isn't what I meant." He angled closer, elbows on the table. "You know I'm not much of a guy for woo-hoo stuff. But that pregnancy-glow thing—there must be something scientific to it. I mean, hell, Rena, you've been in a wreck. Suffered a concussion. Damn near broke your foot, and you're still glowing so bright I could read by it."

Not an intimate touch to her tummy, but he could see his words warmed her nearly as much. Victory chugged through him.

A slow smile lit that glow to blinding levels. "I think there's a compliment in there somewhere."

"I guess so. Wish I'd actually thought to give it. But honestly, I'm just amazed that I could have been so clueless."

"We see what we want to see."

"Putting that psych degree to work?"

"Maybe. Or maybe just one of those side benefits to getting older."

Older. Odd how he could feel so old some days but she still seemed the same woman he'd married.

Only with better curves.

He reached for her hand. "Are you scared?"

Well, hell, that was downright sensitive, and damned if she didn't let him hold her hand. Maybe the Bard was rubbing off on him after all.

"Does it bother me having a baby this late in life? A little. With my job, I know the increased risks with age."

"And that worries you."

"I probably worry less than I did at eighteen. Maybe because I feel more...at peace about motherhood."

"So your fears are...?"

Being alone. He read it all over her face. He worked his thumb over her wrist. Who'd have thought he'd get such a rush out of holding his wife's hand and neither of them was even naked.

"I'm just being emotional. Hormones and all that. The timing's not the best, but I'm going to have a baby."

"We're going to have a baby." He squeezed her hand. "*We.* This is my child, too, so we're in this for another eighteen. At least. Remember that."

He tried to read her again and found...more of that fear. Of him? He deserved a lot of things, but not that.

The back door rattled with a key. Rena jerked her hand away, momentary connection snapped. Chris swung the door open.

Frustration brewed in him. "Where have you been?"

"Talking with a friend." Chris snagged the bowl of chili from the table, found a fresh spoon and started shoveling. "Time kinda slipped away. Sorry."

Rena's hand fell to her son's arm to stop him midbite. "We worry. Call next time."

"Sure," he answered evasively before dropping the bowl

in the sink. Fishing a candy bar out of his pocket, he tore
open the wrapper and tossed broken pieces into his mouth.

Warning bells clanged like an alert klaxon. The kid had
plenty to be edgy about, but was there more?

He had two weeks to find out. Two weeks of nonstop one-
on-one time with his wary wife, where he would be helping
her with her every intimate need while refraining from giving
her the most intimate of touches.

If J.T. didn't touch her, really touch her soon, she would
burst into flames. Or scream. Or do something equally em-
barrassing that would leave her husband frowning pensively,
then helping while giving her a wide berth as he'd done for
the past week and a half.

True to his word, he'd been around whenever she needed
him, all his flights conveniently scheduled at night after she
fell asleep and Chris was already home. But even though J.T.
slept part of the day, his presence still filled the house, reminding her of the good times, until she feared coming down
with a convenient case of amnesia when it came to remembering all that drove them apart.

At least they were out of their too-close quarters, their
home having become a sauna of need. Instead, spring heat
baked the roof of the truck, lunch-hour traffic spewing ex-
haust on the highway leading toward the base. Nausea tickled, but at least it distracted her from her achy foot. Achy,
but no longer throbbing and *sans* stitches.

A cargo plane roared low overhead on its approach for
landing. She fidgeted along the bench seat, anxious to finish
up the drive, get back to work, even for an hour or two. J.T.
wasn't happy about it, but she couldn't juggle this particular
patient to another counselor. And the afternoon would also
offer J.T. the chance to fit in a training class at the squadron
while he waited.

Could he tempt her from clear across base? Seeing him so hot and hunky in his flight suit didn't help.

He'd been doing a mighty fine job of tempting her the past few days even in his favorite Hawaiian shirts and jean shorts. So attentive. So blasted perfect. He carried her up the stairs. Down the stairs. To the shower. Sat beside her on the sofa, shared popcorn, watched chick flicks with her, brought tissues when she cried over the endings because her own life sucked so bad. And never, never once did he make a move on her.

Who the hell was this man and what had he done with her husband?

"We need to talk."

And now he wanted discussion?

The world was totally screwed up. Maybe his trip into base would mark a shift from all those night flights to day flights so he wouldn't be around to entice her during waking hours. "About what?"

He slowed onto the exit ramp off the highway at the base exit during lunch rush hour. "Do you think everything's okay with Chris?"

That sounded more like her husband, focusing on the kids. Safe territory.

She considered his question through an entire traffic light. She'd traveled this familiar parental route with her husband often in the past. He would ask her how he should approach one of the kids. She would give him advice that he always followed. She felt needed.

But he would be parenting alone during his weekends and vacations with Chris. Even though she was close now to help, what if he was transferred? He couldn't pick up the phone every time he had a question about what to say to their son.

He was a loving father, worked hard at being there for his kids. But only now did she realize how he always acquiesced to her way when it came to parenting.

She'd *let* him rely on her. Had she wanted him to need her

on at least some level? A painful notion because then she would have done her children a disservice.

Damn it, she'd tried her best to balance everything. He was gone so often, most of the daily parenting fell to her. They couldn't afford a slew of phone calls. The Internet and e-mails helped with keeping him in touch with his kids, but that hadn't been a major-player option until they were older. ·

She circled her jumble of bracelets round and round her wrist. No use beating herself or him up about the past. Just do the best she could with their present and future.

Concentrate on the present, improving the right now. Instead of giving advice, she would ask his opinion. "What makes you think there might be something wrong with Chris?"

"He was late coming home the day of your accident, then again the night you were released from the hospital. Sure he mouths off sometimes like any teenager, but he keeps close to home."

"Have you asked him what's wrong?"

"He's had plenty of chances to talk and no dice. I know I haven't been around much, but I sure as hell tried this week, worked out with him, jogged. I even showed him how to fix stuff around the house."

So Chris could repair things after his father left again? "Did you ask him what he's feeling?"

His jaw tightened in familiar defensiveness as he downshifted along the pine-lined entry road leading up to the base. "Men aren't into all that touchy-feely emotional crap."

"Lovely."

He rubbed a hand along his neck. "Back down, babe. I respect what you do. God knows, anyone who'd drag her wounded self up there to work is obviously devoted."

Sure he respected her job. Just didn't believe in it and wouldn't touch a penny of her paycheck for so much as a family vacation to blow off steam created by his job. "Some clients could wait a couple of weeks without setting back progress. With others, it's not so simple.''

''Tough one?''

Not nearly as tough as getting through to her own husband, but then he wasn't a patient, and she couldn't heal her family. She knew that. But accepting it? Not so easy.

J.T. flashed his military ID at the security gate and the guard waved him forward. ''I'm not looking for you to break confidentiality. Just expressing interest in your world.''

''Thank you.'' She twisted sideways toward him. ''You know that's borderline touchy-feely.''

''Touch?'' He echoed the word that had been plaguing her all day—for days, actually. Was he a mind reader now, too? ''We probably need to stay away from that subject if we're going to lay some new groundwork for taking care of this little one.''

Of course he was right. She totally agreed. So why was she cranky? She'd won, after all.

J.T. turned off toward her office, red brick building sprawling in front of her, while he hunted for an empty spot in the jammed lot. She was confident in her job, but still her own screwed-up home life made her question her judgment. And, oh, this man did so have a way of jumbling her mind. ''Just as well Chris interrupted last week. We're too old for the over-the-kitchen-counter quickies.''

''We weren't too old for it three months ago. And you sure as hell weren't too old for the table, the stairs, the shower—''

''Sex was never our problem, J.T.''

Steam filled the truck's cab. He shifted the truck into park. The packed parking lot of empty cars offered a pseudo sense of solitude in spite of the public locale, blue minivan on her left, an RV on the right, even a Humvee in front of them. Still, he didn't reach for her.

But his hands shook from the restraint.

Rena launched into his arms. Couldn't help herself. No surprise.

Did he meet her halfway? She didn't know, and with his lips and hands finally on her, she couldn't think or reason. Only feel. Savor. His touch licking fire through her veins.

He palmed her back, molded her against his solid body, soft breasts yielding against hard chest.

And taste, oh, the taste of him as she explored the warmth of his mouth. Talk about cravings. One apparently he suffered from, as well, his tongue delving deeper, sweeping, heating. She could almost forget they were in a public lot.

Rena inched closer, her calf-length skirt tangling around her legs, scrunchy fabric rasping against skin suddenly over-sensitive to the least sensation. How incredible it would be to park somewhere private and toss away inhibitions, pretend they were both twenty-two years younger.

Strong hands gripped her shoulders. Eased her back, broke their kiss, but not the touching. His forehead rested on hers. "God, babe, I've missed you."

Her eyes stung and she knew full well it had nothing to do with pregnancy hormones. "I've missed you, too."

She started to slide her arms around him again. Surely they could hug without getting arrested for a public display. She reached, her bracelets jangling to her elbow. He pulled away.

What?

He opened the door. Where the hell was he going? For the first time in months there was a hint of real emotion and he decided they should head on into work.

She longed for one of his books to throw.

Breathe. Think. Don't let the angry, passionate—pained—emotions clamoring through her reign.

Rena clamped a hand around his arm. "Hold on a minute. Jesus, J.T., you throw that land mine in my lap, clam up and then wonder why I explode."

Tension rippled under her fingers. ''I'm not going to fight with you today.''

''I don't want to fight.'' She really, really didn't want to fight at the moment. But a public parking lot wasn't the place for what her body demanded. ''We were talking. That's good. Why do we have to stop?''

His smoky gray eyes brushed her lips as surely as his kiss, lingered, finally fell away. A long exhale cut the silence before he swung his feet back into the truck. ''Okay, fine. We'll talk. We never did come up with anything concrete about Chris, anyway.''

Her hands clenched. She didn't want to talk about their children. She wanted to hear more about how much he'd missed her. And why. Silly, frivolous words, considering her age and how long they'd been married.

All the more reason they were better off talking about their children. Safer for them. Safer for her heart.

J.T. slammed the truck door. ''I'm not sure what's up with the boy anymore. I *have* tried to talk to him. Guys just approach things…differently.''

''Guess that's why men have more heart attacks than women.''

He draped his wrist over the steering wheel. ''I'll try to talk to Chris. If you have any ideas for conversation starters, I'm not adverse to listening.'' His gray eyes lit. ''Then I can translate them into manspeak.''

''Manspeak?''

''Sure. You've seen those lists that float around on the Internet. Guy says 'uh-huh' and it means—''

''It means, 'I'll agree to anything if you'll quit blocking my view of the football game.'''

''Busted.'' He grinned.

''So if I asked Chris if he's upset and does he need to share what's bothering, you would ask…?''

''Something pissing you off?''

"Or if he's suffering from any anxiety about his parents splitting?"

"You okay about everything?"

Ah. Understanding hummed through her as clearly as the airplane's drone overhead. "Your question is a third as long as mine. And vague. What if he misses the point because of that vagueness?"

"What if *I'm* missing the point and he tells me something I never expected?"

Surprise at his insight stunned her quiet. What else might he have offered up if she'd asked his input on the parenting more often? "Valid thought."

"Yeah, I just made it up."

A laugh snorted free. His dry wit always snuck up on her like that. "But women need those extra words. Otherwise how are we supposed to know when you're in pain?"

"There's your logic flaw. A man's never in pain."

"That he'll admit."

"Bingo."

What else could she pry out of her reticent husband with a few more questions? "So how does a woman know when a man needs something?"

A slow smile dimpled his rugged handsomeness seconds before his smoky gray eyes steamed over her. "Oh, babe, trust me, you'll know."

The truck cab fogged all over again, heavier this time since it sparked the barely banked heat of their kiss moments prior. She wanted so much from him, and she was right in demanding he pony up more in their relationship.

But she'd hit a wall so many times with her clam-up husband. Regardless of whether they stayed together, they would be together in many ways because of their children. She needed to understand J.T.'s hidden emotions if she ever expected to survive without combusting into flames—from both anger and passion. "What does it mean when a guy stumbles on his wife in the kitchen and when she offers to share her precious chili, he says, 'What the hell are you doing up?'''

He stared outside at the red brick building for so long, she thought he wouldn't answer her. No surprise. However, she *was* mega-surprised by how much she wanted that answer.

Finally, he turned, resigned, like a man heading to the gallows, scouring guilt over her for having sent him there. "You want more words, Rena? Here they are. In this case, the snapping then and now means a guy is horny as hell since he hasn't been with a woman except for one weekend in six months. It means he misses coming home from work to his wife, being able to slip up behind her, wrap his arms around her, fill his hands with her breasts. Fill her body with his."

The steam came straight off her overheated flesh this time. He missed her, missed what they had together. And even as she knew they needed so much more to hold it together, it felt so good to know he'd found some comfort, happiness, something in their life together.

He cupped her chin, his touch not quite gentle, but then the emotions stinging through her were anything but gentle. "It means he's damn tired of life being so complicated. But it is. And he's got to deal with it the best way he knows how, which means keeping things uncomplicated."

His fingers threaded up into her hair. "And we both know, babe, sex between the two of us is never uncomplicated." He drew his hand back, gentle, insistent, tugging against tangling curls, long, slow. "Sex for us is intense and messy and mind-blowing."

Her breaths came in heavy bursts of need, nerves along her scalp tingling with awareness. If he leaned forward, she would kiss him again. Let him kiss her, maybe more, because his words touched her as firmly as his hands.

But he didn't kiss her. "And we both need a clear mind now more than ever."

He pulled away. Left her again. A few months ago she would have cried. Or raged. A part of her wanted to now.

Except as she watched him retrieve her crutches from the back of the truck, she couldn't help but wonder what two-thirds he'd left unsaid. And was she really ready to hear what else she might learn from deciphering his "manspeak" when they climbed back into the truck again?

Chapter 7

Who would have thought he'd prefer a chemical-warfare class to making out with his wife in a parking lot?

Saluting a passing officer, J.T. strode up the walkway toward the brick and brown building, late-afternoon sun beating down on his shoulders. Damn it, but Rena had wriggled under his skin and made him say more than he wanted. His trump card in their relationship had always been keeping his cool. Weathering the storm.

Somehow he'd managed to walk away a few minutes ago without giving in to the predictable urge to distract her with sex. Even with that out-of-control kiss of hers, he knew she would do a ninety-degree about-face once they took the edge off their frustrations.

She would start asking more of those chick questions. If he stayed quiet, he pissed her off. If he answered, somehow he came up short of what she wanted.

So he would go slow, soften her up since, no doubt, his prideful wife wouldn't easily get over his leaving. And with a cargo hold full of luck, they wouldn't die from hormonal overload.

He pushed through the glass door into the building, the full blast of air-conditioning catching him in the face. The soft echo of his boots on the industrial carpet echoed along with the low-pitched rumble of voices, ringing telephones, computer chimes.

From one of the rooms stepped Spike, his spiked hair longer than his previous buzz now that he wasn't undercover. In keeping with his regular OSI position, he'd exchanged the flight suit for khakis, a sports coat, and a palm tree-patterned tie that never stayed tight enough. Not exactly the normal look for an OSI agent, but Max "Spike" Keagan got the job done. His way. "Hey, dude. Are you on the schedule for chem-warfare update?"

"Heading that way now."

"Me, too. Thought I'd listen in." Spike slipped into pace alongside him. An easy man to hang with, the guy was as comfortable with silence as J.T.

They'd worked well together during the weeks training the OSI agent to pose as a loadmaster for the infiltration into the American base in Rubistan. Regs kept Spike from holding the crew position solo, but he knew enough to look credible when flying along with another loadmaster. No doubt Spike had picked up some additional tips from his pilot fiancée.

J.T. cleared the door into the room packed with aviators, tables in front of them littered with gas masks. Two more tables lined the front of the room with stacks of training carbon filters, a couple of training chemical suits. A mannequin stood propped in the corner, outfitted in the full gear.

C-17 squadrons didn't fly with set crews except during wartime or special operations, but allegiances gelled all the same, as could be seen by the seating choices. J.T. found his boots carrying him back to the corner with Scorch, Bronco, Crusty, Joker, Cobra...

And, God help him, motormouth Gabby, a six-foot-two-inch wiry guy in constant motion like a kid on sugar overload. Apparently Gabby had raided a Pixie Stix factory today.

"Hey there, sir, glad you could make it. How's your wife? Her foot doing any better? Sorry to hear about your totaled car, but good thing nobody was hurt bad, sir."

Swinging his gas mask up onto the table, J.T. averted his gaze from Scorch—smothering a laugh with his hand over his mustache. For some reason Gabby insisted on calling him sir no matter how many times he reminded the kid he wasn't an officer. Sarge would be fine. Or his call sign, Tag. Call signs were a universal leveler in the air to build a more cohesive team while flying. "My wife's doing better, thanks. She had to pull some office time, so I figured I'd work in the class, after all. Saves me having to make it up later."

Scorch leaned back in his chair, the Ivy League creases in his appearance and flight suit not the least diminished by his casual sprawl. "So she's getting around okay?"

"On crutches, yes sir."

"Glad you've been able to stay on the schedule with night flights." Scorch nodded. "We need you around here."

"I can pitch in extra," Gabby interrupted, "anytime you need time off or whatever. I'm always looking to log more flight time."

"Thanks." J.T. didn't bother arguing because it was a non-issue since the kid didn't have anywhere close to the security clearance needed to fly these missions.

Gabby reached for his Mountain Dew. "Where's Bo?"

Scorch shot over his shoulder. "Had some other appointment."

"Hmm." Gabby's combat boot twitched nonstop against the leg of the table while he banged back a gulp from his soda. "Wonder if his flight attendant's in town?"

J.T. hoped so since it would keep the squadron player occupied if Nikki came home for the weekend.

Cobra, the squadron's previous player but now happily married to one of the flight surgeons, hooked a boot on his knee. "If his girlfriend's not back soon, she'd better hurry. Word from my wife has it that the nurses flocked to the clinic yesterday when he got his cast sawed off."

Scorch swung his gas mask from the floor to the table. "About time he pulled his weight around here again."

They needed all the flying hands up and running. World deployments already taxed manpower, and the current surveillance flights added an extra load. But stopping the terrorist drug activity would put a serious dent in cash flow for the bad guys. Their dirty money bought things like shoulder-held missile launchers off the black market.

Already, their squadron had lost two planes in just that manner. His, shot down by the Gomer in a boat nearly four months ago. Another plane piloted by Cobra later was nailed during an operation to rescue American hostages being held overseas. Cobra's Gomer had camped his ass out in a field three freaking miles away from the runway for the fateful pop.

Gabby whistled low. "Damn, but Bo's got the good life. Women crawling over him. Guess we old married guys have to live vicariously through him, huh?"

Old? Gabby was what? All of twenty? But he certainly was married—to a nineteen-year-old wife who worked checkout at the base commissary to help make ends meet.

J.T. remembered those days well. If life wasn't so crazy he'd have the talkative kid and his wife over for a few meals and mentor him. Except Gabby and his wife would probably run screaming for divorce court with him as a model.

Cobra ducked to the side, lifted a brown grocery sack from under the table and passed it to J.T. "Oh, hey, Tag, when we heard you were coming today, we decided to throw you an impromptu baby shower like we did for Crusty a few months ago when his little half brothers came to live with him. We all chipped in and got you a few things."

Ah hell. If Gabby's goofy-ass grin was anything to go by, J.T. could smell a roast coming. He took the bag from Cobra. Crewdogs cut zero slack when razzing their own. The best way to handle it? Play along.

And plot the comeback.

Already plans formed to ink permanent marker around the earpieces on their headsets so they would walk around for hours after landing not knowing about the doughnut rings circling their ears. And the beauty of it all? Nobody ever suspected him. Usually funnyman Bronco took the fall.

J.T. fished his hand into the bag. "Earplug holder?" He shook the suspiciously light canister. No sound. He cocked an eyebrow at Cobra. "Empty?"

"Bo thought you'd need earplugs to block out the baby hollering, but then Colonel Dawson reminded him that all you old guys are just about deaf anyway from so many years on the flight line. So Bronco stole the plugs out to take home for when his kid's pitching a fit."

Chuckling, J.T. dug in the bag again, pulling out a bottle labeled…Viagra. Ah crap. "Damn, guys, it's brutal around here today."

Gabby leaned forward. "Well, not totally. This bottle's empty, too, since it's mighty obvious you don't need that, either, old man."

At least the kid had a sense of humor buried in all that chatter. J.T. jerked the two bulky remaining items, larger, soft packages.

"Huggies and Depends." Cobra announced the obvious with a wicked grin. "'Cause you'll both be going into diapers at the same time."

"Same foods, too," Scorch added. "Should have thought to add some of that rice cereal and strained carrots my sister feeds my niece."

And the roast got hotter. J.T. pivoted toward Spike. "Just decided to sit in on the class, did you?"

Spike loosened his palm-tree tie. "Wouldn't want to miss out on a good party, even brought along a subscription card for *TV Guide,*" he said, patting along his jacket pockets as if searching. "For all those nights you'll be walking the floors."

More smart-ass quips rippled through the room until some-one shouted over the fray, "Hey, what happened to those Viagra pills? Maybe I can find some use for them."

Cobra snagged the empty bag and dumped the "gifts" in-side like a nice "hostess." "Since Tag didn't need them, we dished them out to the lieutenants for experimentation."

Rolling her eyes, 1st Lieutenant Darcy Renshaw strode across the room and plopped into the seat next to her fiancé, Spike. "Just what those dorks need, more ego inflation."

J.T. dropped the brown bag by his feet. "Well, thanks, everybody. You are all too, uh, generous."

"Ahhh—" Cobra chuckled low "—that's only the begin-ning."

"Seriously, man." Scorch cruised the front legs of his chair to a landing. "We'll be getting together a real celebra-tion later. Just couldn't resist this now. Congratulations."

"Thanks." J.T. thumped his heart, plastering a sardonic smile in place. "I feel the love."

More laughter rumbled through the room as he pulled his chair up to the table beside Scorch.

"Tough crowd today." The aircraft commander smoothed two fingers along his mustache. Rumor held he'd once singed the blond stache in a bar with a flaming Dr Pepper mixed drink, thus his call sign.

"Only the strong survive around here."

Scorch's eyes flicked up to J.T.'s, held for a somber second that affirmed the truth of those words…

From inside the rusted-out jeep bouncing along the rutted

desert road in a convoy, J.T. stared back at Scorch beside him. Both of them resigned. Resolved. Scared enough to piss themselves.

Hands bound behind his back, J.T. tried to brace with a boot on the back of the seat. Shock absorbers shot, the vehicle rocked, threatened to pitch him out. The hemp cut deeper into his wrists, burning like hell, not as bad as his ribs, though. Those flamed like a son of a bitch, but the pain kept him awake.

Could be worse.

Each jolt jarred groans from Bo sitting in front, his mangled hands manacled and swelling. The young lieutenant's teeth chattered, shock setting in.

J.T. glanced back at Scorch. They would have to do something for the kid soon.

Sand caked in Scorch's mustache, the aircraft commander's Ivy League blond veneer dusty as hell. In that moment, they bridged the gap between childhoods of brownstone walk-up and mansion, between enlisted and officer. It was them against the enemy, keeping the bastards off Bo and away from Spike who carried more secrets than all of them put together.

A whistling premonition sounded.

Hell, not a premonition at all. A missile. Crap. "Incoming!"

J.T. ducked a second ahead of Scorch. The missile arced, another, both closer, taking out the lead vehicle, then the last. Explosions, one, two shook the ground.

He propped his shoulder against the back of the seat. "Bo, you okay? Damn it, kid, answer me."

A grunt sounded from the front while J.T. lay in the back seat staring over at Scorch, both of them trussed and unable to help.

Praying the rescue wouldn't end up killing them.

Only the strong survive. The words echoed from Scorch's eyes then and now.

Damn straight. J.T. nodded, shifted front for the start of class. Droning voices dwindled with the arrival of the two chemical-warfare instructors from the Civil Engineering Squadron.

At least the nighttime surveillance flights with the DEA were netting results in figuring out who sold out their flight plan. And J.T. welcomed the chance to be a part of the process to nail the traitorous bastards.

Even if the process was slow as hell.

They'd identified the two military leaks. One guy working in aerial port in Rubistan sent back vehicles to the States with the spare tire filled with drugs. The other Air Force leak—in the transportation squadron back in Charleston—took out the contraband. Their reasons were unclear, as were their off-base connections.

Neither had been picked up yet since DEA wanted to topple the whole operation. The two military links were only a small part of the larger operation.

Both men were under twenty-four-hour watch while the surveillance flights continued. Endlessly. God, the bad guys were good at this, but having closure for the shoot down would go a long way toward easing the roar in his head.

For Rena, for his kids, he would figure it all out. She wasn't the same woman he'd married, a woman who filled his life with plants and smiles and just let him be. Now she wanted things from inside him that he couldn't give. And for a man who already felt he hadn't given her near enough, damn but that blew.

Life was easier when they could use sex to work it out, reconnect while relieving stress.

By the time the training filters were being passed around, he'd decided maybe the parking idea wasn't so bad, after all, once Rena finished up with her client. Even if they didn't actually have sex. Yeah, the needy edge would still be there, but so what? Edgy was good. Didn't mean he had to act on it just yet.

He wasn't twenty anymore. He would control himself now. He would have a chance to make headway with her—without worrying about interruption. And he knew just the thing to romance her with, the last thing he would have expected to use. The toughest for him to utilize. But the only tool in his arsenal with which to breach her defenses.

Words.

Hell, talk about underarmed and untrained. He would have to bring in some emergency supplies for reinforcements to go with his pathetic stash of verbal armaments.

''Don't you want to do some word association crap or something?'' Bo Rokowsky paced around Rena's sparse office space. He tapped a hanging basket in her lone little window, sent the petunias spinning into a kaleidoscope of pink and purple.

Rena tipped back in her office chair with a slow squeak and resisted the urge to tell him not to kill her favorite plant. The guy was wound tighter than the twisted macramé hanger.

For two prior sessions, her patient had tried to charm his way around answering questions. Yet if he wanted to fly again, he needed to clear the mandated evaluation. Today, she hoped for a breakthrough. She'd studied the way he operated, thought she had his number.

Scorch, Spike…J.T., they'd all been okayed after release in the psych evaluations at Ramstein AFB in Germany. But not Bo.

Every person reacted differently to stress, of course. Bo's youth, his greater injuries, his rootless past may have played a part in diminishing his coping skills. Whatever the cause, the initial debriefing called for further psychological evaluation of 1st Lieutenant Bo Rokowsky once his wounds healed before he could be returned to full flight status.

She'd been surprised when Bo requested her as his counselor since she was married to J.T. She had even gone to her boss to discuss the matter. He'd quickly pointed out that in a small base community, it was impossible to schedule around all the work and friendship connections. Doctors and counselors would forever be referring cases elsewhere. There wasn't a technical conflict of interest. The patient felt more comfortable talking to her. Budget cuts had left them short staffed. She needed to be a professional and do her job.

Bo's initial eval indicated time would likely settle his problem. Something she would have to confirm before he could return to the cockpit.

"Word association is one way to find out about you." She dropped her steno pad on the desk. "Honestly, I prefer just to talk most of the time."

"This should be pretty quick though, right? You just need to find out I'm not about to climb into a bell tower or something."

"That's one way of putting it." She flexed her foot on the chair across from her. The simple sprain, aches, immobility from her accident were making her stir-crazy. What more must Bo have gone through during the deliberate injury of both his hands? "Because of the extent of your injuries in Rubistan, the Air Force wants reassurance you're—"

"Not sporting any loose screws before they let me back in the cockpit. Yeah, yeah, I know, I'm already a wild card as far as my commander's concerned, even before this crap shook down." His dark hair gleamed in the late-afternoon sun streaming through the window as he spun the plant faster. "But you can tell the flight surgeon to tell my micromanaging commander that all the screws in my body—currently located in my arm now, by the way—do appear to be twisted nice and tight. I'm more than ready to resume flying. In fact, the only thing making me go batty these days is too much time piloting a desk.''

He abandoned the mistreated petunias for a stroll around the tiny office, combat boots giving off a muffled thud on tile. ''I'll admit, I was pretty messed up when I first got back. That was some scary crap over there. But I'm doing better now. Working. Got a new girlfriend, bounced back fast after the old one and I broke up.''

''I'll take all that into consideration when I meet with the flight surgeon for the recommendation to Colonel Quade.'' She seesawed her pen between two fingers. ''You don't care for your commander?''

Bo stopped short by her file cabinet. ''And you expect me to answer that one? Are you looking to get me booted out the front gate on my ass? Since you're married to one of us, I figured you'd know better than to ask something like that.''

So many threads to pick up on in those few words. And she'd get to them all, in time. ''Our sessions are confidential. The colonel will only see my recommendation. Not the details on how I arrived at it.''

''Since you've seen my file,'' he said, prying a magnet off the file cabinet, a clear plastic cover over a family photo taken ten years ago, ''it's probably no great leap to assume I don't have a lot of experience on how to deal with male authority figures in my life.''

''Why would I assume that?''

''How come you're getting paid for me to come up with all the answers?''

''Great job I have here, isn't it?'' She smiled.

He grinned back. ''All right. I'll play along. It's the government's nickel paying for this anyhow.'' He held up the family-portrait magnet. ''There aren't any photos like this in my past. My old man cut out on us when I was five, cracked under the pressure of paying for all those bicycles and gym shoes. My mother opened a vein rather than live without him.

Cops tracked down my old man, who still didn't want the responsibility of picking up the tab for my Nikes and Huffys.''

Bo's smile, reputed to have charmed women on every continent, turned tight, hard, lending credence to his fallen angel reputation. He slapped the magnet back on the cabinet. "To give him his due, at least the bastard had enough conscience to make sure he dumped me somewhere decent rather than just cut me loose into the system."

"A Catholic orphanage."

"Ah, so you're reading my file after all. Nice work." He sprawled in one of the two government-issue chairs in front of her desk. "The sisters did good by me. I've got no complaints from then on. Guess I just relate better to women because of those hundreds of mothers in penguin clothes taking care of me."

"And that's a part of why you picked me for your sessions, because I'm a woman."

"Maybe." He grinned again, charming without stepping over the line. The guy was gifted at maneuvering.

She was better. "And since I'm married to 'one of you' then you figured I'd be more likely to cut you some slack."

His boot slid off his knee and thumped to the floor. "Hell. You're as good as Sister Nic."

Nikki? Her daughter? "Sister Nic?"

"At the orphanage, Sister Nic, short for Sister Nicotine. She said most of her prayers in the garden so she could sneak a smoke. I never could get anything past her, either. She was one tough lady, just like you."

"I'll take that as a compliment."

"It was meant as one. She's the finest person I've ever known."

"Is she still alive?"

"Oh yeah, raising hell sneaking her smokes in a nursing

home. Just hope she doesn't blow up an oxygen tank with her contraband cigarettes someday.''

''Sounds like the two of you are still very close.''

''We keep in touch.''

''How did she handle your being taken captive?'' Even J.T.'s normally stoic mama had broken down on the phone. Rena's fingers tightened around her pen.

In the most horrific call of her life, she'd finished relaying the rest of the facts to the oldest of J.T.'s eight brothers for him to pass along. The hell of it was, she hadn't realized until then that J.T. hadn't told his family about the split. Of course, she hadn't told hers, either, but they hadn't spoken to her since she married J.T.

''You're good at this talking stuff, yes, ma'am. Got me right where you wanted me in the conversation twice in less than five minutes. The government's nickel is being well spent on you.''

''Only if you answer my question.'' She set her pen aside so Bo wouldn't see her hand trembling.

''I never told Sister Nic. I didn't want to worry her. Since the crew members' names weren't on the news, it wasn't a problem keeping it under wraps.''

She recognized well that macho mind-set resistant to sharing troubles, always protecting the women without realizing the worry quadrupled without information.

And if they were so busy talking in shortened phrases punctuated with macho backslaps, where was the sounding board for what he'd been through? She would be more reassured if she knew J.T.—

Whoa. Hang on. This was about Bo. She would feel better if she knew *Bo* had vented to someone like Sister Nic, who could have perhaps drawn upon religious-counseling training.

J.T. had been cleared, right? He was fine.

Except there were levels of ''fine'' and some of them weren't so ''fine.'' Cleared to work wasn't the same as being a hundred percent when off work. Who would J.T. talk to when the time came to vent?

Jealousy pricked with thorny persistence. "When something as life altering as that happens, you should talk to someone about it."

Bo leaned back in his chair, arms on the rests, so obvious in his primal chest-puffing. "We men aren't big on the touchy-feely chitchat stuff."

Well, now didn't that sound like some other jet-jock she knew? "I've gathered that."

"Besides, while the experience sucked, and I hope like hell never to repeat it, the worst was over pretty quick."

"How so?"

"You know. Don't you?" Defensiveness faded, confusion furrowing trenches in his forehead. "Jesus, I figured J.T. would have told you all this and I wouldn't have to spill every detail."

Lightbulb moment. The real reason Bo had selected her dawned.

Too bad he guessed wrong in assuming her husband told her squat. But then if she let Bo know that, he might well reinvent the past to suit his purposes. If she played along, then at least he would be less likely to lie since he assumed she already knew.

That her husband wouldn't tell her pinched her pride and heart more than her overtight skirt constricting her breathing. "It's always helpful to hear things from another person's perspective. Adds surprising insights."

"Fine. We'll play this your way then if it'll get me out of here quicker."

Unease itched up her spine like the healing skin over her cut foot. She couldn't shake the feeling of disloyalty in hearing what J.T. had chosen not to tell her. Damn it, why couldn't this one have been shuffled to someone else? But even if her boss had relented, the move to a new counselor would mean starting all over again, perhaps delaying Bo's return to flying.

"The part where local warlords got ahold of us at first, was...tense. That's when I got these." He held up his hands. The right could have passed for normal with only one thin scar across the top. But the left shouted pain with fading incisions, the skin pale and peeling after so long in a cast. "Wondering what they would do with us was hell—fearing they might turn us over to one of their terrorist bosses. I wouldn't have made it out alive without your husband keeping them off me."

J.T.'s bruises.

The itch along her nerves turned to a vicious rash—ugly horror spreading through her as Bo confirmed all her worst fears about J.T.'s capture.

The longer her husband stayed silent, the more she'd hoped maybe the images haunting her were just the product of an overactive imagination. So much easier than admitting the worst had happened and her husband wouldn't even tell his wife.

Bo swung his boot back up on his knee, fidgeted with the long black laces. "There were already American hostages over there then, part of what we were checking up on—"

Pausing, he glanced up from his laces. "I swear I'm not being cagey. I can't say more than that for security reasons and it won't make any difference to what's going on here."

"I understand." Understood that her husband was a part of these things he couldn't talk about. Scary things that man-speak translated into the simple word *tense*.

"Anyhow, the Rubistanians intercepted the rebel caravan, and the bad guys turned us over to the good guys."

"Just turned you over?"

"Yep. They knew they were outgunned, so they gave us up rather than die."

More manspeak understatement. No doubt. "What about the days that followed?"

"Consisted of questioning while we waited for international channels to clear, and for the Rubistanians to poke around inside our plane. I don't remember a whole lot since I was drugged up for the pain most of the time."

"Does it help to downplay the events?"

He looked up, his eyes clear of the fog from reminiscing, if not the horrors of what he'd endured. "Yes."

Pain pulsed from him. She couldn't miss it even with the distance of training. The toughest part of her job. And this was a near stranger. The words would be hell coming from J.T.'s mouth.

If he ever told her.

"I don't mean to sound inane, Lieutenant, but you do realize that if you climb back into the plane, this could happen again?"

"I accept that as part of my job."

"And you're okay with it?" she asked, only noticing as the words fell out of her mouth that she'd opted for J.T.'s abbreviated manspeak.

"Only a moron is going to be totally okay with it."

The sanest response he could have given. Rena could all but see him step that much closer to his plane again.

"But I'm less okay with quitting. I owe a debt."

"The time left on your Air Force obligation can be spent in another job."

"That's not what I meant." He pushed to his feet, restless pacing resuming. "I was brought up by people who gave everything for other people, for me. I need to do something to repay that. I figured out pretty damn fast I wasn't meant for the priesthood." He tossed her a roguish wink that almost lit the dark shadows from his eyes.

Bo scooped a crystal paperweight off the corner of her desk, tossing it one-handed in the air. "And I'm too selfish in a lot of ways to go for the self-sacrificing gig. I like my toys. But I have to give *something* back. My Air Force commission allows me to settle the debt with the fringe benefits of some kick-ass toys.''

He gave the weight a final pitch, snagged it midair, then replaced it on her desk. ''I'm not as good as the people who brought me up. And I'm not some genius who can cure cancer.'' He placed his scarred hands on the edge of her desk. ''But once I left the home, I discovered that these hands that were so good at playing music also had a talent for loving a woman and flying an airplane. These hands are who I am. I won't let anyone take that away from me.''

He pinned her with his eyes, direct, no shutters or walls blocking her from seeing the man's burning drive to crawl back into that plane.

Then he spun away, hands on his hips, shoulders heaving. ''Screw this. I've had enough. Isn't the government's nickel spent out for today yet?''

She could have continued for hours exploring the Cro-Magnon implications of what he'd revealed. But that wasn't her job. Instincts told her that while this young man might well have hang-ups, they had no bearing on his fitness to fly.

And about how his hands had been broken? What had happened that day? He'd definitely closed up for the afternoon, but she'd made the break in getting through to him. They would move on to that in the next session.

Still, she couldn't help but wonder, did men really think their entire worth could be summed up with their job and sex? Did her husband think that? With J.T.'s walls so high, she didn't know how she would ever find the answer.

And at the moment, with Bo's recounting of the capture still clanging horribly in her ears, she doubted her ability to keep her own defenses in place around J.T. while finding the answer. Even a hint of encouragement from her reticent husband and she would fall into their old patterns of comforting him the only way he ever allowed.

Naked. With hot, sweaty sex.

Chapter 8

Streetlights flickering on dotted the naked horizon.

Perfect. J.T. shifted gears on the truck, whizzing past their exit. Rena frowned, but stayed silent, the low tunes of the oldies station drifting from the radio.

He'd managed to kill enough time on base to make their drive home dip closer toward sunset. Excellent for his plans. Now they cruised along over the swampy tidewaters, bridges a constant for the waterlogged region. Twenty minutes later, he pulled off onto a two-lane rural road.

"Where are we going?" she finally asked from beside him. Her window down, she tugged the two long black sticks from her bundled hair and let it ripple in the wind.

Now he really wanted that drive.

Hopefully she wouldn't nix his idea before it even took flight. "I figured you've been cooped up in the house for so long, you could probably use time outside. I thought we'd take a ride before we head back to the house."

He could talk to her at home, but not without the risk of

interruption. There were also too many doors to slam. A sunset was romantic, right? Would she agree? His period of romancing her had been so damn short, he wasn't sure what she preferred. They'd spent most of their dating days in the back of her car.

This time he would keep his hands on the wheel and his flight suit zipped.

"Take a drive?"

"Sure. Why not?" Then he would conveniently detour somewhere scenic, overlooking the water where they could talk, away from interrupting teenagers. Already moss-draped oak trees alongside the road grew thicker, more private.

He reached behind the seat and pulled out a Coke.

Rena stared at it as if he held a snake. "You brought a Coke?"

"Uh…" He dropped it between them and reached back again to select a— "Diet Coke?"

He winced. Way to go, Romeo—insinuate she needs Diet when you're already on shaky cheapskate ground romancing her with a one-dollar sixteen-ouncer.

But she would know he was up to something if he started crawling up to her window with a fistful of daisies. A drive and a Coke seemed a safer, nonobvious way to start working his way back into her good graces.

Already up to his ass in the plan, he might as well forge ahead. He arced his arm behind the seat again and pulled out a chocolate Yoohoo. "Or this can count as calcium for the baby with some chocolate for you. You'll have to key me in on what you're craving, because I'm pretty damn clueless about what you'll like."

Would she get the double meaning? Subtext wasn't his strong suit.

She stared down at the bottles resting in her lap. "Have you been keeping a junk-food stash in your car all these years?"

"I stopped by the shoppette before I picked you up." He couldn't see her face clearly enough to gauge her reaction. "That's why I was late."

"You planned this?" Still she didn't so much as glance his way, but her voice went soft.

Progress. Onward. "I wasn't sure what you would want, so I bought a little of everything." He turned off the two-lane road onto a dirt path. "When you were carrying Nikki, you couldn't get enough pizza, but then first time I brought you one when you were pregnant with Chris, you threw up all over my flight boots."

"And then we had ice cream for supper instead."

Made love. Had more ice cream. "Peach ice cream."

"You remember?" Her face went as soft as her voice.

Ooh-rah for Romeo. "I remember."

He slid the truck to a stop at one of his favorite fishing spots, total solitude with a perfect view of the inland waterway. Everything moved slow. The birds. The fish. Even the shrimp boats took their time to cast and draw back nets, cast them again or simply troll to the dock.

Why hadn't he thought to bring her here before?

Hefting the bag from behind the seat, he upended it gently into her lap, releasing a waterfall of food.

Granola bars. Pretzels. Roasted peanuts. Spanish peanuts. Chocolate-covered peanuts. Cashews. Pistachios.

"Ohmigod," she squealed, sifting snacks through her fingers. "You really did buy a little bit of everything."

"I can't take total credit. Something the guys did at the squadron gave me the idea. So do you like it?" He picked up three kinds of peanuts. "Nuts equal protein."

She scooped a bag of peanut-shaped orange candies. "Circus peanuts? And we can call this protein?"

"Hey, whatever works for you, babe."

She clasped the bag of circus peanuts to her chest. "Like

I used to tell myself the gallons of peach ice cream meant healthy milk and fruit.''

Positioning the brown sack below the edge of the seat, he raked the junk food off her lap, and hell but Rena's legs felt good even through layers of her crinkly skirt. He set the bag to the side. "What is it that you need now? Help me out here."

"So I won't hurl on your boots and mess up that nice shine?"

"I'm not talking about Coke and ice cream anymore, but I don't know how to say what you need to hear. We have to find more...neutral ground, and damn, but it was hard before and since I got back..." He shut his eyes, opened them again because the memories kept pushing through anyway. "It seems like we're more screwed up than ever."

She touched his hand. "We've never really talked about what happened to you over in Rubistan."

"There's not much to talk about." Thinking about it sucked enough. "It was scary as hell waiting for the diplomatic channels to clear, but they did. And we all came home."

She wanted more from him. Only a fool would miss that. So much for giving her words, dumb ass. But if those words would upset her? If those words scraped like a blade against his insides on the way up and out?

He would find other words for her instead. "But I made it through since I always knew I would come home again."

"How could you know that?"

"Because there wasn't a chance in hell I intended to die without making love to you at least one more time."

Her chin trembled just before she covered her mouth with a hand shaking twice as fast as that delicate pointy chin of hers. Strategy went out the open window on the marshy wind. He raised his hand, glided his knuckles along the waves of her hair.

All the want tamped down from their kiss earlier, from months, from the first time he laid eyes on her, powered to life. He held himself in check. Barely. Now his hands weren't much steadier than hers, so he let his fall to cup the sides of her neck. Her shaky fingers slid to rest on his chest.

And the next thing he knew, they were kissing again.

Not frenzied, like the out-of-control exchange in the parking lot earlier. But slow. Deliberate. No mistaking the mutual intent.

A growl rumbled low in his chest, the instinctual sound of primal possession he couldn't have stopped if he wanted to—and he didn't want to stop anything.

Apparently, neither did his wife.

She melted against him, her arms slung over his shoulders, her bracelets cool against the overheated skin along his neck. Her body flowed over his while she kissed him with all the sweet passion she'd poured over him twenty-two years ago the first time he'd persuaded her to join him in the back seat of her BMW.

Heaven help him, he would have more restraint now than he'd shown then. Even if her soft hands were crawling into the neck of his flight suit with hungry persistence.

Still in control. He could take this a little further. No problem.

Slanting his mouth over one corner of her lips, then the other, he lowered her back onto the seat, careful to keep his weight off her, for the baby, for her fragile frame. Although her hands felt anything but fragile in their strong grip on his back, his wildcat wife's fingernails digging tiny moons into his shoulders.

He deepened their kiss, explored the warm moistness of her, wanted to explore more, now, sooner, but damned if he would screw up this chance by rushing. She wriggled closer, soft body and softer breasts driving him freaking nuts. He had to touch her. More of her.

Any of her.

He stroked up her side along the loose blouse. No objections from his wife. He skimmed his hand forward and palmed her breast. A groan of contentment rolled though him in sync with the sigh escaping from her lips into him.

She arched to fill his hand, rolled her shoulders so his touch became a firmer caress. Pregnancy plumped her breasts and damned if he hadn't forgotten how it also increased her sensitivity, something they'd enjoyed to the fullest in those early days of marriage.

What a waste not to make the most of it now, and he was anything but wasteful.

He worked his thumb back and forth over the peak straining through even a bra and thin cotton, tugged it gently between two fingers. She nearly came up off the bench seat. Rena's breathy, needy whimpers encouraged him to charge ahead. Her hips rocked up and against him. She wrapped a leg around his hips.

Still in control? Barely. And fast on his way to not at all. Hell, forty-two years old and he felt as horny as at twenty. So desperate to have this woman, so tempted to let the past replay.

But even then he'd known it was wrong. He was wrong for her. Still, he'd lost his hold on reason the first time Rena—totally hot and caught up in the moment—brushed a hesitant touch over the crotch of his flight suit.

Like now. Except not in the least hesitant this time, instead confident in exactly what turned him inside out with wanting her.

Stop. He had to stop if he ever wanted a chance at more. And he definitely wanted more.

He kissed once, again, drawing away in increments, a man addicted to the taste of her and unable to make a clean break. All the more reason to pace himself.

He lifted his head and found a new resting place against

the velvet skin where her neck met her shoulder, a spot he happened to know turned *her* inside out.

Her fingers threaded through his hair, her touch anchoring him and making him fly all at once. She pressed her cheek against his head. "I'd forgotten what a great kisser you are until you reminded me this afternoon. And now."

"I'm not sure whether to be complimented or insulted, babe."

"Definitely complimented."

"If I was that great you wouldn't have forgotten."

"It's just been so long."

"Only three months." And he remembered everything about her from that time. The shape of her hip under his palm. The taste of her skin. The flowery scent of her shampoo that reminded him of all her flowers filling the dark, empty places in their lives.

"We stopped kissing a long time before that, J.T."

Hell. Turbulence ahead. And he didn't have a clue what to say next. He'd pretty much blown his wad on sensitivity with the comment just before she'd kissed him. "I kissed you, damn it."

Crap. Sergeant Sensitivity? Not.

She stiffened under him, shoved against his shoulders. "Obligatory pecks on the cheek on your way out the door don't count. And when we had sex, we pretty much went from smoldering looks to clothes off in under two seconds."

Time to shift tactics. Humor maybe. He angled up and off her. "Hey lady, are you accusing me of being a quick trigger?"

"You know better than that and don't try to change the subject." She smoothed her skirt back into place, running her thumb along the waistband. "I'm actually having a bit of an epiphany moment here and I would like to play it through if you don't mind. Besides, weren't you the one who said you wanted to talk today?"

Bitten on the ass by his own good intentions. Why the hell had he thought he wanted to talk in the first place? He should have gone straight for the one way he always managed to get through to this woman. With sex.

Except damned if she wasn't in the process of telling him how he'd screwed that up, too. "Okay, so you're saying I didn't kiss you enough. I thought I had the foreplay thing covered, but I'm sorry if I—"

"Good God, J.T., would you get your testosterone out of this conversation for a second and listen? I'm not accusing you of anything. I'm saying *we* stopped kissing a long time ago. You know full well you're an incredible lover, generous, sexy."

"Okay, Cro-Magnon level lowering, returning to the modern age." Tension waning, he winked. "And thanks."

"You're welcome." A smile quirked her kissed-poofy lips. "All I'm saying is that in some ways kissing is much more intimate than sex, and somewhere along the line we let that get away from us. It scares me to realize that because then I have to accept that we started falling apart a long time before I saw it coming, which means there's even less hope."

She was hoping?

"Rena, babe, I'm going to be straight up with you. We have our problems. I know that. But damn it, I want us to give it another try. I'm not saying we should jump right back into things. We can take it slow. Keep on like we are for a while. Cokes, circus peanuts and family dinners. More kisses."

"More kisses?"

Ah, he'd breached the defenses. He could read her so well sometimes. He leaned to kiss her again because she'd made her wishes on that clear, even for a dense male like himself. And kissing his beautiful wife was sure as hell no hardship. Her lips moved under his.

Bullet dodged. He could already envision his boots marching across the hall to their rightful place beside her heels lying lopsided, cast off beside their bed.

He skimmed a hand down her satiny arm, linked their fingers, curved them forward to rest on the slight swell of her stomach. "It's gonna be okay, Rena. We'll work it out, make it right, this kid's going to be a new start for us. We'll be there for it just like we were there for Nikki and Chris."

She stiffened against him, even more rigid than before when she'd shoved him off her. "You want to come home for the baby."

What a damn odd question. "Of course."

Her fingers untwined from his. The fading sunset rays cast shadows across her face while somehow showcasing the ones in her eyes. "Did you ever really love me?"

Talk about stunned stupid.

Rena wasn't sure who was more shocked by the question, her or her immobile husband.

He recovered faster, though. "I told you I did."

The tide shushed along the shore, reminding her she should have kept her mouth shut.

"Forget I asked." She'd known he was coming home for the baby, but hearing it confirmed seconds ago hurt even more than she'd expected. "I'm being a hormonal, sentimental pregnant woman. I just want to eat my circus peanuts and go home."

How could she trust his answer now that he knew what she expected to hear? She'd given away her whole hand of cards because of a few kisses. Some things never changed.

She hooked her elbow on the open window and popped a circus peanut in her mouth just as the first stars overcame the setting sun.

"No way, babe." He tipped her chin toward him, his touch gentle, his gray eyes filling with storm clouds, all the more powerful considering how rarely her controlled husband lost his cool. ''You brought this up and there's not a chance you can deny that I said the words. I know I told you. I may not have said it every time I walked in the room, but I know what came out of my mouth.''

Rena swallowed down the lump of sugar too thick for her constricting throat. Did he have to sound so harsh? Pain, betrayal, frustration shifted to anger, mostly with herself for laying her emotions bare before this man. Again. ''Oh, get real, J.T. 'I love you, babe, please, please let me get in your pants' doesn't carry much of a romantic punch once the horniness wears off a couple of hours later.''

''But it worked,'' he snapped, then cursed. ''I'm sorry. I shouldn't have said that.''

She bit back the urge to call him a bastard, since she'd been the one to lash out first with the ''getting into her pants'' comment. Totally unfair since she'd been just as eager to get into his then—now, too.

His chest rose and fell with regulated frequency. Back in control. Overly so. ''I'll try to translate this manspeak into something you'll understand. I gave you the best I had. I know you deserve better, but this baby limits our choices.''

''This is exactly why it won't work, J.T. We haven't even been in the house together for two weeks and already we're tearing each other up again.''

''And about your question...'' He plowed ahead without acknowledging her point.

She didn't want to know. Either way, yes or no, truth or lie, the answer would slice through her. ''I said never mind.''

''But you said something else after that. Yeah, there was nothing I wanted more than to be inside you, and I intended to make damn sure once you let me get there, you wouldn't be sorry or left wanting. And then when we were together, I found all that locker-room wisdom didn't matter. I didn't need it, not when I had those breathy little sighs of yours guiding me if I just listened." He dipped his head to her neck. "Do you still like it when I kiss you right here?"

The edge dulled on her anger, and God, but she resented him, herself, for the predictability of her body's betrayal.

He sketched higher to her ear. "Or when I do this? You usually purr for me when I do that."

J.T. nipped the lobe, continued to vulnerable patches of skin too long neglected. His hands traveled down her spine in a sensual massage that sent her bowing against him again until finally he cupped her bottom and brought her even closer. "And what about that?"

She whimper-purred her assent and frustration.

"Yeah, babe. I heard you." He stared down with narrowed eyes. Pissed. Insistent, and yes, even aroused. "And maybe I was just meeting some elemental itch you had, and I missed the big picture. But at least I was listening and trying my damnedest."

He withdrew his hands, his body, moving away, the muggy air suddenly chilly in comparison to her overheated flesh.

Her muddled brain shouted at her to process his words while her aching heart told her to run. Her flaming body urged her to just jump him so her brain and heart would shut up because everything was crumbling around her.

"I listened to you, Rena, and maybe I'm not as good at understanding out of bed as I am in bed. But I *am* trying, damn it."

As much as she wanted to cry or rage, at least they were talking and she wouldn't let temper or tears shut that down.

She stared into stormy gray eyes usually so steady, constant, ever honorable, and the truth deluged over her like those storm clouds opening up. In his manspeak way, J.T. had answered her question after all. J.T. didn't lie. He gave sparse accountings, but his words counted. He'd told her he loved her then. She'd just never listened.

The truth raining over her chilled to a deeper realization of icy, sheeting sleet. He'd said loved. Past tense.

Today, he hadn't said a thing about loving her still. In fact, he hadn't said those words for a long time. And she couldn't help but notice his love had stopped right about the same time as the kisses.

He'd screwed up.

J.T. lifted the crutches out of the back of the truck in their driveway, sidestepped a bush of pink flowers…azaleas maybe? Or wisteria? Hell he couldn't keep all her plants straight. Or her needs.

He passed the crutches to his silent wife, crickets sawing in the background, night traffic in the neighborhood slow and sporadic. Damn it, he shouldn't have lost his cool. He still wasn't sure exactly where he'd slid off course, but no doubt, his plan to woo Rena had been shot down.

"Thanks," she said without looking at him. She swung trim calves out of the truck, hopped on one foot taking the crutches from him.

He followed while she worked her way down the flagstone path, ready to catch her if a crutch went rogue in the soft lawn. Why did she have to make this so difficult? Everything from a simple trip inside to where he parked his boots.

Not that he intended to ask her. He kept his yap shut, because if she questioned whether he'd said he loved her all those years ago then he must have messed up worse than even he'd imagined. He'd done something seriously wrong and still he couldn't pinpoint what. He'd tried his best to keep the darker parts of his job and himself the hell out of an already strained marriage.

Opening the side door, J.T. followed her into the kitchen. "Son, we're home," he called.

Too bad he wasn't announcing the coming-home deal for real.

Stenciled ivy bordering the walls mocked him with reminders of the time he'd interrupted her painting. He could read her lingering arousal from their kisses in the truck. They could have been upstairs in bed now, together.

Rena rested her crutches against the counter and dragged out a chair at the table. A sign she didn't want to go upstairs with him? Or that she didn't want their evening to end?

She dropped into one chair, propped her foot on another. She slipped her hand into a side pocket on her skirt and pulled out a package...of peanuts. Honey roasted. She tore open the corner with her teeth, poured half the minipack into her palm.

Quiet echoed through the house, dishes on the counter. Two glasses?

One with glittery lip gloss kissing the rim. God, he couldn't be everywhere at once checking on his family.

Chris's footsteps thudded down the second set of stairs leading into the kitchen. "Hey, Mom. Dad. Have fun?"

"Yeah, we had a nice drive." J.T. tucked one glass into the dishwasher, then the other. "Have someone over while we were gone?"

Rena looked up from her snack. "Chris?"

He shrugged, shuffled across the tile floor into the pantry. "Just a friend."

Twisting the setting knob, J.T. started the dishwasher and flipped the magnet from "dirty dishes" to "clean." "A female friend, I'd say, based on the lip gloss on the second glass."

"Just a friend," Chris repeated over the sound of a chip bag tearing open.

Rena nudged peanuts around on the table. "Hon, you know I prefer you not have girls over when no one's here."

"Sure. Sorry."

The phone rang. Lucky Chris.

J.T. yanked the receiver off the wall. "Hello?"

"Hi," a female voice crooned. "Could I speak to Chris, please? Tell him it's Miranda."

At least now he didn't have to make a room search for the girl upstairs. "Son, it's a girl for you."

Chris charged toward the phone.

"Someone named Miranda."

The boy stopped in his tracks, gym shoes shrieking on tile. He shook his head.

Cupping his palm over the mouthpiece, J.T. said, "Your mother and I will leave the room."

And go upstairs where maybe he could regain ground.

Chris stumbled back, tripping over his dragging shoelaces before righting himself.

J.T. raised the phone to his ear again. "I'm sorry, but he just stepped out. I couldn't catch him in time. Do you want to leave a message?"

"Just tell him he needs to come in to work an hour early tomorrow and run deliveries."

"Will do." He replaced the receiver. "She says you're supposed to come in an hour early to run deliveries."

Chris's face paled until acne shone double. Females could do that to a man.

"So you work with her?"

"Yeah, she's one of the hostesses." His gaze ping-ponged from one smiling parent to the other. "It's not like that."

"Okay, son. You're entitled to your privacy." J.T. hefted the transparent garbage bag out of the trash can. "But that doesn't mean I won't be curious as hell."

J.T. started for the door. Rena's gasp stopped him. "What? Is something wrong? The baby?"

"Bring the bag over here," she ordered, standing on one foot. She yanked the clear bag from his hands, tore it open.

Dumped it on the floor? She started rifling through empty cans and wadded napkins.

"What in the hell are you doing, Rena? Careful or you're going to cut yourself."

She knocked aside his hands and pulled free from the rubbish...

A box for an early-pregnancy test.

Chapter 9

Hand shaking nearly as much as her insides, Rena thrust the box closer to her son.

Talk about a visit from the Ghost of Knocked-Up Teenagers Past. Nothing like having her own mistakes come back to haunt her. But she couldn't think about herself or her own fears, not with a more pressing concern on her hands.

Literally.

Chris snatched the empty box from her. "You can both quit with the freaked-out looks. It's not mine. Well, I mean, obviously the test isn't *mine,* but it has nothing to do with me. You know?"

J.T. nudged his toe along the pile of soda cans on top of an empty cereal box. "Then what is it doing in our trash?"

"It was for a good friend." Chris's words tumbled over each other. "Someone you don't know."

His squeaky gym shoes betrayed his attempt to lie, and that twisted more old fears inside her. She'd worked to teach her children the importance of honesty—a trait she so admired in their father.

Even when that honesty broke her heart.

Of course, this lie didn't rank up there with a Mob hit or money laundering or any of the other things her family had been accused of while she was a child. But she was so afraid of unwittingly passing along defective genes and shifty mind-sets to her kids.

To some degree hadn't she taught her son about shading the truth by pretending if she filled her house with plants and overbright smiles no one would notice her empty marriage?

Chris jammed his hands in his pockets. "She was worried she might be pregnant and she came over here to run the test while you were gone since there's, like, never a quiet time around her house. It's a real fishbowl over there. But she's not pregnant, so it doesn't matter, right?"

Not pregnant. Relief took the edge off her fears. If the test had been run correctly.

Rena laid a hand on her son's arm, patted until his shoulder dropped with lowering defenses. "What about false negatives on the test? She needs to be careful and take care of herself, just in case."

"A couple of hours after the test, uh, she found out for sure." Red crept up his face, tipping his ears beneath his dark curls. "She said she figured it must have been stress affect-ing, you know, her cycle."

J.T.'s jaw flexed. "And this makes everything okay?"

"Yeah, of course it does, Dad. She's not pregnant. Great news."

Foot throbbing as much as her head, Rena slid back into her chair, her hand tugging Chris around to face her while J.T. calmed down. "You two were lucky this time. But what happens next time? Safe sex is important for more reasons than unplanned pregnancy. There are diseases out there that can kill you."

"Like I don't know that already? They've been telling us that in school since junior high."

"All right, just doing the parent thing and checking." Rena drew in a shaky breath. "I wish you would have at least brought Miranda over to meet us."

"Miranda? I'm not seeing Miranda. She's just somebody—" Chris shuffled his feet, squeak, squeak "—from work."

J.T.'s shoulders bunched over their son's shoe squeak that chimed like a telltale lie detector. Rena rushed to add, "Okay then, whoever it is, I wish we could meet your friends."

"When?" Chris's deepening voice grew louder. "When's ever a good time around here lately? Besides, like you two have any room to preach to me about getting somebody pregnant even if I had done it."

"Enough." J.T.'s curt edict cut the air.

The air snapped between father and son. Chris's words hurt, but not as much as watching her family disintegrate under the weight of mounting tensions. "J.T., it's okay."

"Like hell it is." J.T. stepped over the pile of trash and stopped nose to nose with his son. "Don't ever talk to your mother that way again."

Chris backed until his butt bumped the counter. "Fine, okay. But I'm not dating anybody. I'm definitely not getting busy with anybody. God. Like anyone would have me. I helped a friend. That's all. You don't want me messing around in your business? Well, stay out of mine." He pivoted on his Nikes and sprinted up the stairs two at a time.

His door slam echoed.

Rena sagged back in her chair. So much for her pride in her mediation skills. Now the evening sucked on all levels. Her hands fell to her lap, peanuts and hope weighing like lumpy cookie dough in her stomach.

Kneeling, J.T. scooped up the garbage, stuffing it back into the bag until at least the floor was clear, if not their lives.

She wadded up the empty snack wrapper and extended her hand to add it to the trash. If only she could back the day up to the start of their drive, just Cokes and kisses. No stupid "Did you ever love me?" questions. "We'll talk to him again tomorrow."

J.T. gave the bag ties a vicious yank. "Damn straight I'll be talking to him. And he'll be giving you an apology shortly thereafter."

She bit back the urge to tell him to go easy on her little boy who wasn't so little anymore. More than ever she needed to let J.T. find his way as a solo parent, too, in case...

The peanuts gained fifty extra pounds of dread in her stomach.

She inched her hand up into her loose shirt and released the waist button on her skirt. She would need maternity clothes soon, new baby things. Would she and J.T. shop for a baby crib together this time? Or would they need two, one for his place and one for hers?

Reaching under the sink, he unrolled a new garbage bag and lined the trash can. He prowled the kitchen, closed an open kitchen cabinet. Smacked the lid back on the airplane cookie jar.

Finally, the kitchen immaculate, he sat, leaning down to untie one boot, then the other. "At least we have a clue now as to why he's been so preoccupied."

"Do you believe him when he says he couldn't have been the father? He's sixteen, almost seventeen. I understand teenagers have sex." She was proof of that one. "But Chris hasn't seemed to go out much in anything other than groups."

J.T. dropped the boot on the floor beside the other. "I think he's telling the truth. Except I can't help but wonder what's up with this friend Miranda or whoever she is. She's obviously sleeping with someone, and she didn't turn to the father. What the hell's wrong with the guy that she wouldn't go to him?"

The unspoken accusation of Rena keeping the pregnancy

secret flicked her conscience. "I know I should have told you about the baby sooner."

"Thank you." He nudged one boot closer to the other with his toe, lining them up before leaning back in the chair when in the past days he would have unzipped his flight suit partway, made himself at home. "There's obviously a problem there. If he's a violent type, then he's not going to like his girlfriend turning to Chris."

"You're thinking about the car accident?"

"Just running through possibilities. I can't seem to get away from the fact that you were in Chris's car, and damn it, that van swerved deliberately. Not some drunken weaving. Once the van hit you, it didn't so much as take out a trash can on its way off. The driving was deliberate and smooth."

"A disgruntled boyfriend?"

"Could be an explanation. Hormones and rage together can be a lethal combination."

"And you need an explanation."

"Don't you?"

"Accidents happen."

"And sometimes they don't." He leaned forward, elbows on his knees. "Look, I don't want to argue with you about this. Especially not now when it seemed like maybe we were making some headway earlier. We never finished our discussion in the truck—about trying to work things out."

Headway that ground to a halt when he'd made it clear he wanted to come home for the baby. She'd gone that route once and ended up with her heart shredded. "We've tried before—"

"Hold on. I'm not talking big plans. Just keep things like they are for a while longer. We still have the weekend before you can drive. There's the question of what's going on with Chris. Why shake things up?"

Because she didn't think she could survive watching J.T.'s broad shoulders walk out of her life again.

"No need to decide now. Tuesday, I have a flight I can't cancel or change. Lots of prep work, too. Why don't we regroup after that?"

Putting off answering seemed easier than discussing anything else tonight with the taste and smell of him still on her. "Tuesday, then."

"Good. This is the right thing, babe, you'll see." He scooped his boots up and stood. "'Night, Rena."

He leaned and kissed her. On the lips, lingering a full two seconds beyond a peck but not long enough for her to gather her thoughts and object.

Then he was gone, the familiar thud of his steps echoing up the stairs.

And thank God he hadn't pressed her for more, because just like twenty-two years ago in the back seat of her BMW, she was afraid she couldn't tell this man no.

"Dad, I want to quit working at the restaurant."

J.T. stared up from the weight bench at his son spotting for him in their garage workout area. "What brought that on?"

"Just don't like it there."

"You're going to have to do better than that." He extended his arms, sweating through his third set of ten reps. His job required less lifting these days as things became more mechanized, but the physical exertion still let off steam. He had steam to spare at the moment, and he needed the time to check up on his son. "A man doesn't quit on his obligations."

Accusatory brown eyes stared back down at him. "Really?"

"There's a difference between divorce and quitting." He huffed through lifts. Muggy gusts of air through the open window by the tool bench provided minimal cooling, merely moving around the scent of sweat and motor oil.

"Sure, whatever."

"Seven, eight," J.T. counted to calm his frustration as well as mark his repetitions. "Nine, ten."

He hefted the two hundred fifty pounds onto the brackets, releasing the bar with a clang. He swung his feet around to the side, snagging a towel from the floor and swiping his head. "So, son? Reason for quitting?"

Chris shrugged, baggy T-shirt rippling. "Exams are coming up. I need to study and, like, with those extra deliveries Miranda was talking about, the job's taking up lots more time. I was thinking I could, uh, quit at the restaurant for a few weeks and then find something else once summer starts."

"Why not ask for a couple of weeks off?" He grabbed the gallon milk jug filled with water and tipped it back, chugging.

Chris swiveled away to adjust the weights, decreasing to one-twenty for his go-round on the bench. "My boss, Mr. Haugen, won't go for that."

"Do you want me to talk to him about time off or cutting out the deliveries?"

He jerked around. "No!"

J.T. set down the jug on the Astroturf covering concrete. "Did he let you go and you don't want to tell me?"

"I'd just like to find something else."

The reasons made sense, but something didn't ring true in his tone. Bottom line, though, he couldn't make his son stay with the job. Chris could just screw up and get fired if he wanted out that much. "Fine. I can't argue with a kid who wants to study more. But I do expect you to find something else once school's out. You're not going to lie around here all summer while your mother and I are at work."

Chris dropped onto his back on the weight bench, feet to the side on the ground. "Is this about the stuff in the trash again?"

"Partly." J.T. stepped in place to spot for his son. "I understand you feel that you can't betray a friend's confidence.

But be careful. If this girl's boyfriend starts gunning for you—''

''He won't.''

''Are you sure, because—''

''He won't.''

O-kay. He wasn't getting any more out of Chris on that one. Although he almost hoped the angry-boyfriend scenario was true, because then there wouldn't be unanswered questions. One angry teen was a helluva lot easier to deal with than original concerns about a gang. Or that something might have leaked about his surveillance flights.

J.T. stared down at his son on the bench. ''You owe your mother an apology for what you said the other night. You hurt her.''

So did you, his son's eyes accused silently. ''I'll tell her I'm sorry.''

Chris hefted the weight bar off and closed his eyes. Concentration or avoidance? Either way, the shutout was obvious.

Two sets of ten later, Chris replaced the bar, ducked around it and sat up. ''No sweat about the summer job, Dad. I got a line on something at the squadron pool party. Spike told me he heard they were looking for lifeguards at the base pool. He said he thought I had a good shot at getting a slot.''

''Ah, now I get it.'' J.T. sat beside his son. ''Bathing suits.''

A sheepish grin twitched across Chris's face, just like the time J.T. had caught him flushing Legos down the toilet.

He hadn't thought much about Chris and swimming, or that his son might have different sport preferences than his own interest in football and wrestling. But since Spike had once been a professional diver during his stint with the CIA, if the guy thought Chris could handle lifeguarding, then it must be so. ''Not a bad way to spend the summer and earn money. Sure a helluva lot more fun than the way I spent my summers as a teenager. I'm lucky now to be doing something I enjoy.''

Chris picked up his water bottle, rolled it between his palms. ''Why did you go into the Air Force?''

''Where I grew up, it was either join the military or work in the steel mill. In my family, when we turned eighteen, we had to head out and earn a living. No hanging around to 'find yourself.' Six picked the mill. Three of us enlisted.''

''But why did you enlist instead of doing what your other brothers did?''

''You're going to college.''

''I know. But why did you decide to join up?''

''If you're thinking about the military, you need to know this isn't an easy job.'' J.T. scratched a hand up his tank top along his ribs where a phantom ache twitched. His eyes gravitated to his tome of Shakespeare's plays, currently tucked sideways between his ratchet set and buzz saw. ''Be sure you're called.''

''Were you called?''

''Not at first.''

''Huh?'' Chris's jaw slacked. ''No way. I thought you lived for this stuff.''

''I do. Now.'' Or God knows he would have never pulled his family through the moves and stress. ''Back then, I just wanted out of that town. I joined for the GI Bill, planned to get a degree, thought after that I'd work in some office. Hell, I'd run the whole damn steel mill.''

''So why aren't you?''

''Because once the airplane took off, I heard the call.'' He could still feel the rush of that first training flight, the lift, the sense of purpose, the chance to make things happen and not just have things happen to him. ''After that, I decided I didn't want to get out for the four years it would have taken me to get a degree. Why should I anyway? I was doing exactly what I wanted.''

He'd had more money, security and benefits than when growing up. He hadn't counted on meeting Rena and wanting to give her more.

"And you met Mom."

Was the kid a mind reader? "Yeah, I met your mom."

"How do you know when you meet her? The one?"

J.T. studied his son, used some of that Rena-insight stuff he'd just started to glean. And ah crap, sometimes it was better not knowing. The poor kid sure as hell wasn't the guy who almost knocked up the girl.

But he loved that girl anyway.

Clasping his hands between his knees, J.T. searched for the words to make this one better for his kid. A hopeless deal when he couldn't even make things better for himself in the woman department. "You've gotta go with your gut on that one, son. There's no clear-cut answer. You just know when you see her."

And wasn't that the truth? Rena had been so hot that day, still was. But honest to God, he'd fallen for her laugh.

"So if Mom was the one, then why did you decide to split?"

"Now, there's the million-dollar question." He tugged his weight-lifting gloves tighter on his hands. "Sometimes right for one person is wrong for another. Sometimes you meet the right person at the wrong time. Sometimes it's the right person at the right time and you do all the wrong things because you're a dumb ass. Basically, it's a real crapshoot getting all the rights lined up at the same time." He glanced sideways at his son. "Any of that make sense?"

"Yeah, it does." Chris stood, crossed to the weight rack, lifted the curl bar. "So what do I do about it…if I have that problem, right person, wrong time?"

"Hell, Chris." J.T. joined him and started alternating curls. "If I had the answer to that one, do you think I'd still be sleeping across the hall?"

"Guess not."

Arms pumping, J.T. thought about telling Chris he didn't have to make any decisions, but hesitated. His son had asked a man's question and deserved a man's answer.

J.T. slowed the reps, replaced the weights and faced Chris eye to eye. "The best I can offer you is the knowledge that you're in the same boat with the majority of the male population. Women are a mystery. And the guy who figures out that mystery could sell the secret for enough money to *buy* the whole damn factory."

Something he now knew wasn't his calling, even if that factory could buy Rena everything she deserved. Damn but he'd wanted to give her more. Yet even as his gut revolted at the thought of a repeat of three months ago, a repeat of what he'd put Rena through, he knew he wouldn't walk away from the Air Force.

"My advice, son? Go ahead and quit the job at the restaurant. Study your butt off for the exams. Then enjoy the hell out of that lifeguard job. I'm betting one of those bathing suits works her way over to your tower by the end of the first week."

He clapped his son on the back, and even though Chris only scrounged a half smile, their talk had gone well. Or at least better than any talk before.

The door into the house squeaked, opened. Rena stood silhouetted, wearing a maternity jumper.

Who the hell sucked all the air out of the garage? Because he damn well couldn't find any.

This baby was real, and getting closer to being born. A dumb-ass obvious thought, still the speed of time ticking away hadn't hit him until then.

She wasn't showing much, but nearing the fourth month, there was no question. The silky green fabric skimmed her tiny bulge. "Supper's ready."

Rena's eyes lingered on J.T.'s shoulders—bared by a

workout tank T-shirt. He could see her pupils dilate from clear across the garage. His heart rate revved in time with her rapidly rising and falling chest.

Chris snatched a towel off the hook. "Great. I'm starving. No surprise, huh?" their son rambled on in the thick silence. "Cool new clothes, Mom. Are you sure you're not carrying twins?"

Twins? Rena went as pale as he felt.

J.T. thumped his son on the chest. "Way to go charming your mother, bud. Are you trying to get us all killed?"

Chris winced. "Sorry. You, uh, look nice, Mom."

Rena gripped the railing and walked down the four steps into the garage with only a slight limp. Time was definitely running out before he would be asked to leave. Soon, she wouldn't need him.

Hell, she hadn't needed him at all since she graduated.

She stopped in front of her son, twisted a dainty fist in his shirt and tugged him down…to kiss him on top of his curly head. "You're forgiven for the twins comment, hon."

"And, uh," he stuttered, straightening, "I'm really sorry for what I said the other night." His thin arms wrapped around her for a rare teenager hug.

She patted his back with the same reassurance she'd given to lull him to sleep after toddler nightmares. "It's okay, hon."

"Thanks. Love ya, Mom." Toddler images aside, the pointed stare he shot his father over her head was definitely all man shouting, *Hurt my mama again and I'll take you down.* He blinked, returning to sixteen. "Catch ya' later, dudes, I'll just grab some food on my way up to my room. I gotta get some homework done. Thanks for the advice about the job stuff, Dad."

Their son's footsteps faded, but neither of them looked away from each other, her gaze still riveted on his shoulders and sweat-soaked T-shirt sticking to his chest. His eyes unable to move from the fertile curves of her body.

The primal need to protect her, have her, surged. The urge to lock that door and find new uses for the weight bench throbbed through him.

She backed, gripped the railing and found the first step. "I'll meet you inside."

The wind through the window molded her silky dress around killer legs and a gentle baby bulge.

"In a minute." Once he willed away the arousal.

Her retreat made it clear. No kiss this time.

At least he'd gotten one thing right during the talk with Chris. Chris would turn in his notice, ditch the extra delivery duties, and maybe they would use the extra time for more talks.

And since the added plans for tomorrow night's surveillance flight should net that final drug trafficking link, he would have a couple of days off to focus on his family. He could step up the pace on the romance crapshoot in hopes that someday he got it right.

Chapter 10

"No hard feelings, pal," Kurt Haugen said from behind his desk, a stuffed swordfish mounted on the wall over his head. Circling around to the front, he extended his hand for a shake. "You've always got a job here if you change your mind. I appreciate a hard worker."

Chris tried not to let his exhale of relief be too obvious. He shook hands, firm, the way his dad had taught him. "Thank you, sir."

"But I'll need you to leave now." Mr. Haugen leaned back against the big wooden desk, crossing one tasseled loafer over the other. "Once someone quits, I prefer they go right away. Not that I don't trust you. It's policy."

"Sure. No problem." Totally. He couldn't wait to get out, and this was so easy he wondered why he hadn't thought of it before. "And thanks for being cool about it. Things are really tense at home, with my mom expecting a baby and stuff."

"I hear you. I live in a house of women." He tipped a

framed family photo Chris's way, the gold rim outlining a smiling trio of Dad, Mom and little girl. "It's important to take care of them, keep them happy. You go easy on your mom, and I promise you it'll all be worth it when you see that new brother or sister."

"Yeah, uh, right." He shuffled his feet, ready to close the book on his crappy first-job experience. The lifeguard gig would have to be better.

Anything would be better.

Mr. Haugen replaced the photo and pushed away from the desk. "Well, no more of my proud-dad stuff. Take care and good luck."

Nodding, Chris backed away. He couldn't haul out fast enough. And best of all, he had some time to kill before his parents would expect him home.

He made tracks into the kitchen, the stink of fried fish sticking to him all the way through the door. Outside, he blinked against the sunlight—still bright even near sunset, inhaled a deep breath of salty air to clear his head.

Maybe he could grab a Big Mac and stop by Shelby's house, hang for a while. She was still pretty wigged out by the pregnancy scare and her upcoming move and the way Murdoch was pressuring her to change college choices this late in the game.

Chris kicked gravel. Didn't the guy realize how lucky he was to have somebody like Shelby? Pushing would just screw it all up. Which might not be so bad if it weren't for the fact Shelby would get hurt. And even if by some fluke she dumped her tall cool boyfriend for a scrawny geek, she was still moving in a few weeks.

It so sucked being a teenager stuck living with whatever the parents decided. Moving houses. Splitting marriages.

Definitely sucked.

He tucked around lines of parked cars, putting more space between himself and the restaurant. Okay, so *something* good had happened today. And the lifeguard job wouldn't be so bad.

But his dad was high if he thought the bathing suit chicks would be hanging out around Chris Price's tower. God, especially not with his bony arms and legs out there and his nose all white from zinc oxide. They'd probably think the base signed on a circus act. At least he didn't have to worry about burning since he tanned like his mom—the one good thing he'd inherited from her.

He rounded the corner to his parking spot—yeah, Dad, away from the ocean and the salt so Mom's car wouldn't rust.

Someone lounged against his back bumper. A girl someone. Shelby? Hope cleared his head faster than the beach air. He stepped up his pace to a jog and saw...

Miranda. Crap. His feet slowed.

Make it official. He now hated Lycra as much as lies.

So much for an easy home free. He'd just talk fast and leave even faster.

Chris threw back his shoulders and walked straight for the car. No hesitation. Ignoring the bodacious bitch, he thumbed the unlock button.

"Hey there, Chris." She arched away from the car and slithered into his path. "I hear you're leaving us."

"Uh-huh. Exams. New job. Less hours. That's life." He reached for the door handle.

Her hand fell on his. Held. Squeezed.

Ah crap, crap, crap. He couldn't push her away, because an honorable guy never got physical with a girl. More of his dad's teaching.

But what was he supposed to do when she got really physical with him?

Miranda slid her body between his and the door. Her cologne wrapped around him and just about strangled off air.

"You're sounding mighty cocky there, Chris. You wouldn't be getting any ideas?"

"Only about getting out of here." He pulled his hand off the door handle, which happened to be a little too close to Miranda's butt. Her gloating smile shouted that she knew it, too.

He crossed his arms over his chest.

She flicked her wavy blond hair over her shoulder. "Your quitting wouldn't have something to do with our little misunderstanding, would it?"

Do ya' think? "Nah. It's just what I said."

"About the misunderstanding part, you misunderstood that, too." She hooked a finger in the chain around her neck, sawed it back and forth, bringing the charm up from between her breasts. "So much misunderstanding going on. I'm not saying anything bad happened, but if you go around shooting your mouth off, people are going to think something *did* happen."

She kept on stroking that chain, the dangling charm swaying, the red circle with a black triangle in the middle a freaking hypnotizing eye magnet straight down to her—

He jerked his gaze away. Up to her face.

"My reputation will be a mess, Chris. Word gets around, doors will close for me. Word will get around about you, too. People will think you just got away with it, but that you're really a mule. A carrier."

He swallowed down fear and a hefty whiff of her perfume. How could he have ever thought she smelled good? "I didn't have any idea what was going on."

"If you go to the cops with what you think you saw, and say there was something bad going on, do you think they're going to believe you're innocent? They're going to think you're trying to save your skin."

She dropped the necklace back to rest against her tanned skin. "And if, just if, something big really was going on, don't you think the people you're dealing with might be smarter than you?''

Straightening from the car, she flattened a hand to his face and patted. ''But guys who play nice don't get hurt.''

Miranda stroked her fingers along his chin on her way past, leaving him standing alone by the car wondering how in the hell he ever could have thought Miranda Casale was hot. She was a freaking snake in Lyrca. His cheek itched where she'd touched him.

As his dad would say, he was in a crapload of trouble.

Chris jerked open the car door, double-checked the back seat to make sure it was empty and climbed behind the wheel.

Locked the doors really fast.

Part of him wanted to crawl away and hide. Okay, most of him wanted to do that, but he'd been hiding for a couple of weeks now. Instead of getting better, things were getting worse.

He felt like puking. But he wouldn't. He would be like his dad. This was the time to be a man.

He would have to come clean.

God, did Miranda really think he was stupid enough to believe nothing was going on? If there had been any doubts before, her little chat cinched it for him.

If he'd been a mule once—his stomach rolled—then they would use that as leverage to make him do other things. Maybe worse things.

Sweat popped on his forehead, feeding his zits. He would have to do something. He would have to talk to his dad after his flight.

Used to be he could talk to his mom easier, but his dad and even Mr. Haugen were both right about keeping women safe. A pregnant chick needed to be protected most of all. No question, his dad wouldn't want this dumped on her. His dad also wouldn't want her left at home alone with this kind of crap hanging over their heads.

The car accident.

Sweat iced. His stomach pitched. Chris scrambled for the handle, stumbling out of the car with half a second to spare before he lost his supper on the gravel.

Doubled over, gripping his knees, he gasped for clean air that didn't stink like Miranda's cologne, fried fish and a screwed-up life.

God. What a wuss. He dragged the tail of his T-shirt over his mouth and staggered back into the car.

He didn't have time to be sick. He needed to get home to his mom. And if he wanted to make it there without more pit stops to heave up his guts, he couldn't think about what might happen next.

Rena flipped pages of her gardening magazine, reclining on the sofa, her head propped by two pillows, her feet up on the armrest. Hot chamomile tea steamed on the coffee table. Cool air conditioner blew through the silence. A totally peaceful way to end the day.

If it weren't for the fact one of those pillows under her head carried J.T.'s scent.

He'd always had a distinctive air. Earthy, sexy. And, ohmigod, how pregnancy heightened her sense of smell, leaving her all the more susceptible to the woodsy soap swirl curling through her with each inhale.

She flipped pages, lingered on an herb garden layout. Odd how smells became associated with emotions. She'd been pruning her oregano plant when she'd heard about J.T. overseas. She still couldn't eat spaghetti.

But a single sniff of J.T.'s soap, and she found her eyes drifting shut so she could isolate that one intense sensation. Remember the very second she'd met the man and he'd bombarded *all* her senses. The magazine flopped onto her chest.

In those days, he'd been a C-141 loadmaster, stationed in New Jersey. She and three friends from her private girls' school had piled into her car and driven over the New York state line for a peek at those flyboys at their air show.

One look at J.T. and she was toast. She still firmly believed she would have fallen for him, no matter what her background. She hadn't felt the same tug to any of the other flyboys that day.

But her past had made her a pure sitting duck for the explosive attraction that rolled over her the first time she saw him. She didn't stand a chance thanks to the combination of her all-girl environment and lack of experience. What teenage boy would risk her father's displeasure by dating her?

J.T. had quietly dared plenty when it came to risking her family's "displeasure," and she would have loved him for that alone.

Still she could remember the feel of his hand on her elbow as he'd steadied her along the back ramp into the plane. And then he'd been waiting for her when she exited the side hatch. She never knew who he'd convinced to take over for him, but suddenly he was free to escort her around the air show.

He'd bought her a hamburger and she totally forgot what fillet mignon tasted like, just knew nothing could be as good as that charbroiled burger mixed with her first taste of love.

The telephone rang, jarring her out of her fog.

She pitched the magazine onto the coffee table, reaching for the cordless phone beside her teacup. "Hello?"

"Hey, babe, it's me." J.T.'s voice rumbled through the receiver.

Her elbow tingled with the phantom memory and damned if she didn't crave a hamburger.

Tucking the phone under her chin, she sank deeper into her pillows, releasing a fresh whiff of J.T. "Hey there to you, too. I thought you were supposed to take off an hour ago."

"Weather delay. We're leaving soon though. Thought I'd check in to see how your doctor's appointment went today."

She stifled down defensiveness. Just because he cared

about the baby didn't mean he wasn't concerned about her, too. The two weren't mutually exclusive. "Everything looks good—really looks good. They did an ultrasound."

"Ah hell, I wish I could have been there."

"I have a picture here for you. It shows so much more than we saw with Nikki and Chris. The newer technology is amazing."

"Then it's probably not a waste, after all, that we got rid of the old baby things, what with the improved stuff on the market."

"Picking out the new furnishings will be fun." Would they do it together?

"I guess it was too early to tell if it's a boy or girl."

"Yeah, in a couple more weeks, though."

"I want to go with you to your next appointment."

The quiet request shouted his resolve. He loved his kids. Her heart ached for him and what she knew he wanted. "No matter how things turn out, I understand this is your baby, too. You should be there."

He didn't answer for a second, the phone lines filled only with background voices from the squadron. Finally, his exhale echoed. "Thank you for that."

Guilt tweaked, hard, as it had done when she'd grieved over J.T. ringing the doorbell at his own house.

He was a good man. Even if he frustrated the hell out of her, she couldn't deny his honor, strength. He deserved better from life.

She could at least give him more today. "If you believe old wives' tales, then the baby's heart rate indicates this one's a boy."

"Another boy, huh? Either way's great by me. We haven't talked about names or anything yet. Do you have any ideas, family names?"

She'd named Chris and Nikki after an aunt and uncle she'd visited, respected, wanting to give her kids something positive from her side of the family. "What about your family this time? Or have you changed your mind since Chris was born about not having a James Taggart Price Jr.?"

"No junior," he answered without hesitation. "Going through school as Price Tag is a tough moniker."

One that stuck through to Air Force days with his call sign. She'd never considered the irony of it before, given his constant worries about money. "Okay, no junior. I'll pick up a couple of baby-name books and we can make lists."

A dangerous little emotion called hope started to flutter inside her. He really was trying. He'd been working hard to relate better with Chris, like during their talk in the garage.

Except she might be better off not thinking about the garage and a half-naked J.T. in workout clothes, arms and legs muscled, bared, sheened with sweat.

"Rena? Are you still there?"

"Oh, yeah, sorry. I was, uh, I don't know. I must have zoned out. No offense. You remember those near-narcoleptic moments of the first trimester."

His chuckle rumbled through the phone line and vibrated inside her. "I'll be quiet when I come in so I don't wake you."

Uh-oh. Too easily she could envision the times he *had* woken her after a flight. His eyes intense, charged, adrenaline all but dripping from him, and then he would pour all that intensity into making love to her, like in the kitchen after his return from Guam.

To this day, she couldn't look at that stenciled ivy without remembering the heat of him moving against her, in her, bringing her to a screaming release at eleven o'clock in the morning. Yeah, she even still remembered the exact time.

"Hey, Rena? I hear Scorch calling for me. Time to roll. See you when you wake up in the morning. Good night."

The line went dead.

"Good night," she whispered, keeping the phone cradled

under her chin for a silly sentimental moment before she thumbed the Off button.

Her eyes drifted closed. She inhaled his scent to mix with the sound of his voice still in her head and drifted into that twilight restfulness, neither asleep nor fully awake, when thoughts took their own direction. Remembering the summer weeks after she'd met J.T. when they'd stolen every moment possible together. Every time they'd said goodbye on her porch or hung up the phone, she'd been certain she would die if she couldn't be with him forever.

Teenage melodrama? Maybe. But also intense and wonderful.

Then one night, parked by the shore, they hadn't been able to wait any longer. Tugging the zipper down on his flight suit, her hands found their way inside.

She'd reveled in being safe and free when he held her, touched her. And yes, he'd said he loved her, those words sending showers of excitement rushing over her because if this honorable man loved her, then she wasn't tainted by her family. She'd believed the words with all her heart back then, not questioning whether or not he really meant them until many years later after too many silences between them.

How safe she'd felt in his arms, safety nearly as intoxicating as his touch, the way he seemed to know just where to stroke until her pulse pounded in her ears. Louder. Louder still until she'd thought she would shatter—

Shatter?

Rena bolted upright. Wind gusted through her front window, through the jagged hole. Glass sparkled on her floor.

Glass surrounding a brick.

Chapter 11

"Five minutes out," Scorch's voice announced through the headset.

"Roger," J.T. echoed from the metal belly of the plane. "Five minutes out."

J.T. stared at the red light posted in the cargo hold, then readied the hatch for the jump. A void of air swirled outside, soon to swallow the four jumpers waiting to hurtle out of his plane. Pitch night. Nothing but ocean below as they flew off the coast of Charleston.

Scorch flew as aircraft commander, Joker as copilot since Bo was out of commission. Their pilot's need-to-know status on these surveillance flights was low. No questions asked, they would fly the routes provided and go through the motions of a training flight as directed. His role in back handling divers and equipment called for more briefing.

Four divers stood, checking equipment, readying for their static line jump, J.T. acting as jumpmaster for the three DEA agents and Spike. The fourth DEA agent who'd been scheduled was currently curled up in the hospital, most likely in the fetal position, thanks to a bout of food poisoning.

Given the DEA's prestanding LOA—letter of agreement—with the OSI regarding this case, Max "Spike" Keagan had been able to step in as a last-minute replacement. Spike's diving skills and inside work on the case from the Air Force angle made him a natural choice for a quick replacement on the crucial mission.

Regular surveillance flights were still netting the same information without pinpointing that critical last link. The drugs were unloaded from the spare tires, then taken off base. The lieutenant from the transportation squadron always drove the same route to the same place at Shem Creek. Parked in the same lot out of sight and waited until a shrimp trawler pulled up.

Undoubtedly, the drugs were being loaded onto that boat. Problem was, the boat never did anything unusual afterward. No long trips. No rendezvous with another craft.

Besides, boats usually *brought* drugs to shore. Strange all the way around.

Thus the divers. The two pairs would drop into the harbor for close-up recon, and hopefully discover what the hell was going on.

"Sixty seconds," Scorch called.

"Roger, sixty seconds," J.T. repeated for the benefit of the jumpers who weren't on headset.

Geared up in a black wet suit, diving tanks, flippers, parachuting gear, Spike stared back at J.T., waiting.

Time to finish this.

J.T. nodded.

"Ten seconds," Scorch called.

"Ten seconds." J.T. listened, counted down, watched the standby light change to—

Green.

"Go! Go! Go!" He gave the first in line the traditional slap-on-the-ass signal to jump.

One, two, three, four, Spike and the other divers launched into the darkness.

J.T. struggled not to fight against the darkness. Only a slight haze permeated the hood the Rubistanians had placed over his head, but it sure as hell blocked the ability to see where they were taking him.

The very reason the Rubistanians had done it.

He kept reminding himself these soldiers couldn't know for sure who they'd captured from the warlords' caravan. Of course they would have questions and concerns about foreign military on their soil. And now that they were in official hands, chances of getting out alive were a helluva lot stronger than a couple of hours ago.

Rubistanian and American relations might be strained, but they weren't outright hostile. Rubistan didn't want to be the next Iraq.

Steady. Focus on images of Rena's face. Think about getting home. Return alive with honor.

Brusque hands guided him out of the jeep. He heard others move with him. His three crewmates?

"Stay calm," *Scorch whispered.* "Be low-key. Remember your training. Everybody here?"

"Roger," *J.T. answered.*

"Here and cool," *Spike muttered low.*

"Yeah," *Bo grunted.*

"Good, okay." *Scorch's voice moved closer.* "Just—"

A hand smacked J.T.'s back. "No talking!" *a heavily accented voice shouted.* "No talking!"

O-kay.

Footsteps shuffled along a dirt path. Or sand. Who knew? The guards talked back and forth, not that any of it made sense.

Hands guided them up concrete steps. Inside. The haze darkened.

The hood swept up and off. J.T. blinked against the stark lightbulb inside what appeared to be a craphole jail. Standard for this country. He hadn't expected any better from these guys than where they would keep their own prisoners.

He stared at his three crewmates, probably the last time he would see them until they were released. The interrogations would start now. Rough. But at least they were in official hands.

One of the foreign soldiers stepped forward. "We question now. You." He pointed to Spike. "We start with you."

They knew what to say, what not to say. Although Spike had the most to cover, and would benefit from more time to gather his thoughts. Hellish luck that they'd decided to begin with him.

J.T. glanced at Scorch. Their mission. Keep the enemy off Bo and protect Spike's secrets. J.T. started to speak, to divert attention and buy Spike extra minutes, but Scorch beat him to it.

"We demand our rights under the Geneva Convent—"

A rifle butt landed on Scorch's jaw.

The aircraft commander slammed against the wall. Blood spurted into his sand-caked mustache.

J.T. winced. But the foreign soldier reacted as expected. He shifted his attention from Spike to Scorch and hauled him off instead.

A minor victory, establishing some control over their situation.

The remaining soldiers led them away, separating them. J.T. watched until the last one faded…from…sight.

J.T. stared out into the dark void of the night sky. Empty. He closed up the hatch along with his memories. "All jumpers clear," he called into his headset. "Door secure."

J.T. strode back up the steel cavern to his station, the instrument panel and seat situated below the cockpit. Their part was done. He'd be home soon. Where his wife waited, something he hadn't fully appreciated until he'd screwed up his life.

He thought about fishing out his book, but found himself staring up at the tangle of cables tracking the ceiling instead. Right now, he wanted to pass out in his own bed with his own wife, against her soft body. Wake up and lose himself *in* her body.

Not gonna happen, of course.

But he would be across the hall. He was back in the house. Progress in regaining his world.

And not being stuck in a cell in some foreign freaking country.

Two hours later, he turned the corner onto his street to find police cars lining the curb. Foreboding gripped his gut in an icy, unrelenting fist. He threw open the door of his truck, boots pounding up the driveway, across the yard, just as hard and fast as when he'd run across the Rubistanian desert, raced to Rena in the wrecked car.

Control over his world shattered in more pieces than his living-room window.

Rena held on to her composure—barely—for once thankful her aching foot offered an excuse to sit in the overstuffed chair rather than stand.

She faced the two police officers in her living room, alone, except for an over-pale teenager shuffling his feet by the piano. She could do this by herself, but damn it, she didn't want to. She wanted to lean on her husband while he leaned on her.

And when this bizarre night ended, she wanted to crawl into the strength of his arms, lay her head on the breadth of his chest and listen to his steady heat thrum under her ear. She wanted him to tell her everything would be fine. It was just coincidence that Chris's car had been hit and a rock pitched through their window all in the span of two weeks.

She needed to hear that their son wasn't mixed up in something bad like her every parental instinct was screaming.

Hell, who was she kidding? She just flat out wanted J.T. with her.

And as if he'd somehow heard her, her husband plowed through the front door. Intense. Focused.

On her.

He stalked straight to her chair, ignoring everyone else in the room. Dropping to his knees in front of her, he clasped her by the shoulders, firm, solid. "Is everyone all right? Are you all right?"

His concern pulsed into her, soothing and exciting all at once. "I'm fine. Someone threw a brick through the window. A scary way to wake up, but nothing overly dangerous. I just thought it was important to report it to the police."

His gaze fell to the splash of glass glinting on the floor, to the harsh gouge in the wood inches away from the couch, then up at her rumpled blanket and pillows. "You were asleep in here when it happened?"

She nodded. Only a few hours ago she'd nestled into those pillows with plans to show J.T. the ultrasound photo.

His fingers bit into her skin. She struggled not to flinch and up his concerns.

"But I'm fine. Really. I wouldn't lie about this, not when it comes to the baby."

Jaw still tight, J.T. stood, turning to Chris. "Son, are you okay?"

"Yes, sir." Chris fidgeted from foot to foot, his baggy clothes rippling with every agitated move. "I was on my way home from work. I would have been home sooner but there was a backup on the bridge. God, Mom, I'm so sorry I wasn't here. Maybe I could have done something."

Horror splashed through her. "You would have stayed

right here in this house with me while we called the police.''
She couldn't even let herself dwell on what could have happened to him out there. ''No more Price heroes for me this year, thank you very much.''

The senior cop stepped forward, hat tucked under his arm. ''Sir, we did a walk around of the yard, had a second car run a quick canvas of the area. There's nothing to report. It's probably just a teenage prank, like rolling a house with toilet paper.''

''I'm not buying that.'' J.T. shook his head. ''Didn't my wife tell you about the hit-and-run two weeks ago?''

The younger female cop thumbed through her notepad. ''We have that report, too, and will follow up. We'll schedule a car to cruise by your house. Unless you have something else to tell us, that's the best we can do for now.'' She flipped her notebook closed. ''You'll want to board up that window tonight, just to be safe.''

''No problem,'' J.T. answered, already looking in need of some physical release for the tension visibly knotting his shoulders.

The police tucked away notepads and started to pack the evidence bag with the brick inside.

''Hold on a second.'' J.T. frowned, stepping closer. He cocked his head to the side for a better look at the brick. Forehead smoothing, eyes icing, he jabbed a finger at a painted discoloration on the side. ''Damn it, that's the same symbol as on the bumper of the hit-and-run car.''

Rena leaned nearer. How had she missed the markings? The inked red circle with a black triangle inside wasn't all that large, still it niggled at her brain with familiarity. Maybe because J.T. had told her, but she'd been too foggy from the accident to process the information?

Until now. Her fears for her child grew exponentially while foreboding smothered her.

"Uh, Dad?" Chris inched forward. "Can we, uh, go in the kitchen for a minute. I really need to talk to you."

Three hours later, J.T. hammered the last nail in the plywood covering the broken window. Pounding nails didn't come close to releasing the anger boiling inside him.

Somebody had screwed with his family. Put his wife's life at risk. Dared try to suck his kid into underworld crap.

J.T. gave the nail a final whack, driving it home.

Chris had given his full statement to the police. For now, it didn't look as if they would need a lawyer, but if things shook down the way J.T. suspected, they would all be spending time testifying in courtrooms before this was over.

His son would have to testify against the people who'd threatened him. The scum-sucking bastards had come after his family, leaving him in his front yard in the middle of the night doing his damnedest to take some precautions for his family while the police looked into things.

Dangerous and scary-as-hell things.

It had taken guts for Chris to come forward, and J.T. couldn't help but be proud of his kid for making the stand. Although he wanted to shake the boy for not doing it sooner. Just thinking about what *could* have happened—

He jammed another nail home.

A cop cruiser drove past for the second time while he'd been repairing the window. Some reassurance. His military web belt now in place with his 9mm holstered provided a little more.

Except there wasn't enough reassurance to douse the fire in his gut. He'd rather be back in Rubistan sweating it out while he waited for an ass-beating thinly disguised as an interrogation than have to worry about his family. He might not have provided the most glamorous life for Rena, but damn it, she was supposed to be safe in her own house.

The hammer thunked to one side. Grazed his thumb.

Crap. He needed to get his head together before he faced Rena again. She would want to talk, and he wanted to pound more nails.

Pound some heads.

At least she was occupied now hovering over Chris. The kid was scared spitless. As well he should be. He could use some coddling from his mom and wouldn't want his dad around to witness him scared and tucked into bed.

Rena's face had been so pale when he'd walked through the door, he'd thought for certain someone had died. She didn't need this. She should be putting her feet up and banging back bowls of peach ice cream.

Instead, they were facing court cases and God only knew what from this Miranda person and her deliveries. Most likely it was a drug purchase.

How ironic. He was busting his ass trying to collar drug runners to stop that very thing from happening to other people.

He'd already left a message for Spike about setting up a meeting with the OSI to report the brick incident. Not much sleep for the OSI agent tonight after the dive, but there were too many coincidences stacking up. Even if this bore no relevance to their investigation, he was bound by his job to report any brushes with possible illegal activities. Hell, even a happenstance chat with a stranger in a bar might not be so coincidental.

Had his family somehow been targeted because of him?

Paranoid? Possibly. But he couldn't be too careful when it came to Rena and the kids.

Crouching down by his toolbox, he tossed in the hammer, nails, and wished life could be this easy to organize. He hefted the box up, nails rattling against wrenches, and strode to the garage door, punched in the code. The door rolled up and open. Inside, he closed the door and double-checked the lock. Checked the window as well, then cranked the fan in lieu of a breeze since that window would be staying shut from now on.

He ditched the toolbox on his workbench—beside his Shakespeare anthology. The book was getting dog-eared from overuse these days.

Thumbing along the edges, he slowed, flipped it open. *Two Gentlemen of Verona.* "The private wound is deepest."

Well, hell. He could use a little less insight tonight.

He smacked the book shut. He'd have to work off his tension in a more basic way. Sex would be great. But not wise. And not an option.

Exercise.

He sat on the edge of the weight bench and unlaced his boots, one, two, tucked them to the side. He unhooked his web belt, placed it within easy reach on his workbench, then peeled off his sweaty flight suit. God, how many hours ago had he put the thing on?

Wearing only his black T-shirt and boxers, he reached for a pair of workout shorts flung over a weight bar.

The door from the house opened—revealing Rena. His hands closed around the shorts. Talk about being caught with his pants down.

She startled to a stop. Tension to match his rippled off her in visible waves. Corkscrew spirals of hair all but crackled with energy.

After a quick flicker-glance down his near-naked body, her gaze met and held his. "I have something I need to say."

Uh-oh.

The determination in the tilt of her chin, he recognized well. The vulnerable glint in her eyes, however, caught him completely off guard at a time when his defenses were already somewhere in the negative numbers.

He braced his shoulders for whatever she planned to tell

him—and wished he had some pants to go along with the strengthened will.

Rena's slim fingers wrapped around the stair railing, queenlike in her garage castle. "Temporary truce."

Chapter 12

Rena gripped the railing until the edges cut into her palm. Swallowing her pride came hard.

Being alone right now was harder.

She moved down another stair, closer to J.T. and the weight bench. "I don't have a clue what we're going to do tomorrow. Or the day after that. I know you want to move back in for the baby, and you have to know I'm still not sure I can live with that. We haven't really resolved anything."

His face blanked, but she'd expected that once she started discussing their problems. He gave her so few glimpses into him, his feelings. She would have to go with her instincts, all of which told her to forge ahead. To take what she could right now, find something solid to hold on to.

"But I also know this is about the worst day of my life, second only to when I heard you'd been shot down."

A vein throbbed along his temple. Not as outward a sign as some of the ones Bo displayed in her office, but she read the tension in her husband well. Her arms ached to hold him as much as her body yearned to be held.

"I can make it through tonight on my own if I have to. But God, J.T., I don't want to. I want somebody to hold me for just a few minutes while that somebody tells me everything is going to be okay. I need for *you* to hold me."

He moved toward her, slow, silent, her big stealthy husband, and yet somehow he was there in front of her before she could blink. His arms went around her, lifted her off the last two steps and clasped her to his chest, lowering her in a glide against his solid body that comforted and excited all at once. Her feet lightly touched ground, if not her senses, which were definitely still flying.

His fingers smoothed over her hair, again and again without stopping, his other hand working a firm massage against her waist that kept her anchored to him. "I can't promise you it's going to be okay. But I can promise I'll do my damnedest to make that happen. And I can most definitely hold you for as long as you need me."

How about forever? she wanted to ask. Except needing him meant more loss if he left again. Not that she expected him to walk out the door with the baby on the way. But she'd learned there were so many other ways to leave. He'd lived in the house with her for years while still seeming thousands of miles away.

J.T. rubbed circles on her back. "Did everything go okay with Chris upstairs?"

She nodded. "He actually fell asleep. I think the fear exhausted him. Is it totally ridiculous that I stood there at the door and watched him sleep as if that could somehow shift things back to when he was five and I used to do the same thing?"

"Not ridiculous at all. The five-year-old was a helluva lot easier to deal with. Bigger kids. Bigger problems." His arms tightened around her.

Frustration sparked inside her, the need to do something,

fix things in a way she could with a little child. "What did we do wrong that he didn't come to us right away?"

"Teenagers don't always see long-term ramifications. I'm guessing he kept slapping Band-Aids on the problem hoping it would get better on its own."

A coping method that sounded familiar. "Who are we to judge on that reasoning?"

"Guess you have a point there, babe." His chin fell to rest on the top of her head. "But bottom line, he's old enough to know better. He understands right from wrong, and whatever is going on with Miranda Casale is very likely wrong."

"He was worried about us. He was trying to protect us. That's not how it's supposed to be. We're supposed to protect him."

"And we are. He did come to us—even a little late—but he came clean on his own. He could have kept trying to bluff. I don't know about you, but I'm proud of him for standing up. He had to be scared as hell."

She turned her head to the side, resting her cheek on his chest. "God, you must think I'm a total mess. I'm okay now though. I only needed a second to find my footing again. Thank you."

He didn't let go.

And she didn't argue.

His hands kept their steady pace along her springy curls and against her back, slowing, shifting from soothing to sensual.

Still she didn't move. Couldn't speak. Couldn't do anything but stand, gripped by his arms and the fire swelling through her as surely as the proof of J.T.'s arousal. "What are we doing here?"

"Nothing yet, babe."

The promise in his deep voice strummed through her. She buried her face deeper into his chest, scent, heat. "But we're going to?"

"I sure as hell hope so." He tipped her chin until she looked up at him. "But not if it means you're going to send me packing tomorrow."

She couldn't stop herself from asking, "You would hold out to stay because of the kids?"

He cupped her face in both hands. "I would hold out so I could stay and have more time to fix this mess we've made of our lives."

Could they be "fixed," like the house or the car? She couldn't sort through it all now with her mind awash with worries for her son, her body craving the reliable comfort only J.T. could provide. And even though he'd avoided answering her question about staying for the kids, the fact that he wanted to try sent hope—and fear—lancing right through her.

Her fingers splayed across the ridged bands of muscles along his chest. "How about we cut a deal?"

"A deal?"

She smiled up at him playfully, even while the magnitude of her risk threatened to buckle her already wobbly knees. "I won't pitch your weights out on the lawn tomorrow, if you'll promise to talk to me. Really talk to me—after."

It wasn't a promise of forever. And the problems would still be there—everything from the lengthy separations brought on by his job, her temper, his hang-ups about her paycheck. But this compromise would pacify her irritatingly insistent logic enough for her to jump this man before she combusted with lust.

"If that's what you want."

She blinked, stunned by his easy acceptance. "You agree?"

His intense gaze shifted to a sensual smile to match hers. "But then I'm a guy. I'd promise to dance down the flight line in a tutu right now."

Much-needed laughter bubbled, a welcome reminder of

one of the things that drew her to this man—the surprise humor he saved for just the right moments.

Even as his blessed sense of timing had attracted her, so did his innate honor. This man would never lie to her. The promise of that talk offered her pride and common sense enough hope to let her body do exactly what she so desperately wanted.

Her forty-year-old pregnant body.

A moment of insecurity flickered. Then his eyelids went to half mast, silvery gray eyes gliding over her with an icy tickle that heated, excited. She knew. He definitely wanted her body, no matter what the age or pregnancy state.

Relief sweeping over her to bury any doubts deep, she brushed her lips across his collarbone. "Do you still like it when I do this?"

J.T. clenched his fingers in his wife's wild curls, the weight bench pressing against the back of his legs a welcome brace at the moment. A jolt of white-hot lust bolted from that patch of skin on his collarbone straight to his groin.

Hell yeah, he still liked it when she did that. His body shouted a resounding *Go for it,* while his brain insisted, *Don't forget how often sex screwed things up.*

And not the good kind of screwing.

He should take his time, do some more of that talking now to be sure she really wanted—

She licked his earlobe.

His brain fogged. The sensuous glide of her moist tongue against his skin proved too damn tempting on a night when the combination of the flight and the invasion of his home left him feeling raw. Basic. In the grips of the elemental need to stake his claim, protect what was his. "Rena, babe—"

"I still remember the first time I did that and how your eyes turned all intense and your lids went to half mast. Knowing what I was doing to you made me shiver. Which sent your eyes even grayer." She sketched his eyebrows with whisper-light fingers. "You still do that to me with just a look."

No doubts. She really wanted this, too.

He dipped his head to kiss her quiet before she could send him over the edge with only her words. The fan behind Rena blew her spiraling hair forward to tangle around his shoulders.

"Do you want to go upstairs?" Where he could give her an air-conditioned room and bed, if not roses and candles and all the things this woman deserved.

"I want here. Now. With you."

She nipped his shoulder, tunneled under his T-shirt, scored him lightly with her nails on a trek down that led her to snap the waistband of his boxers. Her hand dipped inside, found him, cool fingers wrapping around in a single stroke down. Up again.

All right then.

They'd done it in every room at some point, unable to resist an empty house when the impulse hit. But for some reason, they'd never had sex out here, in this place completely his.

Maybe there was his answer. He'd considered it too stark, messy, gritty for his wife. But with her gentle fist gliding along him as they stood right in the middle of the freaking weight room, he wondered if he'd caused them to miss out on something incredible by limiting their options.

Gripping the sweet give of her hips, he scrunched her dress up with crawling fingers, baring her legs to rub skin to skin against him. His fists full of silky dress, his legs against silkier skin, he tugged the dress up, over her head, her hair sweeping, falling free and…

Hell yeah. More creamy skin, lush woman and sensuality filled his gaze while lust filled his body. Her breasts swelled within the purple cups of her demi-bra. Generously. All those extra pregnancy hormones worked their magic. The bikini cut of her panties rode low, drawing a gentle line and attention to the slight curve of her stomach.

Again that primal chord strummed inside him. She was his. She carried his baby inside her. His heart pounded in his ears, his hands gripping tight to the soft fabric still holding the warmth of Rena's skin.

A final question stalled him. "Is everything okay with the baby? You've been through a lot the past couple of weeks."

"Everything's fine." She stepped closer. "Totally fine." Moved even closer until her breasts grazed his chest, beading nipples peaking the lace to tease along his skin. "The doctor said no restrictions. Although I don't think he'd be pleased if we strung up a trapeze."

"A trapeze, huh?"

She traced the corner of his smile with the tip of her tongue. "I'm not particularly graceful right now, anyway."

"I disagree." Something he intended to confirm. With his mouth. Starting now.

He kissed her, deep, moist and so damn hot, hands busy finding their way around purple lace, unhooking, skimming down and off. Passion combusted higher than any fan could combat.

Months of abstinence stoked the flame from red to blue. Bluer still until nothing but white light dotted behind his eye as he remembered how close he'd come to never being with her again.

Rena ripped at his T-shirt, yanked it up and off while he kicked free his boxers. Her body melded to his.

She sighed, damp breath caressing his chest, kisses and nips following. "I've missed this so much, missed you."

They were in total agreement on that. He cupped her breast, thumbed over the beading nipple, tugged, increasing gentle pressure between two fingers until she arched into his palm. "Why can't it all be this easy?"

"Shh." He soothed with his mouth and hands. "Right now it can be."

Creamy skin. All for him. No barriers. He dipped his face to her breast.

She was right. This was so easy, losing himself in the taste, scent, feel of her. No roar in his head other than the blood charging through his veins.

And even as he touched her in every place he knew she enjoyed, even as she reciprocated, somehow it all felt new. As powerful, impulsive—reckless—as their first time.

Without the fumbling.

He stroked down her side, delved past damp lace to trace along her folds, dip two fingers into even damper heat that contracted around his touch. Her nipple grew even harder in his mouth as she moaned.

Flat surface. He needed one. Now. Sooner.

His mind raced with options, the Astroturf floor too rough, the bed too far away. Time for creativity.

Turning, he backed her toward the weight bench, and thank goodness she seemed too absorbed in cupping his ass to question his intent since—oh yeah, her soft hand slipped around front—no way did he want to move his mouth from his current sweet target long enough to explain himself.

Bending forward, he eased her down along the bench, then knelt between her knees.

Her hands glided along and off his shoulders as she relaxed against the padded bench. "So much better than any trapeze."

"Hell, woman, you turn me inside out anywhere, anytime, and you know it."

Skimming her panties down slender legs and off, he flung aside the purple lace. He hooked her knees around his arms, spread her thighs slightly, her upper body totally there and on display just for him. For his hands. For his mouth.

He pressed his lips to her ankle, over to the still-pink scar from her stitches as if he could take all her pain into himself. He nuzzled the crook of her knee, worked his way up, and man, but did she ever sigh and make all those sweet sounds to guide him. Affirmations somehow became clearer, more arousing now that he realized how close he'd come to losing her.

His smile caressed her inner thigh just before he continued his path up until her scent filled his senses—roses and pure her.

"Yes," she sighed.

Again, he heard, agreed, settled between her legs and parted her to drink, deeper, fuller, his tongue circling the tight bundle of nerves. Her next sigh hitched on a sweet whimper-moan that encouraged. Urged. Guiding him to what she wanted, needed now, right now from his hands and mouth.

From him.

And then he heard the sweetest sound of all in her completion. But different, edgier somehow. Torn from her throat in a way he totally understood because this woman tore the breath from him sometimes.

J.T. pressed a lingering kiss that drew another tremble of aftershocks from her.

He may not be able to control forever with Rena, but he could make sure he heard that echoing completion again tonight. And again after that until she was damn near hyperventilating, if he had his way.

But first, he allowed himself a second to look at her— couldn't have looked away anyhow as more of that "first time" sensation rolled over him anew. Instead, he took in the image of her long dark hair spiraling to the floor. Her arms overhead, fingers still clenched tight around the steel grips, her perfect breasts rising and falling so fast, her body flushed from the release he'd brought her.

Her eyes fluttered open. A hesitant smile flickered. "You're making me a little self-conscious here."

He shook his head slowly, kept right on staring his fill.

"No need for that, babe. I'm just…" He paused, swallowing, words scarce for him on a normal day, and right now with so much of the past, present—damn it all—emotion clogging his throat and brain, words came tough. "There are times I can't believe I'm the lucky bastard who gets to sleep with you."

He extended a not-so-steady hand, traced the fragile line of her hipbone up, along the curve of her breast. She gazed back at him, her eyes unwavering, unblinking, glistening with tears when he'd vowed never to make this woman cry again.

She arched up and he forgot how the hell to think. One of the things he appreciated most about losing himself in Rena. She scooched toward him, wrapped her legs around his waist and guided him home. Oh yeah.

Gripping her hips, he steadied her, nudged into the tight fist of moist heat. Waited for her to accommodate, waited for her sigh. Then moved. Again, in time with her, their bodies in sync if not always their minds.

He kept his pace slow, controlled, careful. Her heels dug into the small of his back, urging him deeper, and he let her take the lead, let her body dictate, easy enough since they wanted the same thing.

Eventually, as always, he couldn't tell who controlled anymore. Neither probably, because the driving need had hold of both of them. Something that had controlled them for years.

Eyes closed, his face settled against the damp curve of her neck, his skin equally as slick, growing wetter as she rocked against him. More of that frantic edge slugged through him, the sense that he had to hold on to this moment because he might never have another chance with this woman.

An unacceptable thought.

"Don't stop." Her nails jabbed into his back with urgency. "Not yet."

"Don't worry, babe," he growled into rose-scented hair. "I have no intention of stopping or going anywhere."

Damn straight on that.

She pulsed around him, harder, massaging him in her release that threatened to send him over with her. Still, he held back, took her cries into his mouth, absorbed her trembling, drew out her fulfillment until his body roared for relief. Her cries building, fading, she sagged against him.

Only then did he allow himself the final thrust that would send him flying into the mist. Rena's husky voice and sighs, right there with him, steered him through the haze. Damn, but he loved listening to her.

Shuddering, he gathered her close, his face still in her hair. How long? Who the hell knew? Finally the world, concerns, their son, his work—the promise of Rena's talk—all started echoing through the fog to drag him back. And he would deal with all of it.

He knew his duty, never cut out on responsibilities, always kept his word. But for right now, the world could just shut the hell up, and Rena's talk would have to wait.

He reached for more of the total escape he could only find in his wife's body.

Sprawled on top of her husband on the floor, Rena tried to ignore the dark cloud edging into her brain. It had to be because of Chris's mess. Not because of anything to do with J.T. They'd made progress. They were both on the same page now about talking, working to improve things.

Then why was she afraid of tomorrow?

Their legs tangled, she listened to the percussion of his heartbeat in her ear. "The Astroturf must be giving you a serious case of carpet burns."

"Worth it."

"We could go upstairs," she felt obligated to offer even as she yearned to stay here, in the moment.

"In a minute," he growled, his eyes still closed, hands warm on the small of her back. "Don't want to think enough to walk yet. Not sure I could put my shorts on to head that way anyhow."

She swirled a finger through the hair sprinkling his chest, his skin slick with sweat. "It's cooler upstairs."

His eyelids snapped open. "Ah hell, I'm sorry." Bracing her waist, he sat up. "I didn't even think about how uncomfortable this must be for you. Let's go."

He stared back at her in his lap, his gray eyes intense, resigned and fortified for what would come next.

Déjà vu left her swaying, transporting her to nearly four months ago when he'd worn that exact same heartbreakingly intense expression. Just before their final argument that had sent him walking.

Her throat closed as if to hold back words and the possibility—probability—of a repeat showdown. Something she couldn't face yet with her emotions so bare. Vulnerable.

To hell with getting cerebral right now. Surely she could enjoy the physical nirvana of just lying with J.T. after how many hours she'd dreamed about touching him, tasting him. "No, really. I'm okay. I wanted to make sure you're all right." She tickled his chin with a lock of her hair. "Let's stay here a while longer."

"How much longer?" He nipped the tip of her finger.

She wriggled until her knees landed on either side of his hips. "As long as you can last, flyboy."

"Now, what man could resist that challenge?" He cupped her breasts while she rolled her hips until he throbbed hotter, harder against her. He lifted, shifted, guided her down.

So what if this was a reliable delay to their talk? It was an incredible way. And she would get around to doing the right thing soon enough.

Damn. She hadn't changed one bit in twenty-two years.

She was still totally at the mercy of her body's craving for this man.

Right now she wanted to enjoy the shimmering sensations and connection and a blissful moment when she was absolutely certain they could work things out because they couldn't have something this perfect that wasn't meant to be. They couldn't deny this connection for the rest of their lonely lives.

Yes, she understood it was carnal and elemental, but this wasn't just sex. It was almost as if when reason, defenses, human foibles and stupid, stupid pride fell away, their souls recognized each other at the most simple level, so right. Mates. For life.

She wanted to believe they would make changes this time, but her wary heart couldn't escape a fearful sense brought on by years of experience with this man. That as soon as the sweat chilled on their sated bodies, they would hurt each other again.

Chapter 13

Morning sunlight streaked through the bedroom curtains, throwing lacy patterns on the walls. A familiar enough image for J.T., but one he hadn't experienced in nearly four months. Not in this room, with his wife curled against his side. Naked. Something he intended to enjoy for a few more minutes before life intruded.

J.T. stroked her arm, watching the digital clock blink away minutes. They'd never gotten around to a conversation the night before, and he couldn't say he regretted the delay.

He'd braced himself for the discussion, even to the point of planning where it should take place. At the kitchen table with a bowl of peach ice cream. He hoped the ice cream would remind her of happier times and soften her up before the tough talk.

Only, she'd faded into one of her pregnancy narcoleptic naps. He'd wrapped her in a quilt, scooped her up and carried her to bed. If he'd even considered sleeping elsewhere, she'd put an end to that with a groggy arm around his neck pulling him down to join her.

Fair enough. No need to ask him twice.

His gaze skated from her feet peeking out of the covers, along her curves draped in a sheet patterned with a thousand little flowers, up to the creamy skin of her shoulders and neck.

Damn, but her hair looked good on his pillow.

His hand explored her arm, along her hip. Sighing, she flipped onto her back, landing his hand square onto the tight curve of her belly. Shock stilled him. Longing held him there.

He'd been careful the night before not to touch her stomach. Only a bonehead wouldn't realize she had hang-ups about reconciling because of the baby after their shotgun wedding. Hell, maybe he had a few of those hang-ups himself—wondering if this was the only way to work himself into Rena's life.

But for now, while she slept, he allowed himself a moment to meet his new kid. He palmed the slight swell, turned onto his side until his face rested against the top of his wife's head while he rubbed a slow circle greeting.

Rena snuggled closer, still asleep and warm, mumbling stuff he couldn't make out.

He smiled into her hair. "It's okay, you have a while longer before you need to get up."

"Hmm. Good. So sleepy. Love you."

Sucker punched, J.T. couldn't move. She rolled to her other side, away, and clutched her pillow while her breathing resumed a steady snoozing rhythm.

She was probably stuck in some time-warp dream state from twenty years ago when she'd said those words all the time and he hadn't appreciated how much they meant. But did she mean them now and if so, how would he keep from hurting her this time, too?

Swinging his feet to the floor, he sat on the edge of the mattress, scrubbing his fingers through his hair. Minutes ago he didn't want to leave the bed and now he couldn't haul ass out fast enough. What the hell was wrong with him? The truth blindsided him like a bogey sneaking in from his six o'clock.

He'd fallen in love with his wife all over again.

His head fell into his hands. Hadn't he always loved her? He'd told her so. Sure as hell thought so. But somehow those feelings paled in comparison to the gut-gripping emotion twisting through him.

And that scared the crap out of him.

Now he had to accept the fact that she had been right about demanding more over the years—and about the ways he'd hurt her through a distance he hadn't even known he'd put between them. He had a helluva lot more backpedaling to accomplish than he'd thought.

Okay, so the stakes were higher. At least he had his feelings lined up. He would just tell her when they talked and make damn sure she listened.

Except he couldn't help but wish he had more to carry into this confrontation than three little words he'd used before without realizing their full importance.

Shoving to his feet and away from the temptation to wake his wife up with sex, a reliable connection, he headed for the bathroom and a lonely shower. Maybe the showerhead would beat some inspiration into his brain.

Dressed in a fresh flight suit, he loped down the stairs, his socks making no sound on hardwood. He wasn't sure he wanted to face the garage and all the hot memories there. One look at the weight bench and he would be right back in a world of hurt. But he needed to snag his boots and swap out the Velcro patches off his dirty flight suit onto his clean one.

J.T. paused at the base of the stairs. Maybe he could bring Rena breakfast in bed first. That would start the day on a nicer note.

As long as he didn't pick something that would make her hurl on his socks.

Around the corner, into the kitchen, he stopped short at the sight of his son. "Good morning."

Chris slouched against the counter, spooning a bowl of Frosted Flakes into his mouth, eyeing his dad with confusion. "'Morning."

"You sleep all right?"

"Yeah, how about you, uh, I mean—" Red-faced, he looked down and stuffed his mouth full of another bite.

The bed shuffle hadn't gone unnoticed. Hell, the door to Nikki's old room had probably been standing open. Keeping things low-key for his son had been the last thing on his mind when J.T. carried Rena up to bed the night before.

Still, Chris kept quiet. Shoveled cereal. Didn't ask if his parents were back together, which stung worse than facing the question, because silence meant the kid had stopped hoping.

Breakfast in bed with Rena would have to go on hold for a few minutes. J.T. poured a bowl of cereal and a glass of milk for himself and leaned back against the counter beside Chris, crossing his feet at the ankles. "You okay?"

He stirred soggy flakes. "I'm sorry for screwing up with the stuff at the restaurant."

Not the subject J.T. had been thinking of, but then Chris obviously wanted to ignore the other topic. "I'm not going to lie to you, son. It would have been better if you'd come to us right away."

"Because of Mom's accident?"

No soft-soaping that. His gut burned. J.T. tipped back half a glass of milk, without relief. Hopefully Spike would have some good news for him when they met in a few hours. "Yes, and also as far as having the authorities believe your side of the story."

Nodding, Chris shoveled another spoonful of soupy cereal

into his mouth. J.T. waited, ate, the clock ticking by seconds over the door.

Pivoting on the heels of his athletic socks, Chris dumped the rest of his cereal down the disposal and made an overlong production out of washing the bowl. "When you were over there, in Rubistan, I mean—" he paused, washing the spoon—twice "—did you, uh, get scared?"

Water running, he eyed his dad sideways.

"Yeah." J.T. nodded, the understatement of the century. A dry smile tugged one corner of his mouth. "Sometimes so much I thought I'd piss in my pants."

Chris stared back. Shock sent his jaw slack. He dropped the spoon and shifted to face his dad full on. "Really?"

"Really." He'd always thought children needed to feel parents were invincible. Maybe finding out parents were human might not be so bad, after all. Sure would have helped prepare the kid for the breakup. "Only a fool wouldn't have been scared. Anyone can be brave when the odds are in your favor. It's what you do when you're scared that's the true measure of courage."

"Is that from Shakespeare?"

He hadn't even realized Chris knew he read the Bard's works. "Nope. Actually, it's from my old man."

One of the few conversations they'd had. Right after he'd found out Rena was pregnant. Strange how he'd forgotten about going to his father at that time until just now.

Other talks with his dad shifted around in J.T.'s head. Short exchanges, sure. His parents were just as closemouthed as he was, but they made their words count.

Had he done the same? "You don't have to go to school today."

"Yeah, I think I do have to go."

His son was becoming a man. "Okay, then." The kid was probably safer there than at home, anyway. "But remember, you can call me if you have any problems. I'll be there in minutes."

"Thanks, but I'm okay." He pushed away from the counter and started toward the door.

Make the words count. "Son?"

Chris turned. "Yeah?"

"Love ya.' J.T. hooked his arm around Chris's neck and pulled him in for a hug.

His son hugged back. Thumping. Rena would have laughed over the fact that men had to hit while they were hugging, but hey, guys understood the lingo.

Thunking his son once more on the back, J.T. pulled away. "And you're still grounded 'til the end of time."

Grinning, Chris shrugged, baggy clothes rippling. "I figured as much."

"Go grab your backpack and I'll see what's keeping your mother."

Scooping a muffin off the counter for his wife, J.T. hoped the upcoming talk with Rena could go even half as well as the one with his son, simple, low-key. Otherwise, they were all screwed.

She was so screwed.

Inching back from the kitchen door, Rena steadied her steps if not her pulse. The image of father and son, standing together, white athletic socks on crossed feet side by side, squeezed all those pregnancy emotions until she could barely breathe. Watching J.T. and Chris in sync like that was... perfect, the family she'd always wanted.

Well, without bricks flying through her window.

The fear from the night before quivered through her again. Followed by the oh so vividly red memories of how she'd escaped that fear.

Slumping against the wall by a wrought-iron plant stand, she let herself enjoy looking at J.T. Waking up alone had been disappointing. But then she'd realized J.T. probably couldn't have woken her anyway, as deeply as she slept. She'd squelched down hurt, forced herself to think clearly. He was being considerate by letting her sleep.

Quit thinking with her hormones and start using her brain or she'd never get through this with her heart intact. But oh, as she stared at J.T., freshly showered and shaved in his flight suit, strong jaw and handsome face that only grew more appealing with age, her emotions did so want control over her.

She'd always enjoyed J.T.'s body; however that body became all the more tempting when the man inside was being so incredible. Of course, he'd always loved his children, been active in their care, took his turn walking the floor. But the talking? He'd left that up to her.

Until now.

Seeing him become the father she'd always known he could be made her wonder what their lives would have been like had he shared some of that openness with her over the years. She'd lost count of all the arguments and reconciliation talks—actually mostly *her* talking. And even if he was talking now, too, was it realistic to expect they could patch this up themselves?

This possibility of reconciliation screamed, "last chance." Which meant going for broke on the fix with the one thing they'd never tried.

Marital counseling.

How strange that she of all people should be scared of the prospect. Scared of what she would hear. Could that be why she'd avoided it?

God knows, J.T. wouldn't want to go. Even laid-back Bo dragged his boots at the prospect of spilling his guts and having his brain picked. Hell, she was frightened to her roots just thinking about it, too. But the more she considered the idea, the more certain she became that this offered their only hope.

Of course, that meant delaying any talk for a while longer, waiting for the perfect time rather than some car discussion to and from work. Logical, right?

Not a scared-as-hell stall tactic.

She entered the kitchen before they could come out into the hall and realize she'd been watching them. "Hey, guys. I'm ready anytime."

Chris's gaze ping-ponged from one parent to the other. "Uh, I gotta get something from upstairs."

He angled past and out before she could even hug him.

Rena stopped by the table, couldn't move anyhow. Facing J.T. after making love shouldn't be this…tummy flipping. Exciting. Scary. Much like after their true first time when she realized what they'd done changed everything.

Except after the real first time, he'd held her, kissed her. Damn it, if she couldn't have the holding, she at least wanted her morning-after kiss.

"Hi," she said softly, words suddenly drying up.

"Hi back." J.T. smiled, extending one hand with a muffin, the other with a glass of milk. "Breakfast? I was going to bring it up to you."

Emotions squeezed tighter.

He leaned down over the chair between them while she moved closer and, yes, she had her good-morning kiss even if he couldn't touch her, the chair between them and his hands full of her breakfast. And how sweet was that?

His lips moved over her with a firm, deep, slow kiss as if they had nowhere to go, no real world concerns. A kiss, right in the room where they'd enjoyed a hot encounter after his return from Guam when there had been plenty of sex but, heartbreakingly, no kissing.

His tongue coaxed her lips open, swept inside, connected, explored, sending her tummy into a flat spin. Then he kept right on kissing her so she couldn't say something that would mess this up, and God, but she was relieved.

With a final skim of his lips over hers, he stepped back "I need to grab my boots and change patches." He place her muffin and milk on the table. "Be back in a few and the we can leave once you're dressed."

Watching him stride into the garage where they'd mad such passionate love the night before, she reminded hersel that she had kisses back. That was a positive step. And now she knew what to do to keep them once they both finishe their half day at work.

She also knew how hard her reticent husband would resis her solution. Which scared her all the more because this wa it. Their last chance.

J.T.'s words echoed through her mind. *Anyone can be brave when the odds are in your favor. It's what you do whe you're scared that's the true measure of courage.*

She sunk into the chair. Great.

With the way odds were stacked against her, her bravery points must be off the charts.

J.T. stood to the side while Spike clicked through the ci pher lock at the OSI building. The opening door—thick meta like a safe—hissed with the release of air from the area sealec tight for soundproofing.

He followed Spike through security, down halls and pas a mix of workers in uniforms and civilian clothes—the hear of military counterintelligence keeping base personnel clean. He hated like hell that anyone around him might have a par in drug trafficking.

At least he had the connections here to learn the worst his son could face.

Spike swung a door open to a small interrogation room, sparse, stark and a helluva lot less dirty and dark than its counterpart in Rubistan. They'd already exchanged the basic info on Chris's situation out in Spike's office before the OSI agent had gone silent, then suggested they take the rest of the conversation to a more secure part of the building.

J.T. dropped into one of the unrelenting chairs in the windowless room in a completely windowless building. "Thanks again for coming in early after pulling an all-nighter."

"No problem." Spike sat across from him, coffee cup in hand, dark circles of sleeplessness lining sharp, clear eyes. "Had to come in anyway after how things shook down last night."

"I'll take that as a good sign." J.T. downed the dregs of his java, his fourth cup of the day.

"You'd be right." Spike tipped back his coffee. "DEA cameras confirmed the boats were picking up the drugs and coming back clean. Until last night, we couldn't figure out how they were offloading the drugs. Turns out, they were packaging up the stuff and placing it in the shrimper nets. They cast the net out, but with the webbing loose on one side so the drugs drop into the harbor. Net comes back empty. Looks like a bad throw to the casual observer. They repair the net and keep right on trawling for the rest of the day— or in this case, evening."

"And how's the exchange made?"

"We're still tracking that, but we're pretty certain a small underwater craft, minisub, retrieves it and runs it up the coast. It's freaking genius when you think about it. Without this tip-off, who the hell knows how long it would have taken us to figure it out? Now we just need to pinpoint who's receiving on the other end. We've already connected two independent shrimpers and a market here. We expect more to fall."

"And do you think this ties in to what Chris saw?"

"Could be. Based on your message, I made a few calls before you got here. The young woman, Miranda Casale, has already been picked up for questioning. Everyone at the restaurant will be questioned sometime today. A lot of base kids work at that place. Could be coincidental. Could be someone looking for a new contact. With any luck, that common symbol on the bumper sticker, the brick and the girl's necklace will lock in the final connection.''

J.T. nodded, crumpling the disposable cup in his fist. These bastards had come after his wife and kid. He hoped they fried. His job might have brought stress to his home life, but at the moment he couldn't help being damn glad he'd played a part in bringing down scum like these.

Spike placed his cup on the table. ''Hey, dude, no matter how this shakes down, you're going to be okay and your son's going to be okay. Chris stepped up in time. Plenty of military kids get in trouble—just like anybody else's kids. He gave us a heads up on another lead. He's a good kid who got stuck in a bad situation.''

''Thanks for looking out for him.''

Memories of those days in a Rubistanian cell hummed in the air, whispers of the minor victory they'd all silently celebrated by diverting their captors enough to buy Spike an extra couple of hours before his round of questioning.

Now the time had come for J.T. to buy some of that time for his family. To keep the heat off them until the threat passed.

Spike smiled. ''Hey, dude, it's what we do for each other.'' He drained his coffee and stood. ''Your part's finished here. Go home and hang with your family.''

Chapter 14

Exchanging her work clothes for stretch pants and an over-long T-shirt, Rena turned her back on her reflection in the bathroom mirror. Facing herself and her mistakes wasn't easily done, and she would have plenty of that soon enough.

Time and excuses had run out. She and J.T. would have to come to a firm decision on their future. It wasn't fair to Chris to string things out.

The trip to and from the base had been quiet, as if J.T. understood any talk would require full attention—and likely be too long to accomplish during the short ride.

She tugged her hair free from inside the overlong T-shirt and searched through a basket by the sink for a matching hair scrunchie. Purple? Black? No. Gray, like her mood. Maybe she could just entice J.T. into having a quickie before they opened Pandora's box. Rena gathered up her hair and—

Huh? She focused all her attention inward—

There it was again. The tickle inside her. Gasping, she dropped the hair scrunchie and savored those butterfly whispers of life within her she'd never expected to feel again.

She pressed a hand to her stomach and didn't even breathe for fear of missing repeats. Her baby became all the more real—hers and J.T.'s—this new person who deserved so much more than a couple of parents who pitched plates and stormed out of rooms.

"Are you all right?" J.T. asked from the open door connecting the bathroom to their bedroom.

She hadn't even heard him walk up.

Rena nodded, her hand still cradling the sensation inside her. Her lip trembled. "The baby moved. I'd forgotten what it felt... How incredible... I just..." Her chin trembling, she shrugged. "Our baby moved."

His throat convulsed on a long swallow. His hands clenched and she knew he wanted to touch her, even if he wouldn't be able to feel the flutters yet.

She hated that he had to be hesitant, but if he touched her right now, she would weaken. She would forget all about her resolve and give in when she needed to make a stand more than ever for the baby. For them.

Still, this was his child, too.

She angled past into their bedroom and slid the ultrasound photo from her dressing table. "I never got the chance to show you this last night."

He took the slick black-and-white image and stared at it for so long she grew dizzy holding her breath.

A smile dug dimple brackets around his mouth. "You're right. This is incredible. Even more than I remembered. Thank you."

"There's nothing to thank me for."

Slowly, he set down the photo, his gray eyes somber. "There are many things to thank you for."

Oh God, he could be so sweet sometimes. She walked into his arms, where she'd wanted to be all day anyway. Tension left his bunched muscles, his eyes softening but losing none of their impact.

She guided his hand to her stomach, placed and held it against their child. Cars drove past outside. Trees rustled in the breeze. But they both stood still and quiet for—she had no idea how long.

His hand slid away and up to sketch knuckles along her cheekbone. "I've loved you since the first time I saw you. No matter what happens, no matter what else we might say to each other, I want to make sure you know that."

She melted. Like a bowl of peach ice cream abandoned on the table, she melted into a puddle of emotions. Arching up, she met him as he angled down to kiss her.

With her defensiveness washing away, the hope shone clearer. Tempting her. Maybe things really would be okay this time without pushing him.

But then she remembered his words to Chris in the kitchen about fear and bravery. In the face of J.T.'s strength and courage, how could she be anything less? This was her defining moment. If she wanted to be a woman worthy of this so very special man, she needed to be brave enough to make the tougher choices.

Resolve stronger than her shaky knees and quivering belly, she eased down from her toes, broke the kiss. She caressed J.T.'s bristly jaw up into the silver flecking his temples. "I'd like us to attend marital counseling."

Predictably, he turned stone still in her arms. "Why? Things are back on track now. Didn't you hear what I just said?"

Hear? Of course she'd heard. And it scared the spit out of her because she wanted to chicken out and just take what she could. But she knew now that would only delay the inevitable. "On track? J.T., we had great sex."

He quirked an eyebrow, not smiling. Already she could feel the restrained irritation resurrecting within him.

"Fine. Incredible sex." Better than anything she could remember, sex that touched places of her soul she didn't know existed. "That hasn't helped us before."

Still, he kept his temper reined, cupped her shoulders, his hands on her always a distraction. He almost certainly knew that and was using it, damn him.

"I get your point, babe, but we're talking like you always wanted. Hell, I've talked more in the past two weeks than I did the whole time I was growing up."

He had a point, and she wanted to be swayed as much as she wanted to dig in her bare feet and stand her ground. Problem was, when this man finally decided to speak, he could talk her out of her good sense as fast as he could her clothes and heart. "We need an impartial third party to help us sort through some tough issues."

"I figure we've passed a few landmarks," he continued as if she hadn't even spoken. "Sure we've had arguments, but I haven't walked out of the room and you haven't thrown a dish. That's progress."

"Not funny."

"Yes, it is."

Her lips twitched. "Maybe a little."

"So what's the problem? We've got a good thing going. Let's roll with it."

"Yes, things are improving. We both still have feelings for each other." She kept her eyes on the neck of his flight suit rather than risk falling into his smoky eyes. "But we're deluding ourselves if we think everything's magically going to get better. This—" she waved her hand in the general direction of their bed—a bed that was waiting too conveniently close for her peace of mind "—is wonderful, but it's a Band-Aid fix. What's changed to keep us from landing back in the same hurtful place?"

"We're older. Smarter."

She snorted. "We're older, anyway." Grabbing hold of her resolve while sticking strong to her decision not to grab hold of him, she stared straight into his eyes. "Jesus, J.T., can't you see that even with progress, we're also still making some of the same mistakes?"

He exhaled long, slow, pissed. "So use the counselor degree and tell me what I should do."

She forced her own arms to stay at her sides as much as she wanted to cross them, close herself off. "It's not you. It's us. And you know I can't do that, anyway. It's like telling a doctor to diagnose and treat herself. There's no way to obtain impartial distance."

"You're great just the way you are."

"Quit BSing me, J.T." She resisted the urge to stomp her foot, which would only hurt and not accomplish squat except to give away her frustration level when it came to this infuriating, sexy, heartbreakingly wonderful man. "I may not be able to heal my own family, but I know enough to realize it takes two to make or break a marriage."

"We can't afford it," he said, thumbing the ultrasound photo off the dresser, "especially not with a new kid on the way."

"We can't afford not to, especially with a new baby on the way."

He replaced the photo, sliding a crystal ring dish to the side and out of her tossing reach, a smile playing with his dimples.

Damn it, she would not be charmed by his quiet humor. Not now. His dimple deepened.

Maybe she was a little charmed.

She closed the distance between them and flattened a hand to his chest. "It's free at the base clinic, covered as part of your benefits. Family Advocacy is there for a reason."

How could dimples turn to a scowl so quickly? "I'm not putting my problems on record there."

"Confidentiality applies."

"Yeah, right. Until someone sees me walking out of there. Fliers can't afford a hint of personal problems."

"And a broken marriage isn't a hint?"

"No."

Deep breaths. She toyed with straightening his collar while she regulated her breathing and organized her thoughts. "All right, you have a real problem with counseling. I'm trying not to be insulted that you think so little of my career field."

"Don't look for a fight." He lifted her hand from his chest and pressed a kiss against her wrist, playing havoc with her heartbeat. "Let's both take time off from work, spend it with the kids and each other like you wanted before. I'd already decided during my flight tonight to take leave."

His concession surprised her, big-time, since it would involve dipping into her paycheck to finance the trip, a definite step forward for them. Enough to relent? Hoping that she could soften him up later on the counseling issue?

If only he weren't nipping at the sensitive inside of her wrist in an obvious, calculated effort to distract her. "And we would go somewhere. We would use *our* money to pay for it."

"Yeah, sure." He dropped her hand and made a big freaking production out of brushing away a few dead leaves from around the base of a begonia plant in the window. "Let's rent that cabin like you wanted to for Christmas. We can have that family time together once Nikki and Chris finish up exams."

He'd agreed, even if the prospect left him looking itchier than one of her kids after a roll in poison ivy. Why couldn't she stop reading something into the fact that his restless movements straightening things in the room took him closer and closer to the hall?

The vent by the door captured his attention and he stretched up to adjust the open/shut lever. "Or if the cabin thing doesn't appeal for summer, make whatever arrangements you want. Anything's fine by me.''

His left foot landed in the hall.

''Since you're walking out the door, does that mean I get to throw something?''

That stopped him. He looked back over his shoulder. Turned. ''Real funny, Rena. I'm trying to be accommodating.''

''Accommodating? Sounds to me like you're trying to placate me so you can get the hell out of the room.'' Deeper breaths. ''This is exactly what I'm talking about when I mention marriage counseling. We could probably use some family counseling, too, with Chris's situation.''

''Well, hell,'' he snapped. ''Didn't we get anything right?''

Old habits slid into place too easily and she refused to let them take over. ''I'll ignore that comment since I'm trying here. But it's obvious you're only agreeing to the vacation to placate me.''

''You won.'' He crossed his arms over his chest. ''Be happy.''

Bad-body-language alert. And her temper was sparking, ripe and ready for anything to fuel it to life. Two weeks of holding her tongue, walking on eggshells, terrified to hope and terrified not to, all sliced at her paper-thin control. ''I *won?* Good God, do you hear yourself? It's not about winning. It's about both of us being happy.''

''I'm happy if you're not pitching plates.''

''You deserve more than that and so do I. I want us to go to marriage counseling.''

His arms unfolded and he gripped the top of the door frame, the hall sealed from sight. ''Oh, I see how it is. I agree to what you ask by talking—like how I'm finally agreeing to the vacation you wanted so damn bad last year. So you up the request until I say no. Then it's my fault things fell apart.''

Was there truth in that? Maybe. But if so, then it only solidified her surety that they needed help. "How could you think I would wish for this hell? Don't you realize how much our split hurt me? More so the second time, even, coming so close on the heels of what happened overseas. Do you have any clue what it was like thinking you'd died? Imagining what was happening to you if you hadn't?"

His hands fisted against the frame.

"We were both a mess when you came home. And as much as I want to hope nothing bad ever happens to us again, that's unrealistic." The fear of a repeat swamped her until she used the excuse of her sore ankle to sit on the edge of their bed. "We need to be rock solid to face the future. We need to be open with each other, not just winning and losing. Do you realize you still haven't even told me what happened over there yet?"

"We already covered that in the truck."

"Do you actually believe that constitutes a real conversation on the subject?"

"You already said imagining it hurt you. Why would I want to make that worse?"

She flattened her hands to the giving softness of the quilt as if pressing the wedding ring patch pattern could somehow imprint the premise and promise into her. Talk about a Freudian slip in buying the thing in the first place. "Because being married means sharing burdens. And if you won't share yours with me, then I can't share mine with you. I need someone to lean on, too."

"More upping the ante to make me walk?" Hands falling from the door frame, he reentered their room, one step, two. "You want to hear all about it? Fine. We were in Rubistan on a mission that looks like one thing but really is about something else. We were stressed. Ready to get the hell out and back to our families."

He paced the room, back to the ultrasound photo. "We

figured we were almost home free once we crossed out over the water. Instead, we took a missile hit that would have sent us into the gulf if anyone other than Scorch had been flying the plane.''

The reality slammed into her as if she'd been hit, too, but she forced herself not to sway, an outward sign that would make him stop.

God, she still couldn't quite believe he was actually talking after all this time. She wasn't sure whether to be relieved or more scared than ever.

''But we made it, landed. Got picked up by some tribal warlords who beat the crap out of us, broke Bo's hands.'' He glanced sideways at her. ''Bo's great act of resistance? Looking up.''

She blinked down the tears clogging her eyes and throat, air heavy. Heart heavier for the young pilot not much older than her own children. For her husband.

''Lucky for us, the Rubistanians arrived within a couple of hours and shot the hell out of our caravan so we could have the marginally better option of being interrogated by them instead.''

She flinched, couldn't hold it in anymore, but stayed silent, her hands digging deeper into the quilt.

''You want more from me?'' He stalked toward her, toe to toe. ''A pound of flesh like in that Shakespearean play? Well, I'll just cut myself wide open for you, babe.''

Scrubbing a hand over his face, he spun away on his boot heel, stalked, glanced back over his shoulder. ''Scared? Hell yeah, we were scared. Scared of dying.'' His feet took him clear across the room to the window shrouded with lace curtains. ''But most of all, I was scared of what you and the kids would go through when you got that front-door visit.''

His fist met the wall.

Tears burned acid paths from her eyes and down her face. As a counselor, she knew this outpouring was the right thing for him, pain concealed being far more lethal than pain released. But as a wife, God, she hurt for him.

Familiar features assumed a stranger's cast with harsh angles. "Is this sharing deal working for you? Are we closer now? Do you feel better about us? I hope someone's happier, because I sure as hell am not feeling at all better."

A thousand words jumbled through her head, a thousand different ways to try and make this better for him, except what if she chose wrong and hurt him worse? Objectivity wasn't even an option at the moment, but the pain in his eyes was killing her. She had to do something.

Rising, she reached to hold him.

His hands shot up. Backing, he shook his head. "You want me to make this easy for you? No problem. I can do that just like I did a few months ago."

Pivoting away, he walked out the door.

Her eyes flooded, and she wanted to run after him and hold him. Not that he would let her.

Which frustrated her all the more and left her itching to throw something. No dishes though. She'd grown beyond that. Her hand settled on the pillow sham made to match her spread and she allowed herself the outlet of a hefty pitch.

Whoomp.

The pillow thudded against the door frame, slid, plopped, quilted linking rings mocking her from the floor.

Damn it.

J.T. descended the steps two at a time, boots pounding hardwood and releasing none of the roaring tension kinking every muscle in his body. He shouldn't have lost it.

Duh.

But somehow that woman always knew how to crawl under his skin and peel everything away until his emotions lay out all raw and exposed for the sunlight to burn. He should have just agreed to her counseling suggestion and made nice with the shrink of her choice.

So why hadn't he?

Hand on the end of the banister, he stopped, truth delivering a helluva gut punch. He'd shut her down because he was half-certain a shrink would tell them they didn't have a chance. At least this way, he kept control over the situation.

Control?

Then how had he ended up out in the cold again like after his return from Rubistan? His fingers closed around the wooden knob at the end of the banister, light slanting through the hall window like the open load ramp of his plane.

J.T. clanked down the belly of the C-17, the Charleston sunlight blinding through the open hatch. Almost bright enough to wipe away the darkness of days spent in a hellhole cell before diplomatic channels cleared for him to come home.

Home.

An efficiency apartment not much bigger than his cell, except he had no one to blame but himself for landing there. He'd let his stupid-ass pride propel him when Rena tossed his crap on the lawn. How could he be so proud of her and so freaking pissed at the same time over the fact that she didn't need him?

J.T. slowed his steps, not in much of a rush to get out of the plane now, after all. He paused alongside Bo's litter. The flight surgeon, nurse and techs worked the transfer while the kid groused about not being allowed to walk out under his own steam—as if he could anyhow, all drugged up and casted during their layover and assessment in Germany.

As J.T. waited and watched through the open load ramp, Scorch cleared the load ramp first. Steps steady, the five stitches along his jaw the only visible sign of their ordeal. His sister, brother-in-law and baby niece met him with hugs

*and crying and a quick hustle off to leave all this behind for
a family reunion.*

Spike, in civilian clothes now that he was back on base and
not in his overseas undercover role anymore, strutted straight
into his waiting fiancée's arms. 1st Lieutenant Darcy Renshaw kissed him hard, unmoving and eyes shut tight while
tears streaked free and fast down her face.

Happily ever after around this place still came with heart-
aches along the way. Only the strongest relationships survived.

Damn, but he'd hoped his and Rena's could be one.

He looked down at Bo, the lieutenant pale but outwardly
cocky on the stretcher. "Do you need somebody to hang with
you until you're settled at the hospital?"

"Are you kidding? Have you seen the hot new flight nurse
over there? I'm figuring I'll need a bed bath before supper."
He winked up at the flight surgeon keeping pace alongside.
"Right, Doc?"

Bo laughed, a hoarse croak but damn clear about the need
to keep things light, superficial, something J.T. totally understood. Too much emotion, adrenaline, anger rumbled around
to be processed yet.

Spike and his fiancée broke apart. Arms around each
other's waists, they strode away. Clearing sight lines to reveal something J.T. hadn't even dared let himself hope to see.

His family.

He'd been fairly certain Rena's big heart would bring her
here, as well. But on the off chance it wouldn't happen, he
hadn't let himself think about it. He didn't have room in his
head to process even one more emotion—especially not disappointment.

He left Bo to the tender ministrations of the flight nurse
and walked forward, his boots landing on the tarmac. American concrete. Relief tingled over him like the start of a sun-

burn. He was pretty sure his feet kept moving, because his family drew closer.

Then they were all in a group huddle of hugs and words he couldn't hear because the buzzing in his head was so damn loud.

One thing about that afternoon stayed clear. How Rena trembled, those emotions churning through them all, multiplying until it even rattled his teeth. If he hadn't been holding on, Rena probably would have fallen off her high heels.

Right then, he knew. He couldn't put her through this anymore. She'd wanted him gone and maybe that was the best thing after all.

But not just yet. He hated himself for being a selfish bastard, but he couldn't walk today. The kids deserved this homecoming, Rena, too. And, damn it all, he couldn't make himself walk away from the chance to lose himself in her body one more time.

They would have their homecoming, before he left for good.

And what a homecoming it had been, so perfect, and somehow he'd felt like a freaking black cloud walking through the clean light of his house. Like now, standing in the hall, wanting to go back up those stairs and wondering if staying away was better for her in the long run.

He glanced upstairs, frowning. Had he started to understand, then, this deeper love he felt? God knows it confused the hell out of him now, and he'd been too much of a mess then to process much of anything.

Holy crap. He slumped against the wall, bracing his foot on the banister across from him for support. He hadn't walked away to protect her. He'd left because the dawning realization of how much he loved her scared the hell out of him.

He couldn't reconcile it all then. Still wasn't sure he could.

Except now, he wanted to.

At least he was home. Alive. He could—and damn well

would—deal with the rest. Once he got his head on straight. He needed five minutes to pull it together again and then he'd go back upstairs for damage control.

He opened his office door.

To find a man dressed in black and a ski mask sitting at his desk, rifling through drawers. What the hell?

The man looked up, eyes narrowed in the ski-mask slits.

Anger, rage, raw emotions still stark and ugly on the surface roared to life. J.T. launched forward.

The man's hand slid into sight—holding a Glock, the big nasty-looking 9mm stalling J.T. quicker than a brick wall in the face.

The dark eyes blinked from inside the mask. "Well, hello, Sergeant. I was hoping to finish up here before you came in, but now we're out of luck."

Options raced through his head. If he called a warning, Rena would come downstairs. As much as he hated having made her cry, at least it might keep her safely upstairs.

One-on-one odds he could handle. Hell, right now he welcomed the chance to fight back, better than being stuck in a cell with his hands tied behind his back.

The man's attention shifted. J.T.'s muscles bunched for action.

The gun twitched. "Well, hello there, ma'am."

Ma'am? Rena? Adrenaline turned to icy heat. A trick? Maybe, but with that gun possibly pointed at Rena, J.T. couldn't afford to act until…he…looked…

At his wife standing red-eyed and horrified in the doorway. *Oh God, babe, I'm sorry.*

Pain exploded in his head. J.T. managed a half turn toward his attacker before…

Everything went dark.

Chapter 15

Rena screamed. Ran forward. Tried to catch J.T. as he fell toward the ground. God, he was heavy. She crumpled to the floor with him, hard, but at least she'd kept him from cracking his head on the desk on the way down.

As if he hadn't already taken a hard enough hit to the skull when the guy looming in dark clothes and a ski mask had knocked J.T. out with the butt of his gun. Bile bubbled up, scalding her throat.

She cradled her husband's head in her lap, fear snaking through her, gripping, like poison ivy to fertile ground. "Take whatever you want. I'll tell you where everything is in the house, the keys to the car. Just take it all and go, but please don't hurt us."

Don't hurt J.T. again.

Gun level, the lean man skirted around the corner of the desk. "I need your husband's flight schedule, ma'am, for tonight and tomorrow, and then I'm out of here. Out of your hair. It's really simple, actually. I have everything under control."

What the hell did this guy want with a flight schedule? His flat accent gave her no hints of his background other than that he sounded educated, not some street thug in search of a quick pawn. Something niggled at her about his voice, but she couldn't place him as anyone she knew well.

Rena studied his clothes for clues, black pleated pants and T-shirt, nice cut and make on a tall, fit frame. Not someone she had any real hope of taking out.

Her world had gone crazy in a couple of weeks.

She didn't know why this man had a gun pointed at her, but she knew enough to realize this was bad. Really bad. "And if I find whatever schedule it is you're looking for, you'll let us live?"

"You don't have a choice but to believe me. Of course, I could start by killing your husband, and then wait for your son to come home. What do you think?"

She thought all the options sucked. Him knowing she had a son scared her even more. Was he someone they knew? Maybe his voice sounded familiar, after all, or maybe her frightened-as-hell mind was playing tricks on her.

That she didn't have any idea where J.T. might have a flight schedule made things worse. She feared he didn't have one at all, because hadn't he talked about taking leave? That his schedule was clear now?

What did this guy need a flight schedule for, anyway? If she was sure she would live, she could give it to him and then let the base know it was gone.

But if she gave it to him and then he killed them… She would have put crew members' lives at risk. Furthermore, giving it to him would constitute treason. A line neither she nor her husband could cross.

Think time. Start with the truth, about her only option since what more could she do? Bash him over the head with her begonias? "We don't have it. J.T. is starting leave now. There's nothing in this house for you."

"Like I believe that. Try again, ma'am."

Apparently this overpolite scum didn't recognize truth. She burned to take this guy on with a lamp or ashtray upside the head for a chance to protect J.T. and Chris. Too bad she hadn't pocketed the crystal dish she'd longed to lob at J.T.

Except she also had to protect the baby she was carrying. She needed to buy time for J.T. to regain consciousness.

If he regained consciousness.

Oh God, she couldn't even think about that.

Time to pile on the lies. Because no way would she let J.T. die before they'd worked things out between them and until he'd apologized for walking away from her again, bless his stubborn soul. They deserved forever.

"Okay, fine. What I said was true, but there's more. The schedule isn't here—yet. J.T. had to leave work early to bring me home. I'm on half days because of a car accident—and I'm pregnant," she rushed to add in hopes that even if this slime didn't respect her condition, he might fear the harsher legal ramifications if he killed a pregnant woman.

She watched her assailant for hints of his personality, weaknesses, anything to provide an edge. If only she could see his facial expressions. Instead, she had only body language and flickers of emotion in those narrow eyes peering back at her through the slits in the knit mask. Gun steady, he smoothed his other hand along the wrinkles in his black T-shirt.

Fastidious? Obsessive-compulsive? Or just plain freaking amoral that he would think he could break into her home, hurt her husband.

She frowned, watched. "J.T. left early, and someone from work is supposed to bring his schedule by later."

Geez, that was lame and so not how things worked, but hopefully this person would buy it anyway, the best she could come up with while under so much crushing pressure.

"Why don't they e-mail the schedule to him?"

Why hadn't she thought of that? "Because the computers were down today. One of those out-of-control virus things. You'll probably hear about it on the news in the morning."

She'd never tested her aptitude for her family's shady penchant for lying, but obviously she'd picked up some of the skill by osmosis from years of exposure while growing up. One thing to be grateful for from her childhood.

His eyes squinted in the mask. "Okay, I'm not saying I trust you, but what you say sounds possible. You're going to help me tie up the big guy here and then you're both going to hang out secured in a closet while I look. If you're actually telling the truth, I'll let one of you get the schedule at the door. But I'll be holding a gun to the other one's head. Understand?"

Rena nodded. God, had he actually stolen a glance of himself in the windowpane as he walked? She was worried about dying here and he was checking himself out?

Rage threatened to blind her. Come hell or high water, she was taking down Mr. Narcissist.

He looked around the room, knelt, unplugged a short extension cord. "Now tie his hands behind his back with this. And do it tight, because I'll be watching."

Rena hefted her husband's limp body to his stomach, stalling as best she could, an easy enough prospect since he was heavy. Gently, she pulled his limp arms behind his back. How long had he been out? Was he awake now, faking to listen, plan, establish an edge?

If so, he was doing a helluva good job with the act.

Once she finished, she glanced up, exhausted, scared. And determined not to fail.

Mr. Narcissist waggled the gun toward the hall. "Drag him into the closet."

"You have got to be kidding. There's no way I can manage that. No way." If she could get him to put down his gun…

"I see your point. But I want you to sit there."

He pointed to J.T.'s recliner in the office, a butt-ugly green chair she'd made fun of just before she'd jumped her husband's bones on the eyesore.

"And don't move, ma'am," Mr. Stuck-on-Himself added. "I'll be able to see you. One twitch from you and I'll crack your husband's head open this time."

She shivered. Nodded. Started to move for the chair, but suddenly found herself reluctant to leave J.T. She pressed a kiss to his head and whispered, "I love you."

"Touching," Mr. Narcissist mocked. "Now get in the chair while I lock this guy up. Then you're next."

She inched away, careful to keep her moves smooth, predictable. Her captor tucked the gun in the small of his back, in his belt, his gold buckle and design catching the light...

A red circle with a black triangle inside.

What did Chris's mess have to do with someone wanting J.T.'s flight schedule? And damn, damn, damn, why couldn't she figure out why that symbol looked so familiar?

The man rolled J.T. onto his back again. He gripped under J.T.'s shoulders, dragging him into the hall, straining and scooching backward.

What a dumb ass. He should have put her in a closet first so she wouldn't be free while he maneuvered J.T. Not that she intended to mention the oversight. Instead, she processed the new insight. The man wasn't as smart as he thought.

Rena studied him closer, saw sweat seeping through his mask. Stress or heat? His hand fidgeted with his belt—again. Stress. Definitely.

While that edginess could be dangerous, it could also be her weapon since it impaired his logic. Playing him, outsmarting him would be a tightrope walk, but he had her on size and firepower.

When he turned his back to open the door, she snatched a paperweight off the edge of J.T.'s desk and tucked it in her pocket.

Mr. Narcissist shifted back, huffing. He tugged his gun out again. "Okay. You next. Closet."

At least she would be with J.T. again. She crossed into the hall.

"Are you nuts, lady? You get your own closet."

No damn way could she let that happen. She needed to talk to J.T. when he woke, update him, reassure him. She extended her wrists. "Tie me up before you put me in there, but I'm not leaving him. You're the one with the gun, all the power."

"You're damn right." He pressed the gun to her temple, a cold, lethal kiss. "And you'll do whatever the hell I say."

Childhood memories shivered over her, visions of the soulless eyes of her father's friends who carried weapons like these. Panic thrashed against reason, threatening any hope of calm. She had maybe three seconds to figure something out. Her gut churned. The baby somersaulted.

The baby. The man had seemed to shift his focus when she'd mentioned being pregnant.

"I have to go to the bathroom," she blurted.

"You're joking, right?"

"I'm pregnant." And damn, but this might work. "I swear there's no way I can hold it a minute longer. If my husband doesn't come to in time for delivery of the schedule, don't you think it'll raise a few questions if I answer the door with wet clothes, not to mention the smell, and it's not like I'll have time to change my clothes once the doorbell rings—"

"Okay! Okay, lady, I get the point." Gun waving, he grimaced. "You can go to the bathroom, for God's sake."

A small victory, but she'd take it. Plus, every time she pushed and won, she discovered more about her enemy.

"But I'm going to search you when you come out."

She pulled a weak smile. So much for the paperweight she would have to ditch now.

He kicked the door shut on J.T.'s prison and followed her to the half bath around the corner.

Rena stepped into the bathroom and closed the door. Exhaling, she sagged against the door, searching for ideas. But there weren't any convenient guns in the toilet tank.

She considered writing Help on the window in lipstick, but he might check the bathroom and she couldn't risk triggering his anger.

Yanking open the medicine cabinet, she scanned the metal shelves. No nifty drugs to drop in his drinks. Nothing but a soap refill and the nail-care products from Julia Dawson's gift at the hospital a couple of weeks ago.

Rena snatched up the metal nail file, bent it into a curve and slipped it into her bra down near the underwire. Uncomfortable as hell, but not visible in the mirror. At least her swollen, tender pregnancy breasts offered better hiding.

Wouldn't that make an interesting headline for tomorrow's television news flash? Pregnant housewife takes down abductor with her killer bra…more details to follow at eleven. Stifling a hysterical laugh, Rena ditched the paperweight in the trash.

Rena flushed the toilet and turned on the faucet. She needed to get a grip.

She twisted off the water, gripped the doorknob. Fear sliced through her with every tight breath. What hell J.T. must have gone through overseas. She'd known, of course, but hadn't really *known* until this moment.

Guilt crawled over her. She hadn't been there for J.T. when he needed her. Sure, she'd gone through the motions when he'd lumbered off that plane. But when he'd walked out of the house a couple of days later, she should have chased his ass down. Dogged him until he came home where he belonged, until he had time to come to grips with his hellish experience.

He'd braved her family, offered her safety, a haven. Love. He deserved the same from her.

She'd fought for her marriage. She'd fought for herself. Now it was time she fought for J.T.

J.T. fought the fog.

God, his head hurt. Groaning, he rolled to his side, off his numb hands. Still they wouldn't move.

He was tied. Ah hell.

He blinked against the dark, his eyes slowly adjusting with the help of a thin bar of light slanting under the door. Small space. Hands tied. Rubistan? His brain logy, he battled with now and then. Wrestled down dread. Forced even breaths in and out to stuff down the swell of nausea. From a concussion?

He filled himself with air. Smells, too. Smells of home. Rena's cologne. He struggled to sit, canting up closer to the scent wafting off…wool dangling overhead.

A coat. Hers.

He was in a closet, not a cell. Relief washed away nausea. Memories blasted through of the man at his desk. Rena walking in. And then… What?

J.T. jerked against his constraints. He had to get out. To his wife. He couldn't allow thoughts of what might be happening to her.

And then he heard her. Her voice pierced the door, growing louder.

He slumped back against the wall. She was alive. For now.

With slow, controlled moves, he worked to free his hands as he grounded himself in the husky, vibrant—alive—sounds of Rena's voice.

"I'm telling you, if you put me in another closet and my husband wakes up without me there, he's going to flip out. He gives new meaning to the word *overprotective*. You won't have the chance to convince him I'm all right or bring him to me, or me to him. He'll cause a ruckus that will alert anyone who's anywhere near the house. Then there's no way you'll get that flight schedule you want.''

Flight schedule?

Realization dawned through his clearing brain. She was feeding him information in case he was awake. Warning him. Damn, he loved this smart, spunky woman.

''Your best bet is to put me in that closet with him. You can tie me up. But you need to keep things level until the guy from the base comes with the finished schedule.''

What the hell? She had to know that wasn't true.

Of course she did. She must be stalling. She had to be scared to death and still she stayed calm. Pride for her clenched inside him, a welcome break from the other emotions pummeling the hell out of him.

''We really shouldn't wait much longer to open the door,'' she continued. ''Do you think he's hurt badly? I should check him. Since you're wearing that mask, I'm hoping that means you genuinely want us to live. So why not—''

''For God's sake, lady.'' A male voice cut through. Familiar? Tough to tell with the pain and door muffling. ''Will you please just shut the hell up for a minute so I can think?''

A smile so damn incongruous with the nightmare situation tugged at him. God love his wife's ability for gab.

''Okay,'' their captor conceded. ''You can go in the same closet. But you will be tied.''

''Fine. We all want to get out of this alive. You're making—''

''Tied *and* gagged.''

The bastard was dead.

For now, he needed to make the most of the window of opportunity Rena had bought them. J.T. slumped back onto the floor and waited.

The doorknob snicked. He closed his eyes, forced his muscles to relax.

Light flooded through his eyelids. Rustling sounded. N‹ more talking from Rena. The son of a bitch had truly gagge‹ her. A tic tugged at J.T.'s eye.

More rustling. The heat of another body drawing close‹ Settling against him. Rena.

Tension seeped from him.

More heat, another person. "So, Sergeant," said their cap‹ tor, hot breath blocking out the scents of home. "Yo‹ wouldn't be faking, would you? I should probably check."

Ah crap. J.T. had one second to prep himself before—

A fist slammed into his ribs.

Pain rocketed through him. A moan slipped free, from him, from Rena, too. He forced himself to relax again in spite of the pain howling inside him.

"Guess he's still out, after all." The sounds of popping knees creaked as the man stood. "I'll be close by and check-ing. Often. So no tricks or stupid heroics."

The door slammed shut.

J.T. listened for the sound of retreating footsteps, his head and ribs throbbing. He blinked to adjust again, swallowing back the reflexive need to vomit. He didn't dare risk more than a whisper, and damn it all, she wouldn't be able to an-swer. But at least they were both alive. In the same place.

He wasn't alone in the cell this time.

"Rena? Rena, babe, I'm okay." He angled up to sit, the pain nothing in comparison to the need to comfort her. "We're okay. We're going to get out of this."

She wilted against him with a whimper.

Glancing down, he could almost make out her face in the murky closet. Best he could tell, she wasn't hurt, other than a bandanna tied tight around her mouth.

He wanted to put his arms around her so damn bad. "You did good. Real good, getting him to do what you wanted and feeding me information. I'm proud of you, babe." Understatement. "Now, here's what we're going to do. Are you listening?"

She nodded against his chest, nuzzling deeper as if she wanted to burrow inside him.

"We're going to shuffle back-to-back and untie each other. Can you do that?"

She nodded again.

Shifting, scooting, trying like hell not to make noise, he moved. His feet bumped old gym shoes, rain boots. An umbrella toppled.

Crap.

He froze. Stopped breathing, waited. The umbrella rolled down his arm to a whisper rest against the floor.

J.T. inched again until his fingers touched Rena's. She linked hers with his for three precious seconds before she picked at the binding.

He searched by touch along her wrists...hell. She was secured tight with some kind of rope. How she made her fingers bend and maneuver along his binds he couldn't even imagine. Her hands must be numb. And then there was the baby, too.

Damn it, he needed to do something, but all he could do was talk. A wry smile kicked in. That's what she'd always wanted from him, after all, and he could come through now, reassure her if nothing else. Say all the things she needed to hear.

Say all the things *he* needed to say to her in case he never had the chance again. "I still remember the first time I saw you. It was like somebody colorized a black-and-white movie. A hokey thought, huh?"

She melted against him a little and he thought maybe it wasn't so hokey, after all. Too bad he'd never thought to say it before.

"I'm committed to my job, don't get me wrong, and I love the hell out of it. But there are parts that are...tough. Dark. The things that we do and places we go, it's so—" he struggled for the word "—opposite of home. I don't know how else to describe it. Even when I'm enjoying the job, the whole time that I'm away I still look forward to coming home, flipping the switch that shifts from there to here, dark to bright colors."

Her breathing grew quieter, her fingers slower for a second before she picked at the cord around his wrists again. Her smaller hands pried at the knots better than his fumbling ones, much the way she'd always been able to work free those strings of knots that seemed to build into a chain on the kids' gym shoes.

He leaned forward to give her better access to his bound wrists. "Problem was, sometimes the switch got stuck, my head was there even though my body's here. And I don't know how to be in both places at the same time." A low laugh climbed free. "I can already hear you asking me why the two have to be separate. But there are things I don't want in my house. Things I don't want touching my family. Or touching you."

The cord fell free from him. His fingers burned with the rush of returning circulation. He tried to flex, but couldn't order his hands to move yet. Kinda like how he'd known he should act and say certain things when he'd returned but his body just stayed…stuck.

He couldn't afford the luxury of time now.

J.T. shook his arms and gritted through the fiery pain. "It's not because I didn't think you were strong enough. God, babe, what you do holding this family together year after year while I'm gone… How you held it together today…"

His fingers twitched, clenched, slowly listened to his brain. He reached behind Rena to untie the bandanna gag. "You're the strongest person I've ever met, but you shouldn't have to be." He fumbled, yanked, untwisted the knot. "You didn't sign on for this. I did."

The bandanna slipped free and landed around her neck.

Rena leaned forward, forehead to forehead, tears glinting even through the dark. "J.T.? I didn't sign on for a job. I signed on for you, wherever you are, good or bad places, I want to be there, too."

Her hands still bound, she toppled forward to kiss him and he thanked God for the chance to hold her. A privilege he wouldn't throw away again.

Rena skimmed her lips over his once more, then rocked back on her heels. "Now, what are we going to do to take out that bastard before our son comes home from school?"

Chris flung his backpack onto the ground by the park bench outside school.

Okay, he was trying not to be an ungrateful brat. Geez, he was already lucky his parents hadn't killed him for holding out about what happened at the restaurant. But like, couldn't they at least pick him up on time? As if it wasn't bad enough everyone would see his "mommy and daddy" drive up to get him.

At least no one had tried to pound him today while John Murdoch was absent and couldn't stick up for him.

Chris slouched lower on the bench. He was really, really trying not to screw up and piss off his folks. He'd actually turned down four different rides because, if his dad didn't think it was safe for him to drive himself, then he shouldn't take rides with others his age—even if one of those "others" was this really cute babe from his Spanish II class.

Nope, he'd called Bo. A mature choice. Right? Since that's who Dad picked to stay over when Mom was in the hospital.

And at least Bo drove a cool Jeep with the top down most of the time rather than a dorky parentmobile.

"Hey, Chris?" Shelby leaned over the back of the bench into his sight line. "What's going on? I thought you were using your mom's car 'til everything works out with buying you another one."

Geez, her dark hair smelled good swinging right there beside his face. He could even remember how soft it felt when he'd hugged her while she cried.

He looked away, down, scuffed his gym shoe over gum stuck to the concrete. "Dad drove me in today. He's late picking me up."

She slung her backpack over. "Do you want a ride home?"

Make that *five* ride offers and one of them from Shelby. And he couldn't accept even one. The day just got suckier by the second. "Nah, thanks. I already called Bo to come get me."

"Bo? He's cool. Great Jeep."

"Yeah. He got a Jet Ski to celebrate his cast coming off."

"Really cool." She circled around to the front and plopped down beside him. "How about I wait around with you?"

There wasn't any reason he couldn't talk to her. School was safe or his dad wouldn't have let him come. "Sure. Thanks."

A bus chugged by. Arms hung out the windows. The shouts and laughs and we're-free noises carried on the wind.

He lifted his shoe off the gum, a long stream of hot sticky pink stretching. "Everything going okay?"

"Great. Really great." Turning, she hitched a knee up onto the bench, a megahot knee pressing against his thigh. "Listen, Chris, I just want to say thank-you for being there when I needed a friend. I mean, I don't know who else would have been so cool about everything and not judged me and just helped me—"

He kissed her.

Oh God, he was really kissing Shelby Dawson. He didn't remember leaning or even deciding to do it. But her face was right there and Murdoch—the lucky bastard who got to do it with her and probably didn't appreciate her—wasn't around.

And her lip gloss was all shiny and he had to know what it tasted like before she moved or he would die.

Strawberry.

Her breath hitched. He heard it. A tiny gasp thing that said maybe this was okay and she wasn't saying no or pulling back. Her mouth softened a little and he leaned forward, angled his mouth over hers more fully.

She jerked away. "Ohmigod."

Crap.

Her eyes widened. She touched her lips with a hand that shook.

Double crap. He was so screwed. "I'm sorry. I'm not sure what I was thinking by—"

"I had no idea."

No idea he liked her or no idea she would like him? His heart shifted from double time to triple, pounding like the bass drum rallying the football crowd.

"Chris, you are absolutely one of my best friends in the world."

Thud. Stop. The friend word.

His heartbeat started again, slow, pushing against the ache in his chest. "Your friend, huh. Gee, thanks."

"I'm so sorry if I did anything to lead you on."

Get it together, Price. Salvage some pride. "Hey, chill. It's no big thing. I totally understand. Just thought I would see, if, well, before you move—"

"Stop, please." She clamped her hand over his mouth and blinked back tears. "God, Chris, I'm really sorry."

That she felt this bad over trampling his heart to bits notched his pride up a little. He clasped her wrist to pull it away from his face and tried not to get too hyped by the way her pulse throbbed so fast against his fingers.

He placed her hand on her knee and gave it one more hinting try. "Since you and Murdoch are hardly together anymore, I wondered—"

"Uh, Chris?" Her gaze shot down to the sticky gum before coming back up to him. She winced apologetically. "John's not here today because his dad took him for a late registration at the college I'm attending. He changed schools for me."

That was it then. Shelby was moving and John Murdoch was going with her and the guy deserved her because he'd made the tough choice to be with her. "I'm glad for you two that everything worked out."

"Are you okay?"

"Of course I'm okay. It's not as if I was in love with you or anything. I like you, all right? And I thought if Murdoch was out of the picture I'd better make my move fast before some guy moved in ahead of me. I mean, Geez, Shelby, you're hot."

She gave him a watery smile. "Okay. Enough. Stop it. And thanks."

"Sure." He tracked his eyes back to the Bazooka bubble-gum blob, not a big fan of seeing her pity-stare right this minute.

Yeah, the tree, bus stop, road hurt less to look at, especially now that he saw a Jeep rounding the corner, a guy in a flight suit driving who—the black vehicle revved closer, clearer— was Bo Rokowsky. "Hey, there's my ride. I gotta go."

Chris hooked his arm through his backpack on the ground by the bench and stood.

Rising, Shelby stopped him with a soft hand on his arm. Her eyes went from sad to kinda confused. "And Chris? About what happened just now, you know, with the kiss." Confused changed to—surprised? "For what it's worth, you're really good at it. I mean *really* good."

Pink popped along her cheeks before she started looking over at the tree, bus stop and road before her gaze fell some-where short of his face, more like his shoulder. "Well, uh, I need to go, okay?"

"Sure, catch up with you later." Chris shuffled backward

toward the Jeep, watching until she got in her car and drove away. His dad's words niggled to the surface, bringing understanding, if not peace.

Right person. Wrong time.

He pivoted toward his ride. "Thanks for coming over, man," Chris called out. "My folks aren't answering at home or on their cell phones."

Bo downshifted to a stop. "No problem. I'm still flying the desk. Just tapped someone to cover me for a few." Snagging the green flight bag from the front seat, he pitched it into the back. "Hop on in and let's get you home."

Chapter 16

"Ready whenever you are." Rena clenched her fingers in J.T.'s flight suit.

His heart pulsed steadily against her fist as she sat with winter coats and sweaters tickling her head. At least they weren't helpless anymore. They had a plan, a chance, hope. The nail file had even helped saw and pry at the persistent knots binding her wrists. They'd kept the ropes loosely in place, would soon slip her gag back up too so their captor wouldn't be alerted.

Part of her wanted to stay inside the closet until the very last second possible to stretch her time with J.T. But they couldn't afford to wait much longer and risk Chris coming home. Already, he must be questioning why his father hadn't arrived. Please, please, please, Lord, let Chris be irresponsible and just go hang out at a friend's house.

Not something they could count on.

J.T. tunneled his fingers into her hair, locating the knot in her gag. His hands hesitated, stroked along the sensitive nape of her neck. "I'm proud of you, babe, and how you handled that bastard out there. We have this chance because of your quick thinking."

"I hope it's enough." She allowed herself one precious last minute to look at J.T.'s face in the dim light, checked that he wasn't hiding some injury from her. His pupils appeared evenly dilated...but his eyes seemed different somehow, distant. Not cold, but focused, steely.

Ready for battle.

And finally she understood about that mental switch of his. How could she have lived with this man, slept with him for twenty-two years, carried his children, and never have seen such an integral part of him?

How utterly ridiculous to think that even though her mind had always understood he served in the military, until now she'd never known the warrior. She'd prided herself on her love for this man, only to find she'd missed out on half of *who* he was.

Footsteps sounded.

Rena startled.

J.T. lifted the bandanna. "Time's up, babe."

Panic, adrenaline, resolve washed through her like sheeting rain. She wanted to shout for fate to wait. She needed another moment to process these new emotions, just one minute.

Thudding steps grew closer, louder.

Eyes closing, J.T. slumped back against the wall, but with adjustments, angled to spring faster.

The door jerked open. Their captor's body blocked the bulk of the light, only a few beams streaking around him. Even so, spots danced in front of her eyes, finally clearing.

"You." He pointed the gun dead center toward her chest. "Get up."

Why was he coming for them? Although this certainly worked better than concocting some reason to kick the door and draw him over.

Rena shifted awkwardly, as if straining for balance but in reality shielding her body from the gun's line of fire, shielding her baby. Giving J.T. a clear path to launch.

She could see J.T.'s muscles bunch. Anticipation pulsed from him.

"Damn it, come on," Mr. Narcissist barked, all mannerly pretenses gone. "Apparently you weren't lying, after all about the schedule. Some guy from base just pulled up in your driveway."

What?

He waggled the gun, gesturing for her to rise. "The door bell will be ringing any—"

The back door opened. "Mom? Dad? Everything okay? I tried to call."

Dread pierced her more effectively than any bullet. In seeking to protect one child, now she had another just as precious in danger.

Mr. Narcissist jerked to look—the perfect chance to jump him. Except now he had his gun pointed at Chris, her son standing pale-eyed and swaying in the archway from the kitchen to the hall, with Bo stunned to a stop a few steps behind him.

Damn. Damn. Damn.

"Chris, get back," she shouted.

"Don't move, pal." Gun level, the man reached down and jerked Rena to her feet. Her hands still tied slackly, she stumbled up, her knees protesting after so long folded. "I'll put a bullet right through your mother."

"Mr. Haugen?" Chris gasped.

Chris's boss? Hadn't that guy already been questioned in regards to the Miranda Casale issue?

And likely released. Hell *and* damn. Their hope of getting out alive evaporated now that they had a name for their attacker. He couldn't let them live. And obviously everyone would know that.

An exasperated sigh slid through the mask right before he peeled it off, sandy-colored hair standing on end. "You never could learn when to keep your mouth shut, could you, pal?"

Kurt Haugen pitched aside the mask, grabbing her arm again before she could inch more than a whisper away. The barrel of the gun cut into her side. She didn't dare risk more movement even with his attention focused on Chris and Bo.

She stole a quick check on J.T. in the closet. His eyes opened, not much but enough for her to know he was awake and plotting. He stared straight at her, two fingers flicking. She frowned. He repeated the flicking gesture until she understood.

He wanted her to lead the man away, keep him occupied. Give J.T. a chance to slip out and catch him unaware.

At least that's what she hoped he meant.

They had a single edge. Haugen didn't know J.T. was awake and untied—an edge that wouldn't last long once Haugen regrouped.

She prayed Chris wouldn't ask about his father and remind the man. "Hon, I'm okay. Everything will be fine as long as we stay calm. And now that Bo's here, maybe he can help Mr. Haugen with the information he needs. Is your flight bag in the kitchen or the Jeep?"

"Whoa. Hold on a minute," Haugen interrupted with an easygoing smile, as if doing nothing more than asking friends to wait up for him on the golf course. "Nobody goes anywhere unless I say so. And I say we go to the kitchen and figure out what the hell's going on."

He jerked her forward—without sparing so much as a backward glance at J.T.—and ushered them all into the kitchen.

"I had a good thing going, pal," Haugen tsked at Chris, "until you opened your mouth." Frowning, he glanced back over his shoulder.

J.T.

She had to keep this guy talking. Narcissists loved to talk about themselves, right? "What do you mean, a good thing?"

"The drug running, of course. Well, until your kid got weirded out by moving a little money for us. Geez, we would have paid him well. The two military dudes were more than happy to figure out a way to pay their maxed credit cards."

"Why not leave the country? Why take a chance breaking into our house, holding us this way? It sounds like you're smarter than that." Keep talking. Cover noises.

"Because I can't just run off, even if there was somewhere to hide from my boss. I'm accountable to people, people who expect something from me on this end—which I will have once I have the flight schedule. The feds are getting a little too snoopy after those surveillance flights. Once I have the schedule in hand, we can reroute our guys' paths and times accordingly for a final big payoff. Then the family will relocate me."

Like a kaleidoscope, his words and images jumped in her mind—drugs, family, threats, emblems…

Her gaze dropped back to his belt buckle. Finally she remembered why it had seemed so familiar painted on the brick. "Ohmigod."

The red circle, black triangle inside.

Revulsion shuddered through her. She knew exactly where she'd spotted those markings before, symbols that were well-kept secrets known only to those on the inside. This insignia represented one of the most powerful Mob families.

A perverted coat of arms she'd seen as a child while peeking through the banister rails at her father's "business" guests.

Voices fading with footsteps, J.T. shook his hands free of the loosely wrapped cord. He crouched low, peering through the thin gap between the hinges of the open door.

Haugen stood in the kitchen archway with Rena at his side. He jammed his gun deeper in her side.

J.T.'s hands fisted. He channeled the rage, training never more important than now.

Instincts. Breathe. Assess.

Rena asked Haugen some question that left the man furrowing his forehead in concentration. Good job, babe.

Sliding into the hall, J.T. kept his observation peripheral now. No looking at the bastard and setting off the internal radar that might cause him to check his six o'clock.

Haugen chuckled. "So you recognize my belt buckle, Mrs. Price. Not many would. Maybe it was a little egotistical of me to place it on my calling card through your window, but I figured your son would make the connection with Miranda's necklace."

J.T. processed the periphery view. Rena and Haugen in the doorway. Chris by the table. Bo, to Rena's right, by the refrigerator. Moving infinitesimally. Trying to work a rescue solo? Or had he seen J.T.? And what about Chris?

Come on, somebody. Get back to distracting Haugen. J.T. wound his way through the hall, grateful for the clutter and oversize plants that provided a helluva lot more cover than desert. This was his turf, damn it.

Chris backed until his butt bumped the counter. "You've been running drugs? And now you're going off with Miranda Casale?"

"Miranda?" Haugen's face whipped up, his body moving forward, deeper into the kitchen—way to go, Chris. "God, no. Aside from the fact that she's the don's niece, I love my wife. Why would I screw around with Miranda Casale? Besides, she's too young and too obvious. She was sent down to keep an eye on her uncle's interests."

Rena leaned on her right foot, the gun barrel inching out of her side. "If you love your wife, how could you leave her like this?"

Damn straight, Rena. Good men don't leave their women behind. He heard the message loud and clear, and wouldn't be repeating his mistake.

"I'm taking my wife and daughter with me."

Bo stepped closer. "Your wife's a part of this, too?"

J.T. flattened his back to the wall. Angled around a picture frame. Only five more steps and he would be hidden on the side of the archway. Out of Haugen's sight line.

"Of course not." Haugen looked past Rena to Bo, the man's gestures growing more erratic as Rena, Chris and Bo had him ping-ponging responses around the room. "They think it's a family vacation. No need to worry them. I'll explain things when we get…where we're going. They'll realize I did this for them, to give them the things they deserve. I'd do anything for them."

Two more steps. Past a plant stand.

Bo inched closer. "Even sell drugs and pump money into terrorist accounts?"

"If I don't do it—" Haugen shrugged, his gun pulling out of Rena's side, but his grip on her arm still tight enough to dig into her flesh "—they'll only find someone else."

Bo's chest expanded with outrage, bravado, as he strutted closer, an arm's reach from Rena. "That's a bullshit excuse to justify your own greed and you know it."

In place, J.T. nodded to Bo. Knew the young officer caught the movement even though he was smart enough not to alert Haugen by looking away.

"Are you an idiot or what to tick me off this way?" Haugen advanced around Rena.

No, Bo wasn't an idiot. But Haugen was. This time, the enemy was going down.

Bo sprung toward Rena. Body blocked her out of the line of fire. J.T. launched through the cleared archway, tackled Haugen. They hit the tile. Hard. Teeth jarring as they skidded across the kitchen, bashing into chairs, the table. He pinned Haugen's gun hand to the floor.

Rena? He wanted to check. Didn't dare lose focus.

Haugen arched, swung his other fist. J.T. blocked. Slammed Haugen's hand against the saltillo tile floor, once, again and again until the gun clanked free.

J.T. channeled the roar, instincts honed and focused. This was home turf and damn anyone who threatened what was his.

Haugen panicked, bucked, tried to twist.

J.T. coldcocked the son of a bitch with an uppercut to the jaw. Haugen's head smacked tile, lolled to the side. Chris scooped up the gun, his too-long legs and awkward teen body never exhibiting more speed and grace.

That fast, it was over. Battles often were, and thank God this one ended with no shots fired. Rena? He searched, saw her shielded by Bo's body behind the pantry door.

Rocking back on his haunches, J.T. shook out his aching fist and extended his other arm. Rena untangled herself from Bo, shook loose her ties and flew forward. She landed against J.T.'s chest. Into his embrace. Covering his face with kisses.

"Ohmigod, J.T., you did it, holy crap, you really did it." She reached for Chris. "Come here, kiddo."

J.T. glanced over her shoulder to their son. "You okay?"

"Yeah, Dad, I'm cool." The teen passed the pistol to his father. "I'm okay, Mom. Geez, no need to pump out the tears."

"Shush up." Her arms closed around both of them. No arguing with a determined Rena. "I'll cry over both of you as much as I damn well please. And Bo, too, oh God, thank you."

Bo's face creased into his best bad-boy grin. "No problem. And as much as I'd enjoy a hot lady like you crying all over me, I'm not overeager to meet up with Tag's right hook."

Winking, Bo yanked up the phone, dialed, relaying clipped details for 911.

J.T. trained the gun on Haugen's prone body while keeping Rena tucked close.

Adrenaline still surged through him, but aftermath stripped away the numbness of battle focus. Emotions blazed through him—good, bad, some raw primal, some even downright Shakespearean poetic. And yeah, the force and collective roar still scared the crap out of him.

But not enough to make him run for the quiet of cover anymore. Not now that he understood exactly what he'd been missing by closing himself off from the full power of his love for his wife. Her love for him.

With the joint forces of Rena's indomitable will and his determination, they could accomplish anything—even rebuild a marriage made to last a lifetime.

Lounging against the porch post, J.T. sucked in a drag of pure night air as the last cop cruiser pulled away from the curb. Adrenaline still singed his insides, but tonight he would find peace with his wife rather than through the Bard.

Once he thanked Bo for a debt he could never repay.

The young officer leaned against the opposite post, flexing his fingers. Yeah, crap like this brought back some bad memories.

Crickets and june bugs hummed above the minimal traffic. Street lamps glowed into empty yards, lights flickering off in the windows of a neighborhood going to sleep. Chris, upstairs being fussed over by Rena, would likely be asleep soon, as well, the teenager exhausted, relieved. There would still be trial testimonies, but the badasses had been nailed.

Rena's surprise ID of the circle/triangle symbol even offered Spike the final link he'd been seeking. Now authorities knew where to look in tracking the drop-off point for the drugs once they'd been run up the coast.

And all without a bullet fired.

J.T. rubbed his hand along the tender knot on the back of his head. A small price for putting this all to rest. One of the flight surgeons had even made a house call for him, checked him over, deemed him perfectly well thanks to his thick head.

And hadn't Rena laughed at that pronouncement?

Damn, but her laughter sounded good. God willing, he was through making her cry. "Thanks, Bo, for everything today. You really put your butt on the line for my family."

"I owed you."

"Well, we're definitcly even."

"Nobody's keeping score. It's what we do for each other," Bo said in an echo of Spike's same words, not surprising since the credo ingrained itself in all of them.

Bo studied his bootlaces. "Besides, it felt damn good to strike back at the bad guys on this one. Makes everything that happened to us over there mean something."

"Yeah, I hear you." Understatement. It had taken them nearly four months, but finally, they'd completed their mission.

J.T. drew in a little more of that magnolia-scented air to ground himself in home.

Home.

It was time to return.

Bo pushed away from the post. "Well, man, I should hit the road. I'm betting I can milk this for a little TLC from someone of the female persuasion. What do you think?"

J.T. thumped the young officer on the back on their way down the flagstone path. "I'm thinking that you better stay the hell away from my daughter, *sir,* or I'll tell people your real name."

"Yeah, yeah, I know." Bo swung up into the front seat. "No crewdogs for your little girl."

"No players."

"A player? Who me?" Winking, he cranked the Jeep. "Catch ya' later, dude. I'm off to romance my lady friend."

Bo revved the engine, shifting into reverse and roaring out of the driveway into the night.

Romance. Chuckling, J.T. shook his head. He and Rena had pretty much skimmed over that part, jumping from shared hamburgers to a shared kid, family, apartment, day-to-day get moving with life.

More lights along the rows of houses switched off, reminding him of his explanation to Rena about his work/life switch, his inability to blend the two worlds.

Had he somehow segmented his relationship with Rena, as well? Dating, one switch. Flick the switch to husband, another mind-set, being a provider like his father.

Recreation had never played a big role in his life. He'd found a job he enjoyed, productive hobbies like rebuilding his house or his car. And for smiles? Light? He had Rena.

But what had he given her for light in return?

Well, hell. He stared down the empty road. A few weeks ago he'd been beating his head against the wall at the prospect of entering the "dating" world again. But now, the idea sent one helluva thrill through him—when the right woman was involved.

The romance gig wasn't a crapshoot, after all. As much as he wanted to present Rena with diamonds and fancy vacations, the incredible woman he loved enjoyed circus peanuts, too.

He wasn't giving up on draping her in a diamond or two someday. But he'd finally learned he could also drape her in plenty of romance now.

J.T. fished into his back pocket for his cell phone. After twenty-two years, it was about time he asked his wife for a date.

* * *

Rena rapped two knuckles against her son's open bedroom door.

"Yeah?" Chris called from his bed, pitching a magazine to a floor already covered in clothes, a towel and schoolbooks.

Her heart rate still thumped an extra couple of beats every time she remembered how close she'd come to losing J.T. and Chris today.

Rena tiptoed over a discarded backpack on her way to her son's bedside. "Are you okay, hon?"

"Still a little wigged out, but it'll be better in the morning. Just need to sleep. Maybe swim some laps tomorrow. Get my head together."

She perched on the edge of his bedside table. "Swimming laps is a good way to relax."

"Yeah. Gotta work out the stress somehow." He crooked both arms behind his head. "Dad's probably down in his office veging with the Bard."

"Excuse me?"

"You know. How he always reads Shakespeare and junk like that to chill."

But she didn't know.

How could she have missed that about her husband? A sad commentary on how little she and J.T. had communicated over the years. She would have cried her eyes out over the discovery a couple of days ago. Now it only fueled her resolve to learn more about this fascinating man she'd married. And along the way let him learn some more about her, as well.

"'Night, hon." Rena leaned to skim a good-night kiss on her son's forehead. "I love you."

He hooked an arm up and around for a hug. "Love you, too, Mom." He pulled back, mock surprise on his face. "Gee, when did you get so little?"

"When did you get so big?" She grinned.

Laughing, a deeper sound these days, he flopped back. "G'night."

"Good night, hon."

Clicking off the overhead light, she left, closing his door on her way out. Finally, she and J.T. could be alone. Would they talk? Or just cut straight to mind-blowing sex? Or pass out from exhaustion?

Her tummy tumbled in nervous flips.

Rena padded down the stairs, toward the computer room, refusing to let the ghosts of their afternoon horror haunt her home. She peeked into the office. No J.T., but sure enough, right beside the butt-ugly green chair rested a thick tome.

She stepped closer, her hand falling to rest on the volume of Shakespearean plays. She thumbed through, some pages highlighted, her husband's spiky scrawl beside passages. She let the book fall open as if it might give her a glimpse into J.T., a hint for what she should do next.

"Our doubts are traitors, and make us lose the good we oft might win, by fearing to attempt." *Measure for Measure.* Rena traced a finger along the words. No more waiting. She knew exactly what she needed to do and finally had the confidence in herself to go for broke.

Rena snapped closed the book. She had a husband to welcome home.

Making tracks back up the stairs, she headed straight for the bedroom closet. First on her welcome-home agenda, clear room for his flight suits and Hawaiian shirts.

A swoop of her arm smooshed her work dresses to the side. She didn't intend to give up pushing for marital counseling. But in the meantime, she could still go on her own, work through some of her issues from her childhood. Straighten out her insecurities and need for control.

A starting place.

Kneeling, she lined her heels up in double rows to empty space for his boots and gym shoes.

The phone jangled from beside the bed.

A call? This late?

She eased to her feet and rushed to scoop the cordless phone from beside a pot of mini-mums. "Hello?"

"Hi, is Rena there?" her husband's deep voice rumbled through the line.

Huh? Had he hit his head harder than she'd thought? Maybe she should have insisted the flight surgeon take another look at him. "J.T.? Are you all right?"

"I'm totally all right. In fact, I've been more than all right since I saw you at that air show."

Okay, now she was really getting worried. "J.T., where are you?"

"Turn around."

She spun—to find him lounging against the hall door, cell phone at his ear. One black leather boot pressed to the wall, his knee bent. His flight suit stretched across mile-wide shoulders. "I was hoping you'd remember me, because since the second I saw you, I've been hoping like hell you'd go out with me. So, I decided to give you a call, see if you're free this Friday for a date with a local flyboy."

God, as much as she drooled over those shoulders of his, he really took her breath away when he smiled. Damned if she didn't feel eighteen again.

Phone pressed to her ear, she smiled back at him, flicked her hair over her shoulder, played along. "I might be free, if the right flyboy asked."

"Well, babe, I'm asking." He angled away from the door frame, ambled closer, his big, muscled body drawing nearer, filling her eyes and her heart. "And I intend to keep right on asking until I can convince you to go out with me."

He stopped inches away.

She clicked off her phone but kept it cradled against her neck, soaking up the silly romantic gesture a little while longer. "You are so crazy sometimes."

"Not often." He set his phone on the end table. "And only for you, babe. Only for you."

He reached for her phone, as well, and placed it beside his before lifting her hand, kissing her palm.

Definitely eighteen again, but with a forty-year-old's wisdom on how to do things better this go-round. "I want you to come home. For good."

"That's where I want to be." He folded her hand against his chest, against his heart thumping along at a pace as fast as hers. "Not just because you're pregnant, but because I can't stand the thought of living the rest of my life without you beside me."

She gathered the beautiful words up into her heart with surety and happiness, because, by God, J.T. never lied.

He stared down at their linked fingers and rather than pushing him to talk, she knew now to wait. He would come around to filling the silence if she simply gave him the chance.

"I spoke with the flight surgeon when she checked out the lump on my head."

Her racing heart stopped. "You're okay?"

"Totally fine." The twinkle in his eyes jump-started her heart again. "Although you'll have to keep me awake all night."

She sagged closer, her hips rocking against his. "I think that can be arranged."

"Thank God." His forehead fell to rest against hers. His chest expanded with two hefty sighs before he continued, "About my discussion with the flight surgeon. I asked her to recommend a marriage counselor."

Rena's throat went as tight as her chest. She'd been prepared to wait, work, hope, pray that things would work the way that she wanted. But to have him make the huge step on his own... Oh God, she loved this man.

Steady gray eyes stared down at her with no doubts to

cloud their beautiful-sky appeal. "Up the stakes as high as you want. I'm not walking again."

Sometimes hormones were a wonderful thing. Letting all those happy tears well up and flow free, Rena flung her arms around his neck. "Oh God, J.T., I love you."

J.T. felt her words rocket right into him, straight for his heart—where she belonged. He wrapped his arms around her and pulled her against his chest—also where she belonged. "I know, babe. And I don't ever intend to take that for granted again."

He dropped a kiss on her head while her sighs caressed through his flight suit, still so damn stunned and glad to see over her shoulder where she'd made room for his clothes in their closet again.

"Hell, I can't believe I'm the lucky bastard who stole your heart when you could have had anybody." His fingers tangled in her hair. "There are so many things I wanted to give you over the years. Still things I wish I could give you. But you can be certain I love you. Always have, and it only gets stronger with time."

"Things?" Her stunned response drifted up.

"Yeah, a bigger house, trips, a grocery budget that didn't include coupon clipping."

"I never asked for any of that."

"But you deserve it all."

She angled back, hints of her fiery temper sparking in her chocolate eyes. "Do you really think that little of me?"

"What?"

She thunked his chest. "Do you believe I'm so shallow that I would only be happy if we had more money? I think I'm insulted here, J.T."

Rena clasped his flight-suit collar in two determined hands, strong hands that nurtured, loved and, yes, even demanded. "Do you have any idea how proud I am of you, hell, of myself, too, for that matter, and everything we've built over the years?''

The words rolled out of her, ringing with a conviction he couldn't fight even if he tried. And he definitely didn't want to fight with her anymore.

Her soft hands caressed up to his face. ''We started with nothing, and in twenty-two years you've risen to a rank most in your profession never see. You've given me three precious babies, and we've brought up two of those children. They may not be perfect, but then neither are their parents and I'm still proud of who Nikki and Chris are becoming. Even our house, we did this from the front porch you replaced to that ivy I stenciled.''

Those words rolling from her settled into him with a rightness that brought peace. Yeah, he still wanted to give her more, but now knew he could keep her happy while they waited.

He turned his face to kiss her hand again. ''I'm partial to that ivy.''

''Me, too.'' Her arms looped around his neck. ''You've given me something I never had as a child. The chance to hold up my head. To be proud of who I am.''

Studying her dark eyes, he found flecks and sparks of pain he'd seen reflected in the mirror and in the eyes of his crewmates. He'd understood about Rena's upbringing and had been determined to take her away from the ugliness of that world. But he'd never realized until now that his wife had also spent time in a war zone. With guns. Deceit. Danger. What a scarring way for a child to grow up, now that he actually thought about it.

In flipping his switch, maybe he'd closed off the chance for his wife to share some burdens with him, too. Something he now knew to fix.

Rena's arms slipped forward and she lifted his hands, kissed each palm as he'd done to hers. ''I love your hands and what they do for me, but I need you for so many reasons that have nothing to do with what your body can provide." She tapped his forehead. "What are you thinking?"

A thousand things, about their past, her past, all things they could share later in bed. And with the counselor. And on moonlit nights by the shore.

For right now, he'd settled for the obvious, most important answer and a piece of himself to share with her. "You reminded me of a quote from a Shakespearean play, *A Midsummer Night's Dream*, I think. It goes something like, 'Thou art as wise as thou art beautiful.'"

"Wow. Am I ever one lucky lady or what?" She arched up against him, whispering against his mouth. "I get love, a hunky flyboy and sensitive poetry all in one fella."

His mouth found hers, settled, held while relief over their new start swept through both of them.

And then the chemistry soared. Ooh-rah.

Her lips parted or his mouth opened. Who could tell what happened first? And what the hell did it matter? Because he was too busy exploring the warm, moist heat of Rena.

She tipped back, tugging him down onto the bed with her. Definitely ooh-rah.

He caught himself with his elbows against the bounce of the mattress, careful of the baby, of her. "You still haven't answered my question."

"What question was that?" She tickled her fingers along the nape of his neck.

"Will you go out with me this Friday?" Gathering a fistful of her hair, he kissed along her jaw, her ear, not at all averse to using a little persuasion. "We could catch a movie, go park by the shore afterward."

"Yes, I would love to go out with you, anywhere, anytime. Surprise me." She stroked her delicate foot up the length of his leg, slow, deliberate, until her leg hooked around his hip. "And it's a sure bet you'll get lucky on the first date."

Epilogue

How could a guy get so lucky in one lifetime?

Smiling, J.T. followed his wife up the stairs to their bedroom, the gentle sway of her hips, the swing of her spiral curls along her back drawing his eyes as always. Framed pictures of kids marked the years. And soon, another photo would be added to the collection once the hospital's newborn picture taken just last night was developed.

He cupped his hands around his son's tiny back, securing the baby to his shoulder with a seasoned grip. Like riding a bicycle. J.T. remembered the parent-hold well. One hand cradled under his son's bottom, the other hand cupping Jamie's dark, curly head.

Jamie. James Renard Price. Not a junior, but rather James for J.T. and Renard as a masculine form of Rena. Their two names blended for this baby who had brought them together.

He and Rena had come a long way in the past few months with the help of their marriage counselor. Not always easy, spilling their thoughts, but well worth the effort in the payback of a solid relationship. He'd learned to open up more. She'd learned that his quiet moods didn't mean distant. Rena had even told him she'd gained all the more faith in her abilities now that she'd seen how effective counseling could be from the *other* side of the desk.

So much love flowed freely these days, for his wife, for his new son, his other children, too. Life was good.

And about to get even better once Rena saw the surprise waiting to welcome her home.

Like a teenager ready to impress his first girlfriend, he followed her up the last stair, down the hall, to their bedroom. He stopped his wife before she could open the closed door. "Wait right here."

"How come?"

He sealed a quick kiss on her lips. "Trust me."

Her smile caressed his mouth. "All right then, flyboy. I'm waiting."

Tucking inside their room, he placed their sleeper-clad son in the middle of their bed, on Rena's favorite quilt with rings. He tugged Jamie's tiny foot. "Hold on for just a second, little man, while I go back for your mama."

J.T. made a quick sweep of the room to ensure everything was in place before sprinting to the hall where his wife waited with suspicious, but twinkling eyes.

"Okay, babe. Ready now." Gently, he swept her up into his arms.

Her hair trailing over his wrist, she laced her fingers behind his neck with a squeak and laugh. "I really can walk."

"I know you can." He settled her closer, enjoyed the scent and softness of her. And yeah, he wanted to pamper her a little. He'd forgotten how tough childbirth was on a woman, even with a quick four-hour labor like Rena's. He needed to hold her close. "But can't a guy be romantic?"

Ah, he loved how she melted against him. Hell, he just loved *her.*

Sighing, she relaxed in his arms. "By all means, then, carry away."

He stared down into the dark eyes of this woman who'd stolen his heart at an air show nearly twenty-three years ago. "I love you."

She stroked his face. "I love you, too." She nestled her head under his chin. "Now let's enjoy the peace and quiet while we can."

Amen to that. Nikki would be home soon to meet her new brother, and Chris would be bringing his girlfriend over to see Jamie as well.

Since his older friends had graduated and left for college, Chris seemed to have come out more, found his footing, especially once the police had fully cleared him. The lifeguard job had brought a girlfriend to his tower and into his life. He was calmer, more settled.

Knowing the possibility of a swim-team scholarship loomed in Chris's future calmed a part of J.T. that would never totally stop worrying about money. Of course, he worried a little less now that he'd made Chief Master Sergeant.

J.T. shuffled aside other thoughts, focused on his wife instead. He didn't want to think of anything except the homecoming surprise he had planned for Rena. Romancing his wife was turning out to be fun as hell.

Since folks from the squadron would be showing up to drop off dinner soon, he needed to get moving with his plan. He toed the bedroom door open wide and waited for his wife's reaction.

Flowers bloomed on every surface along with her potted plants—all mixed among candles. By the bed, bottled water perched in an ice bucket beside a plate of strawberries and grapes.

Rena's gasp of surprise, of happiness, told him all he needed to know. Romance rocked.

"So, Jamie," he called to his son, the little guy pumping

his tiny feet in response to his father's voice. "Do you think your mama likes the flowers?"

"She most definitely does." Rena snagged a pink rose from a vase as J.T. carried her toward the bed and inhaled the flowery scent. "Who says you can't have kids *and* romance? Thank you."

"My pleasure." And he wasn't done yet.

Carefully, he placed her onto the mattress against the piles of pillows, pulled her shoes off. J.T. stretched on the other side of the bed, while they watched their baby as they'd done in years past with Nikki and Chris.

His wife cooed and conversed with their newborn son, adjusting his lightweight blanket, tickling his toes and glowing even more than she had while pregnant. She would enjoy these next couple of months off before going back to work part-time.

Rena tugged the loose tail on J.T.'s Hawaiian shirt. "I think Jamie likes the crazy colors."

"Seems so." J.T. reached into his back pocket for the small box tucked away and hidden beneath the loose overshirt. "Remember how Nikki and Chris used to track things with their eyes early on?"

"I sure do."

Behind his back, he flicked open the box and pulled free the gift. He brought his hand forward and let the chain slowly slide loose, pendant swaying. "What do you think of this, little man? Will your mom like it, too?"

Her eyes glinted with tears. "Just when I think my heart can't get any fuller, it stretches even more."

J.T. winked at his son. "I think that's a yes." The jeweled charm continued its pendulum swing above the entranced baby. "I saw this while I was TDY to Spain a couple of months ago. The stones aren't as big as I would have wanted to get to celebrate something so damn awesome. But I actually put some sensitive-guy thought into it. Thank goodness the kid was born on time so I didn't have to change the birthstone.''

He looped the chain up to show her the circular mother charm crafted to look like a woman holding her children, each child a jewel stone. Their three children-gems winked back—a diamond, sapphire and topaz.

She touched each of the jewels with a trembling finger. "It's perfect. You're perfect."

Leaning over Jamie, Rena kissed J.T., a warm kiss, nothing passionate given her recovering state, but warm was good, too. Especially when there was the promise of so much more in a few weeks.

And judging from the glint in his wife's eyes, she was already anticipating six weeks into the future as well.

Ooh-rah.

She sagged back onto her pillows, the necklace clutched in her hand to her heart, the rose resting in her lap. "God, it's good to be home."

Home. Rena. Two words with the same meaning for him now.

He'd found that just as it was okay to bring darker parts of his military career into his relationship with Rena, into his house, he now always carried a part of her with him wherever he went. It had been a long journey across the years, across an ocean, but finally he was where he belonged.

"Yeah, babe, it sure is good to be home."

* * * * *

*Watch for Catherine Mann's next two
releases coming from Silhouette Bombshell
and HQN Books this November.*

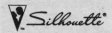
Silhouette®

INTIMATE MOMENTS™

From reader favorite
SARA ORWIG

Bring on the Night
(Silhouette Intimate Moments, #1298)

With a ranch in Stallion Pass, Jonah Whitewolf
inherited a mysterious danger—a threatening
enemy with a vendetta against him. When he
runs into his ex-wife, Kate Valentini, in town,
he comes face-to-face with the secret she's kept—
the son he never knew. With the truth revealed,
Jonah must put his life in peril to protect his
ranch and his family from jeopardy. But can he
face the greatest risk of all and give himself up
to love a second time around?

STALLION PASS:
TEXAS KNIGHTS

*Where the only cure for those hot and sultry
Lone Star Days are some sexy-as-all-get-out
Texas Knights!*

Available June 2004 at your favorite retail outlet.

Gaining back trust is hard enough…but especially when you're being set up for murder!

USA TODAY bestselling author

MARY LYNN BAXTER

Divorce attorney Hallie Hunter can hardly keep her composure when Jackson Cole walks through her door, begging her to represent him in an ongoing murder investigation in which he's the prime suspect.

Never able to deny her ex-fiancé, Hallie is thrust toward a dangerous underworld as she helps him confront a devastating truth—and must decide for herself if she can ever live without him again.

WITHOUT YOU

"The attraction between the hero and heroine sparks fire from the first and keeps on burning hot throughout."
—*Publishers Weekly* on *Sultry*

Available in May 2004 wherever paperbacks are sold.

New York Times **Bestselling Author**

LISA JACKSON

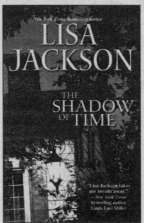

THE
SHADOW
OF TIME

After four long years, Mara Wilcox had finally accepted that her
lover, Shane Kennedy, had been tragically killed overseas. But
now, inexplicably, he was back—as handsome, arrogant and
sensual as ever! Can Mara and Shane overcome the shadow of
time and give in to their long-denied passion?

"Lisa Jackson takes my breath away."
—*New York Times* bestselling author Linda Lael Miller

Coming in June 2004.

Where love comes alive™

Visit Silhouette at www.eHarlequin.com

PSLJ824

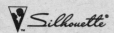

INTIMATE MOMENTS™

**A new generation begins
the search for truth in...**

A Cry in the Dark

(Silhouette Intimate Moments #1299)

by Jenna Mills

No one is alone....

Danielle Caldwell had left home to make a new life
for her young son. Then Alex's kidnapping rocked her
carefully ordered world. Warned not to call for help,
Dani felt her terror threatening to overwhelm her
senses—until tough FBI agent Liam Brooks arrived on
her doorstep, intent on helping her find Alex. Their
clandestine investigation led to a powerful attraction
and the healing of old wounds—and the discovery
of a conspiracy that could unlock the secrets of
Dani's troubled past.

The first book in the new continuity

FAMILY
SECRETS

THE NEXT GENERATION

Available June 2004 at your favorite retail outlet.

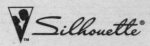

COMING NEXT MONTH